THE RAPE OF APHRODITE

THE RAPE
OF APHRODITE

Arden Winch

HEADLINE

First published in 1988 by
HEADLINE BOOK PUBLISHING PLC

To Elena and Polly

British Library Cataloguing in Publication Data

Winch, Arden
The rape of Aphrodite.
I. Title
823'.914[F]   PR6073.I4755

ISBN 0-7472-0063-7

HEADLINE BOOK PUBLISHING PLC
Headline House
79 Great Titchfield Street
London WIP 7FN

Printed and bound in Great Britain by
Richard Clay Ltd, Bungay, Suffolk

Chapter One

His wife was stroking his thighs as he sat on her bed when his bleeper went; the little transistorised miracle of modern science that tied him like an umbilical cord to the State he served. Bleep, two three, bleep.

Phone in. No panic, but phone in.

He reached up behind his lapel, and pressed the tiny button on the base of the little instrument. It was all no bigger than a thumbnail. Message received.

Barbara said, 'What did you give her to make her contact you now?'

'Who?'

Her face changed, and she snatched her hands away. 'How the hell should I know her name? Whoever it is you're screwing! What did you give her? So she'd get you on that bloody thing while you're with me!'

Joshua said wearily, 'You know it's not like that. They just want me to phone in.'

She said, expressionless, 'There are no other women. Is that what you're telling me?'

'You know there are no other women.'

God knows, there could have been, but there hadn't. All that time, and there hadn't been another woman.

He rose to his feet. 'I'll just call them.'

'Will you come back?'

'I expect so. It wasn't the emergency signal. But it depends what the message is.'

He went out into the corridor, with its carefully spaced tables each with their perfectly arranged flowers, all so immaculate you would have thought they were plastic if you had not known they arrived fresh every two days, a fact that was reflected in the nursing home's charges.

There was a pay phone by the entrance, opposite where the girl sat and smiled at relatives. As he dialled she said, 'Mrs Doyle seems to be getting better all the time, don't you think?'

She was lying, and he knew she was lying, and she knew he knew.

'You're the experts,' he said, then listened to the phone. He recognised the voice of Jimmy Ames, who must have been the Duty Officer.

'This is the Snowflake Chinese Laundry,' said Ames. 'This is a recorded message. There is nobody here at the moment, but if you will leave your name, address, and telephone number after the tone –'

What would happen if someone had misdialled and actually tried to leave a message? There was no record of it ever having happened.

'Doyle.'

'Did the shirts ever reach you?' asked Ames.

Have you got access to a secure phone?

'No. They might be at home, but I'm some way away.'

'Oh. If you could drop in later, I know Mr Woo would like to see you.'

The Old Man wants you.

'You mean today? On a Sunday?'

'He happens to be in, catching up on the underclothes. He suggests oh-twenty-one hours.'

Bad mark, thought Joshua. If by any chance there was a crossed line and someone was listening to this bizarre conversation, what sort of laundry used the twenty-four hour clock?

'Is Mr Woo inviting a lot of people to sort out anything that's missing?'

'No. Just you.'

Joshua glanced at his watch. Twelve minutes past five.

'Okay. If you could tell Mr Woo I'll be there.'

'He has an eye that flickers. You should see it when he's ironing ladies' blouses,' said Ames, who had a collection of George Formby 78s, and rang off.

Twelve minutes past five. Say an hour and a half if he went straight to the office, allowing for the fact that there wouldn't be much traffic on a Sunday. No. Better go home and have supper, then on to the office.

No real excuse for leaving Barbara in her sterile room. He replaced the phone, smiled at the girl who was smiling at him, and walked slowly back to his wife.

6

She looked up as he came in. 'Lock the door,' she said.

He knew what she meant, because her face had changed again, and there was the mad look in her eyes.

He managed a laugh. 'You can't lock these doors. Least, you can, but they've got the keys.'

Momentarily he thought, do all the visitors notice things like that, or is it just me, because I am what I am?

'Then put a chair under the knob!'

'Darling, they won't like it if we start turning hospital wards into honeymoon suites!'

'Then you can tell me what they do to you!'

He knew what was happening, but he hoped she would go through another of her mercurial changes.

'Do they wear kinky clothes? Do you undress them? Do they undress you like I used to? Tell me! I want to know! Do you have more than one of them at a time? Tell me!'

He sat on the bed again. 'There aren't any other women,' he said wearily. 'You don't really believe there are, do you?'

Her eyes were full of tears. 'Couldn't we . . . you know . . . here?'

He took her hands. 'When you're better,' he said.

'Will I get better?'

'Of course you'll get better! They keep telling me how much better you are every time I come.'

I don't believe them, he thought, but they say I have to give you every encouragement. That was the phrase. Every encouragement.

Then he thought, do I really want her to get better? Isn't it already too late?

'When you're better. When you're back home and we're a family again, all together.'

She smiled, and for a second he loved her as he had always loved her when she smiled.

'Family.'

'Yes.'

'How is Joanna?' Then, suddenly hard, 'Where is she? Why isn't she coming to see me?'

'You know where she is. We talked about it all half an hour ago. She's on this trip with some of the girls from her school. I told you. She phoned me from Athens on Friday night.'

Her face went blank, and she turned away.

'What day is it today?'

'Sunday.'

7

'Yes. Sunday. That's right. You told me all about it. Greece and all those archaeological sites. And going on a ship to the islands. You told me about it, and I'd forgotten.'

She looked up at him. 'I really am mad, aren't I?'

He said, 'I saw her off for the airport. Luton. They went from Victoria Coach Station. God what a place! But the very last thing she said to me was to remind me to give you her love.'

It wasn't quite true. The last words, and he could still hear them, and all the girls round had heard but she's still said them, she'd said, 'Daddy, I do love you so much.'

But she had said to pass on her love. She'd said it earlier.

'She's deserved it, that trip.'

Barbara smiled, again that bewitching smile. 'I remember, I was almost angry with you when you said she could go on the trip if she got a scholarship. I thought, if she didn't, it would be awful. All her friends going, and not her. It would look so mean.'

'I always knew she'd get the scholarship.'

It was true. He had faith in his daughter as he no longer had faith in anything else.

He said, 'Miss Bickerstaff, she took me aside at the bus station and said she thought Joanna was the sort of girl who'd get a First.'

'Who's Miss Bickerstaff?'

'The physics mistress. You know. The one with the glasses like the bottoms of a couple of wine bottles and the extraordinary figure. The one the girls all call Boobs.'

'She's not called Bickerstaff. She's called Bellamy. No. Not Bellamy. Burnett. Bessemer. Enid Bessemer, that's it!'

'Boobs.'

'Boobs. We know who we mean.'

They laughed, and for a moment it was as it had been a long time ago, the two of them relaxed, happy, at ease with each other.

Then she said, 'Now Joanna isn't home, it'll be easier for you to bring your women back.'

He was about to speak, but he realised it would be pointless.

They waited in silence, and then a nurse came with the usual allocation of pills. They all smiled at each other, and he had his excuse to leave. He nodded to the nurse, kissed Barbara on the forehead, and walked out of the nursing home into the warm, clear sun of the late afternoon. The forecasters had been promising a heatwave, but it hadn't happened.

He had left his car, without thinking consciously about it, so that he could get out of either of the exits from the car park without risk of being obstructed. He hadn't thought about it, just as he didn't consciously check the windows and the doors and the exact position of the wheels, to make sure that nobody had tampered with it. It was habit, done without thinking, like other men put out the milk at night, and then wondered if they had remembered to do so.

He was home by ten to six. He went through the routine that always surprised the Doyles' few visitors when they first met it. Someone had once watched Joshua countering all the assorted alarm systems and unlocking the first of the three locks on the front door, and remarked that now he knew what was meant by an Englishman's home being his castle.

Unsmiling, Joshua had said, 'Colditz was a castle.'

The house, without Joanna, ached with emptiness. On the mantlepiece in the living room there were photographs of her, first as a baby, then tracing her to young womanhood, but they only added to the emptiness. There were photographs of Barbara, too. There was one of the two of them on their wedding day; Joshua tall and gawky in the hired morning coat, Barbara radiant, waving to someone behind the cameraman. Then there was a studio portrait which she had laughingly called her passport photo for a charm school, and one taken in Prague a few days before he had had to send her home because she was becoming a security risk; and two of her with Joanna. Then there was the one of her laughing during a reception in Washington. That was the first time he had had to use force on her, to put her to bed and lock the door. Ironically, she was holding a glass of champagne. At that time he had had no idea of the other drinks, the gin in the clothes cupboard, the whisky in the lavatory cistern. She was holding a champagne glass and laughing, and it was noticeable that of the four men who were also in the photograph, three were looking at her and there was desire in their faces.

There were no other photographs of him, because it was policy to avoid being photographed whenever possible. He only kept the wedding photograph on view because he was barely recognisable, and because Barbara had once said, 'Don't ever move that. That is there to remind you that you are married to me!'

He switched on the televison, then switched it off again. There was very rarely anything in the early evening programmes that appealed to him. He opened the freezer chest, and selected a packet that promised *Gourmet's Choice, Tender Breasts of Chicken with*

Rich Cheese Stuffing, All Wrapped in Golden Crispy Crumbs, Two Servings. In Joshua's opinion, single servings were for anorexic dwarfs. He checked the instructions. Forty minutes at 450°. He switched on the oven to heat, and returned to the drawing room. He had a microwave oven, but it worked too quickly. It didn't kill enough empty time.

He cooked and ate the chicken, and put the plate into the dishwasher. It was still only a quarter to eight, but he wanted to get out of the house. It was a beautiful evening, the sun dipping down behind the oak tree his neighbour was so inordinately proud of. (He had changed the name of his house from Mayfield to The Oaks, although there was only one of them.)

If he arrived far too early, there was always the Unicorn, the pub favoured by the organisation because it had somehow maintained a degree of Victorian chaos that meant that people could meet, quite naturally, in smokey darkness and reasonable privacy. He didn't like it as a pub, and they didn't know how to keep their beer properly.

But the alternative was another three-quarters of an hour alone in a house haunted by a daughter who was somewhere the other side of Europe, and a wife lying quietly mad in a nursing home.

Anything was better than that.

Chapter Two

He left the grassier reaches of suburbia, and turned down towards Putney Bridge and the river. It was the only aspect of retirement that appealed to him; getting away from suburbia. He was not yet near retirement age, forty-two, but he knew that he would be regarded by Them as too valuable to be risked doing the things he enjoyed doing, the work he was best at.

He had seen the signs, younger men entrusted with the riskier, more challenging, more exciting operations. They had even dropped hints. Not quite buttoned-up, old man. Can't risk you on a thing like this. But it had been the challenge that had lured him into his world in the first place, and had kept him there ever since.

When the time came, when he directly requested to be put on an assignment only to be told that someone more expendable would be doing it instead, then he would resign.

One thing about Them. If you didn't try to trick Them, they looked after their own. They'd find him a job, something very confidential, probably quite important. Whatever it would be, it would certainly be a great deal better paid. It just wouldn't be the same, and Joshua hoped the day of decision would not come too soon.

The streets of London were nearly empty, handed over to parked cars and the litter that would be removed before the capital awoke in the morning. There was a pigeon pecking something in the middle of the road which didn't even move as he drove round it.

He turned off Northumberland Avenue into the little street behind it where JBH was based. The building, undistinguished early Victorian at the back of Northumberland Place, had a number of name plates of firms and professional associations on either side of the main door. The names could all be checked. The companies were registered at Company House; the two firms of solicitors were registered with the Law Society; Alderson, Cooper and Ware

11

were on the membership list of the Institute of Cost and Management Accountants; even the United Kingdom Waterways Trust was accepted by the Charity Commission. The fact that none of these organisations actually existed was known to few; but collectively they provided every reason why so many disparate people should use the building. Fewer people still knew of the corridor that linked the basement car park of Huber House, two doors away, with the main headquarters, a corridor reached by opening a door out of sight of the car park itself marked Fire Exit, a door that only opened if an unlikely combination of pressures were applied simultaneously to the door and the box which said Break Glass in Case of Emergency. The building itself was known to its normal users as JBH, because the top left-hand name plate happened to be for J.B. (Holdings) Ltd., supposedly a firm of property developers, based in Guernsey.

As he expected, he was early. He parked his car in his reserved space under Huber House, and went up to the Unicorn.

It seemed to have undergone a transformation. Whereas he had always known it as a haunt of people he vaguely recognised, albeit not, for the most part, people he wished to know well, it was now full of Japanese drinking whisky. From somewhere in the gloom a man was saying, dogmatically but untruthfully, 'This old inn was a favourite of Charles Dickens, a famous English author, 1812 to 1870.'

The Unicorn had clearly become part of some Sunday tourist itinerary. Joshua wondered fleetingly how much the landlord paid the guide, and backed out without buying a drink.

He looked at his watch. Eight forty-two.

The Old Man disliked people who turned up early almost as much as he disliked people who kept him waiting. If Joshua went into JBH, simply to have somebody to talk to, there would only be the minimal staff on duty, and if they weren't too busy to chat to a superior, they ought to be.

That was one of the handicaps of his chosen life, the inevitable loneliness: nobody except his family he could really talk to, and now, since Barbara's illness, not even that.

It had always been a lonely life. There was not just the loneliness of a policeman, a man different from his fellow men. There had been the extra loneliness as subtly, almost imperceptibly, it had become clear that he was being singled out. The police college at Bramshill, then the string of attachments and special assignments:

12

the undercover work investigating corruption in the Met itself; the year spent with the FBI in the States, and the other year going from British Embassy to British Embassy, checking the security, which really meant checking the personnel; the courses on terrorism and political corruption; the work in collaboration with MI5. Finally, unexpectedly, not the move that everybody had been predicting, into the Anti-Terrorist Squad, but a sideways move into JBH where his salary was paid by the Force as cover, but where his rank was never referred to, and where most of his colleagues seemed to have no police background at all.

The establishment knew that it needed a strong sword arm, and unwittingly, a long time ago, Joshua had been chosen. The State had benefited. The price, paid in stoically accepted isolation and loneliness, had been paid by him.

Seven minutes to nine. He walked down into the Huber House car park, and entered the corridor. As the actual JBH building was supposed to house only activities that would not work on Sundays, the main entrance into the headquarters itself was always kept locked after one o'clock on a Saturday afternoon. For the same reason the offices that were staffed during the weekend all looked inwards, over the courtyard.

At the second door (with *Danger: Fallen Masonry* hand-painted on it) he said 'Joshua Doyle one, one, one.' The Voice Identification worked immediately – occasionally it did not – and the door swung open, closing automatically after him as he broke the infra-red intruder detector.

In JBH he went into the main Duty Office, where Ames was recording an encoded message, and nodded acknowledgement to Joshua in the doorway. When Ames had finished, Joshua asked, 'Any idea why I'm wanted?'

'Not a clue, sir,' said Ames.

'What's come in?'

'Nothing much. Did you ever know someone called Hector Boulez?'

Boulez. A fat little man from the DST.

'Met him. In fact, he was supposed to be cooperating with us on a GRU defector.'

'He won't be cooperating any more. He's been shot. But the report is he was naked at the time in a girl's bed, so the DST are looking for the girl's boyfriend.'

'Hm.'

13

'Not the GRU.'

Ames flicked through some papers in front of him. 'Then there's an unconfirmed report of some British subjects kidnapped in Cyprus.'

'I didn't know they went in for kidnapping in Cyprus.'

'They probably don't. As I say, it's unconfirmed, and only graded C4. There's an Iranian student who's blown himself up in Manchester. Or else somebody else blew him up. Or else he was having a bath and the geyser exploded. We're waiting for details. And the only other thing of any interest is a CIA query about our checking procedures at GCHQ. But they know them anyway.'

'Yes.'

'Just, why are they asking?'

'Yes.'

Ames pushed the papers away. 'So I'm sorry, sir, but why he wants you upstairs, I've no idea.'

Joshua glanced at his watch. Two minutes to nine. 'I'll go and find out,' he said.

The Old Man's office was right at the top of the building; old servants' quarters in the eaves turned into a pair of offices, some sort of residential accommodation, and two or three other rooms whose role was not known to most of JBH. There were various rumours why whoever headed the Department had this eyrie. Some said it was to do with security; others that there had once been a Head who had gone insane, and had been locked up there until he died because he was too much of a risk to release; others that one of the first Heads had messages arriving by carrier pigeons who were trained to return to one of the offices which then served as a pigeon loft. Whatever the explanation, from the window, over variegated intervening rooftops, the tower of the Houses of Parliament could be seen: and it was understood that when the Old Man looked out in that direction and pronounced, he was, unofficially, unattributably, but unmistakably passing on orders and instructions that he had been given, orders and instructions he did not necessarily agree with, but which he had to accept.

The secretary who guarded the Old Man, and always reminded Joshua of the black bombazined concierges that the KGB put on every floor of Russian hotels, glowered up at Joshua, but was expecting him and let him pass without the tiresome formality of checking the identity of someone she saw every day.

The Old Man was peering vaguely out of the window, and turned as Joshua entered.

14

'Sit down,' he said. 'Sorry to drag you in on the Lord's day.'

Joshua sat in one of the chairs that were positioned so that the light, whether from the windows or from the electric light, fell on the visitor, and the Old Man, if he wanted to, could watch every expression.

'I'll start at the beginning,' said the Old Man. He pulled his pipe from his pocket and examined it thoughtfully.

'We've had a report from Cyprus about some half dozen – the figure isn't certain yet – some half dozen or so British subjects who've been kidnapped.'

'Ames downstairs mentioned it.'

The Old Man nodded. 'I was expecting you'd ask what had come in. Why I'd want to see you. Well, obviously, in a thing like that, normally I wouldn't. Want to see you, I mean.'

'No.'

'Despite the fact that, in my opinion, we haven't got a single agent in that part of the world I'd trust to send out for a pastrami sandwich, I wouldn't involve an operator with your experience on a bloody little kidnapping. But I've lined up a briefing session for tomorrow morning, oh-nine-thirty, and I'd be grateful if you'd attend.'

Joshua waited. The Old Man sucked noisily at his pipe.

'The background is that there was a cruise ship. Docked at Limassol. Everyone got off. Naturally, that sort of thing, all the different travel companies have laid on activities. Unless it's what they call free time, which means the customers have to find their own food. But among the various parties there were a couple of school parties.'

He had stopped sucking the pipe, and was looking straight at Joshua.

'It was one busload of school children who are provisionally reported to be missing.'

Joshua whispered, 'Joanna . . .'

'We don't know.'

Unexpectedly, gently, the Old Man put his hand on Joshua's shoulder. 'We have no names yet. But it was her school. You filled in the normal SOH form about her . . .'

SOH. Special Operational Hazard. The form that listed the everyday activities of himself, of his family: the everyday activities and also the breaks in routine, the holidays abroad, Barbara's nursing homes, that summer when Joanna had been an au pair in

15

France. It was all there somewhere in the building. When you were an official SOH, when the details were on the computer, you'd made it. You were officially recognised as important enough to be in real danger. You and your family.

'On the form you gave the dates and the name of the ship. The *Classic Dawn*. The computer threw it up.'

'Yes.' It wasn't real. It wasn't happening.

The Old Man said, 'I have to say again, we don't know. We haven't any details. No names. We should know a bit more by the briefing. But on the face of it, there doesn't seem much to be gained by kidnapping a few English schoolgirls. Not financially, I mean.'

'No.'

'But politically. Terrorists. If what they were really after was the daughter of a senior man in JBH . . .'

Chapter Three

'The position,' said Brigadier Lucksey-Hart brusquely, 'is unclear.'

They were in one of the two conference rooms on the third floor, a room too large and under-equipped for normal purposes, and therefore rarely used and smelling of dust. The Old Man had presumably picked it because of the presence of the man in the Wykehamist tie on his right at the head of the over-sized table, a man introduced as Sir something Joshua didn't catch. From the Commonwealth Office.

'Unclear,' repeated the Brigadier. 'Inadequate information. But what we have you know.'

Joshua glanced down at the pad in front of him on the table, a pad with his notes from the Brigadier's lengthy summary. He had long ago decided that Lucksey-Hart was a second-rater; one of those British soldiers destined to lose every battle until the last, by which time, with any luck, he would have been rumbled and replaced, slid-off sideways to something like Northern Command or JBH, where his shortcomings either didn't matter or could be overruled.

In fact, in his inadequate way, Lucksey-Hart had something that JBH could, and did, use. He was an incorrigibly hard worker, and convinced, like Mr Gradgrind, that facts alone were wanted in life. (Not that he would ever have heard of Mr Gradgrind.) The problem was that the world was full of facts, and Intelligence involved evaluation. Lucksey-Hart was quite unable to distinguish between wood and trees and it was left to his colleagues in JBH to assess the mass of assorted timber that he offered them.

The summary had taken some thirty-two minutes. Joshua knew that he could have given it in six.

The facts were, despite the Brigadier, simple and unquestioned. A modest cruise boat called the *Classic Dawn* had sailed from Piraeus at eight o'clock on Saturday morning. On board were two

17

hundred and eighteen passengers including two school parties total-
ling twenty-seven children and four adults. The children came from
St. Hilda's School, Guildford, and a school in New Hampshire. The
ship belonged to a Greek shipping line registered in Panama, and the
tour was organised by Classic World Educational Tours, a division
of Sunswept Holidays PLC of London. The voyage out had been
occupied, according to Lucksey-Hart, mostly in lectures about the
classical world the passengers were going to see, and must, Joshua
thought, have been pretty boring.

The ship had docked at Limassol, Cyprus, at approximately ten-
forty on the following morning. The passengers had been taken to
different buses. They had then set off to various destinations, to
avoid overcrowding the various sites. The bus carrying the girls from
St. Hilda's together with one member of staff and a driver who was
also a guide had headed north towards the capital, Nicosia. There
they were to visit the Cyprus Museum, the Museum of Folk Art, and
the Culture Centre, and take a brief look at the impressive Venetian
walls of the old town. At one o'clock they would meet children of the
other school for lunch at the Sans Rival Hotel.

But after the bus had left Limassol on the featureless road to
Nicosia, it had not been seen again.

At first nobody had noticed, because there was no over-all guide in
Nicosia. But eventually someone had told Sunswept in Nicosia, who
had phoned Sunswept in Limassol, and when it became clear that the
bus had certainly left, enquiries were made through the Tourist
Police. As it happened one of their number reached Limassol as the
phone call was taking place, a man who had just driven down from
Nicosia. No, he said, there had not been a stray Sunswept bus on the
road or he would have noticed it, because that was part of his job.

The police were told. Sunswept's representative in Nicosia phoned
his office in London, who told him to take a hold on himself and find
the missing bus. This was at three-twenty in the afternoon Cyprus
time, one-twenty English time. With some initiative, the Nicosia
agent hired three taxis, took one himself to drive to Limassol, and
ordered the other two to explore any of the comparatively few roads
that led off the main road between the port and the capital. At four-
fifteen Cyprus time he phoned London again from Limassol, and
made his third call at five-twenty, three-twenty English time, after
the taxi drivers had also reported failure.

There were those at the time who thought that the Cyprus police
were over-reacting when they sent out search parties, and were,

18

frankly, panicking when they telexed London. As events were to prove they behaved very wisely. The routine message reached JBH at two minutes past six Cyprus time, two minutes past four at the rear of Northumberland Avenue. The computer operator, bored as he expected to be on a Sunday, fed the machines, and to his total amazement came up with the link with one of the organisation's most senior officers. It had been just four minutes after that that Joshua had been contacted at the Brookside Hospital.

The Brigadier reached his peroration. 'And the odds are, obviously, that the damn fool driver has simply got lost and doesn't dare admit it. On the other hand . . .'

He paused and checked his notes. Joshua thought, here is a man who says, 'on the other hand,' when he can't think what he is going to say next.

Lucksey-Hart found his place. 'On the other hand, Cyprus is a very vulnerable place. Important. To us. And the possibility of the disappearance of some British citizens, in particular British children, could well be a matter we should take seriously.'

He put the sheet he was reading from to the back of the stack in his hand, found that the next page was blank, and stopped abruptly.

There was a long silence. The Old Man was sitting under a crude Ministry of Defence sign saying Smoking Forbidden. He lit his pipe and puffed on it thoughtfully.

'Two things,' said the Old Man. He had a strange voice, unusually deep, but unusually soft. 'One, if indeed we are talking about a bus that is at this moment tucked behind the donkey shed of the driver's mistress, the schoolgirls being entertained to sweetmeats while the driver pleasures the woman, then we all wasting our time.'

He paused, then said, 'I personally don't think that is what has happened, and I can't think of any other comparatively innocent reason for the bus to have disappeared. I happen to know that road . . .'

It was a source of continuing surprise to JBH just how well travelled the Old Man proved to be. (There had been a moment once when he had thrown in the remark, 'Of course, nobody in their senses would use the northern route into Lhasa.') He went on, 'If I had to use a word to describe the road, I would use the word, boring. Nobody could have an accident on it unnoticed. And I can't recall anywhere a vehicle could stray off accidentally. Point two, let us suppose the worst.'

There was a sudden sharp pain across Joshua's chest. For a

moment he thought, Christ, is this a heart attack, then it went away.

'Let us suppose,' said the Old Man, 'that someone, some people, some group, have kidnapped these children. We in this room would tend to assume political motives, but that is only because we naturally think like that. Did whoever took those children know which bus would hold which school? If I were a kidnapper . . .'

He chuckled gently at some forbidden memory, then continued, 'If I were a kidnapper I would more likely choose a busload of American children. I would think, rightly or wrongly, that their parents and their governments would be more likely to pay up. The American Air Force might well wipe out some wretched city in revenge afterwards, but they would be no danger to me personally. The kidnapper. So did they pick on this bus by chance?'

He puffed reflectively on his pipe. 'Or did they know that among those children there was the daughter of . . .?'

He vaguely waved his hand towards Joshua.

Joshua felt them turning to look at him. He knew he should say something, a stiff upper lip message, something about duty and responsibility, or perhaps a half-laugh and an easy dismissal of the whole matter.

But he couldn't speak. He had nothing to say. He knew, quite simply, that there was no choice for him.

Finally it was Ames who spoke. He was perhaps the most junior officer in the room, but he seemed at least to understand Joshua's silence, and Joshua was grateful.

'Assuming it is a kidnapping, sir,' he said, looking respectfully towards the Old Man, now hardly visible behind his pipe smoke, 'if it is political, what do we know about groups active in the area?'

It was a generous move on Ames' part to help Joshua. It was a stupid question, because the answer was not in the room, but in the files and the computers; and the Old Man was not the person to ask.

But perhaps the Old Man sensed the reason for the question. For a moment the smoke cleared, and he inclined his head to the right.

'I think Sir mutter could give us the background,' he said. Joshua realised that he didn't know the Wykehamist's name either.

The Wykehamist, a man of about forty with the complexion of a baby and the gravitas of a Chinese philosopher, leant forward, his elbows on the table, the tips of his long fingers touching.

'The secret of Cyprus is Aphrodite, the goddess of love,' he began incomprehensibly. 'It was on Cyprus, near Paphos actually,

20

that Aphrodite stepped from the sea, borne ashore on, not to put too fine a point on it, the sperm from the severed testicles of her father.'

Joshua had a sudden sense of unreality. His daughter was missing. She might be in the hands of terrorists. And he was sitting in this stuffy room listening to a man talking about mythology.

The Wykehamist's eyes were closed. 'She was beautiful as Cyprus is beautiful. Everybody wanted her. Hephaestus, Ares, Hermes, Adonis, Phaeton, gods and mortals, they all lusted after her. Even Zeus. The Egyptians, the Phoenicians, the Romans, the Assyrians, the Persians, the Franks, the Knights Templar, the Venetians, the Ottoman Empire, the British – everybody except the Greeks themselves – they have all ruled the island of Aphrodite.'

His eyes opened, very pale blue eyes, almost colourless. Joshua got the impression that the world of mythology was not only more interesting than the twentieth century, but also more real, to the man from the Commonwealth Office.

He continued. 'The British effectively took over Cyprus in 1878, and legally in 1914. You must realise that Aphrodite is not a demanding goddess. Not particularly intelligent, rather cowardly, not particularly difficult to control. She does not ask to be fought over, only to be loved and seduced. So we did not send the elite of our manhood to serve her. We sent officials for whom it was thought that St. Helena might be too taxing a posting. Because Aphrodite smiled so wantonly perhaps we underestimated what she had to offer. Besides her fair hair and silver feet, her rose-tipped breasts and a *mons pubis* that promised ecstasy, she offers two reasonable harbours, two airports, two sovereign bases with a total area of ninety-nine square miles, and most important of all sites for radio-monitoring stations that cover most of southern Russia.'

He glanced around, perhaps expecting questions, but nobody spoke so he went on. 'The population consists mostly of Greeks and Turks in the ratio of roughly four to one. The Greeks are regarded by many mainland Greeks as rather provincial, not terribly cultured, and with the most dreadful accents. Rather as some English regard, say, the British of South Africa or Ulster. But they saw themselves as standard-bearers of the great Hellenic dream. The Turks were really what you might call pre-Ataturk Turks; the last residue of the Ottoman Empire. But many other men have tried to win Aphrodite. In the population there are also Armenians and Maronites, Lebanese and Egyptians, Jews talking of Jerusalem and English talking of taxation.'

21

The room was getting warmer and warmer. No air circulated. But it was impossible to open the windows because the microphone sensors would have been disturbed.

'In the last war the Cyprus Regiment played a long and undistinguished role on the Allied side. Then the Greeks in Cyprus began agitating for Enosis. Union with Greece. We didn't take it very seriously because Greece was having a particularly nasty civil war, reflected in Greek politics in Cyprus, so we argued that they were bluffing because if they *did* get Enosis, then fifty percent of them would be shot depending on who won on the mainland. The Turkish Cypriots were on our side, because they were a pretty inert lot, and the last thing they wanted was to be governed by pushy Greeks in Athens. Anyway, such Turks as didn't spend two thirds of the daylight hours asleep tended to be in the police force, which remained loyal.'

His voice acquired a sing-song tone as he said, 'It seemed to be as it always had been, Aphrodite asking for trinkets she didn't really expect to be given and could well live without.'

Then back to his normal tones. 'The craving for Enosis, which never interested the mainland Greeks much, led to the EOKA terrorism. The Germans would have put this down in a week with a section of SS, but we're different, and we failed to put it down over four or five years. In 1960 we made Cyprus an independent republic within the Commonwealth. There was a Greek Cypriot President and a Turkish Cypriot Vice-President. It was a typical compromise of the sort the British are so good at; sensible, rational, fair, unworkable and totally unacceptable to all the people of Cyprus. You can't tell Aphrodite that she will love one man on Mondays, Wednesdays and Fridays, and another man for the rest of the week.'

He gave an almost imperceptible shrug. It was difficult to tell what his own point of view was, except in terms of mythology. 'So instead of trying to kill us in a rather half-hearted way, they started killing each other. Not in very large quantities by modern standards, but enough to cause ill-feeling. Since 1964 there has been a UN peace-keeping force in the island, keeping the peace. More or less. In '74 the Junta who ran Greece at the time installed an ex-EOKA lunatic as President in a coup d'état. The mainland Turks invaded the island. Somebody seemed to have been expecting it, because the main danger the Turkish paratroops ran into was getting castrated through falling on a TV camera's telephoto lens.'

The Old Man asked, 'Who made sure it was expected?'

'I don't know. If I did know, I would be forbidden to tell you. At a guess, whoever ran Greece and Turkey at the time. I mean, effectively ran them. Not the governments.'

From his expression the Old Man knew the answer to his question before he asked it. 'Meaning?'

'The Cousins.'

Joshua looked up. He had not expected a man from the Commonwealth Office to use the rather dated Service slang for the CIA.

'The Turks occupied roughly the northern third of the island,' the Wykehamist continued. 'In '75 they proclaimed northern Cyprus as an independent state. Nobody recognises this state except Turkey. To be fair, due to a misunderstanding, Bangladesh recognised it for half an hour. Literally.'

There was a murmur of amusement, but the man from the Commonwealth Office looked round the table and he wasn't smiling.

He said very quietly, 'The island is divided by walls and minefields. In the north the villages are nearly empty because there aren't enough Turks to fill the houses that used to be Greek. The hotels are mouldering because you can only get there through Turkey, and in any case they have no idea how to run a tourist industry. The south is over-crowded, riddled with refugees, booming vulgarity, none of the beauty of the old towns of the north. Vengeance hangs in the air like the scent of lemon blossom. Most bitter of all, the two sides conscript their young men, Aphrodite's future lovers, to glare across the barbed wire and prepare to fight the only possible enemy, which is each other.'

He looked round the room. 'But love is not a rational emotion. It was Pallas Athene who was wise, not Aphrodite. It is unreasonable to expect Aphrodite's admirers to see both sides of an argument. And Aphrodite has been violated. Aphrodite was not seduced. She was raped.'

Unexpectedly he turned to Jimmy Ames. 'You asked about active terrorist groups,' he said. Ames blushed. Ask a silly question and get a diatribe in answer.

'Because of its geographical position Cyprus is quite abnormally full of Intelligence agents.' The hands came apart to indicate the scope of the problem. 'We have our bases, and the KGB and the GRU have their agents to penetrate them. And penetrate the RAF operating them, if one believes what one reads and is later denied.

The Americans, of course, are there. And the French. And Mossad, in rather large numbers. Plus a lot of part-timers. The reason for this is that after the last war a great many people who thought that somebody might be looking for them got washed up in Cyprus, and the habit of incompetent espionage stuck and spread among later generations. Then there are groups which are in that fringe area between espionage and terrorism. For example, some of the old EOKA terrorists were tied to Communist groups on the Greek mainland who were in turn partly run by the KGB. Other EOKA terrorists were on the right, and had links with the Greek Junta, who were run by the CIA. Mossad has in place on the island, or can get them there in a matter of hours, enough Shin Bet to make up a hit team to cope with anything the PLO plan to put up against them. Plus, no doubt, the legacy of the Jews who were attached to the American Jewish Relief during the days in the forties and fifties when Cyprus had camps full of what were called Illegal Jewish Immigrants, who were mostly let out of Eastern Europe by the Communists, financed by the Americans, and run by the Irgun Zvai Leumi and the Stern Gang, who were in turn the nucleus of Mossad. Not to mention the Israeli Government. But we don't mention that, because it's not in anybody's interest. In addition you will recall that Gadaffi from time to time identifies Cyprus as a particular target. In terms of ordinary terrorists you can take your pick. They're all there, either resident or in transit.'

'So we won't know until and unless we're contacted,' said the Old Man.

He looked round the room, his eyes passing over Joshua as just another member of JBH. 'I think it's pretty obvious that we play this as close to our chests as possible. If we announce that there are possibly – I say possibly, because we've no hard evidence as yet – possibly a group of English schoolgirls missing, we'll have everything from the Provos to the Red Brigade claiming them.'

Lucksey-Hart said gruffly, 'As you say, we've no hard evidence.' He obviously resented the virtual dismissal of his suggestion of a lost bus-driver.

'Usual bloody business of waiting.'

From the corner of the table furthest from Joshua, Paul Delacourt asked, 'What's our position with the Cyprus Government?'

Delacourt had come into JBH through the Diplomatic Corps, or rather, after a scandal that made it advisable for him to leave the

24

Diplomatic Corps. He knew exactly what was, and what was not possible in that arcane society; his combination of ability and charm had been easing his way upwards when it had also eased his way sideways into the bed of the wife of a GCMG.

'Complicated,' said the Old Man. 'They all have to say they're still committed to Enosis, though they'd really rather be independent. They think we ought to pay for our bases in the island, but they know damned well they'd be another Lebanon, only with the Turks, if we weren't there. We lent them the SAS over a hijacked plane, so they owe us one. One of their Ministers is KGB and two juniors are CIA. We can lean on them, if only because they want tourists. But we mustn't be seen to lean.'

'Sounds a familiar story,' said someone Joshua didn't identify.

'Yes. They'll do anything to keep their noses clean.'

'Including keeping quiet?'

'Especially keeping quiet.'

The Old Man vaguely waved his pipe towards Mike Berrisford. 'I know it's a bit early for your blackboard and chalk stuff, but . . .'

Berrisford smiled. He enjoyed the title of Assessment Coordination Officer, a title deliberately vague even by JBH standards. In fact, on more operations than not he was the link between whoever did the planning in JBH and whoever carried it out in the field. As the Old Man explained to new members of JBH, it was not normal policy for JBH officers to endanger their lives; not, he then added, because anybody thought they were particularly valuable, or that anybody liked them very much, but because it took longer and cost more to train them than it did a Sandbagger or a volunteer in the SAS or the SBS.

'It's far too early yet, yes, sir,' said Berrisford. He spoke clipped military English, which he had learnt in an elocution school, determined to hide his Birmingham origins. The same deep-seated insecurity was reflected in the Rifle Brigade tie he always wore, the shoes with the soles polished, and the MC and bar that he had won before he was wounded and transferred to JBH. 'I've had a chat with a couple of contacts on the island, in the services, and also with an Irish major with the UN peace-keeping people who's anxious to help because we know a bit about him. They all said more or less the same thing. Interesting, that. They said they didn't see how anybody could make the bus disappear. Sunswept are about the biggest tour operators in the island, and their buses are bright orange and green, would you believe. Hardly inconspicuous. And Cyprus has a

25

pretty big standing army for its size, plus the British forces, plus the UN. And damn few roads, considering. So the bus'll turn up. Not much doubt about that.'

The Old Man said quietly, 'And the girls?'

'Yes.' Berrisford hesitated, then said, 'The way I see it, sir, either they're still with the bus, or they aren't. Perhaps they are, just . . . well, lost. But when I suggested that to the people out there, they didn't actually flip about it. But supposing they're kidnapped, they're either in the bus being moved somewhere – and they should have got wherever they're going by now, because they've had twenty-two hours and the bloody island's only seventy-five miles by thirty, excluding the Turkish bit – or they've been taken somewhere and hidden. In which case presumably they'll send a ransom note. The only other alternative is that somebody is making a political gesture and – '

He stopped abruptly, remembering that Joshua was sitting at the table.

'Yes,' said the Old Man smoothly, and continued with the briefing. Joshua listened as Section by Section the requirements and degrees of readiness were outlined. It was just like any other briefing: except that they were not talking about kidnapped British subjects, they were talking about Joanna. In many ways it was a much less urgent briefing than most, and at the back of his mind there was the suspicion that it was only taking place at all because of him. Why? He forced himself to ask the question and worry out an answer. There were two possibilities. One, the girls were in greater danger because one of them was his daughter. Two, the briefing was a gesture of sympathy towards him.

He knew how JBH worked. JBH did not operate on a basis of sympathy for anybody.

Finally the Old Man looked round, eyebrows raised. Nobody spoke, and he rose to his feet. He murmured something to the Wykehamist, who nodded, and then came over to Joshua as the rest of them started to head towards the door.

'I don't want you to think we're all quite inhuman,' he said quietly. 'We'll do everything. You know that.'

'Yes.' Then because it sounded a little flat, Joshua added, 'Thanks.'

'I know what you're going through,' said the Old Man. 'I lost a daughter myself.'

Joshua watched the Old Man leave, his juniors imperceptibly

parting before him. He realised that although he was as close to the Old Man as anybody in JBH, this was the first time he had ever mentioned his family.

Then Joshua realised something else. The Old Man thought that Joanna was already dead.

Chapter Four

The telex arrived at eight minutes past eleven, and was decoded within five minutes. Just before midday Joshua was summoned to the Old Man, and was surprised to see the Wykehamist still there, sitting beside the desk.

Silently, the Old Man handed Joshua the telex. FROM HEAD-QUARTERS SECOND BRIGADE GREY WOLVES STOP WE DEMAND IMMEDIATE RECOGNITION OF REPUBLIC OF NORTH CYPRUS BY BRITISH GOVERNMENT STOP IF RECOGNITION NOT GIVEN WE WILL EXECUTE SINGLY BRITISH SUBJECTS NOW IN OUR HANDS STOP NAMES OF BRITISH SUBJECTS FOLLOW STOP ENID BESSINGER JOSEPHINE COWLES PENELOPPY BAKER APRIL EDGE-WORTH JOANNA DALE PALINE TROOP HELEN OAKES COSTAS GAVALAS STOP FURTHER INSTRUCTIONS WILL FOLLOW.

'They've spelt some of the names wrong,' said the Old Man quietly, 'but the school confirms those are the ones who are missing.'

Joshua put the telex down on the desk in front of him. 'The first one's a teacher,' the Old Man added.

'I know,' Boobs, he thought. They call her Boobs.

'And they assume that Costas what's-his-name must be the driver of the bus. The drivers also act as guides, apparently. But they're checking that.'

Joanna Dale. They'd got her name wrong. Perhaps that meant they didn't know who she was. Perhaps they knew and just got it wrong. Perhaps it didn't matter anyway. They were just going to do what they said they were going to do.

He felt himself distancing from the problem. Incredibly, he was seeing it as he would another crisis. There had been many, and he was assessing it just like the others. He knew this feeling wouldn't last, but it was happening and he was grateful.

'Who sent this?' he asked.

'Ankara,' said the Old Man. 'One doesn't ask how they got it.'

'No. Do we know what language it was originally in?'

'English.'

That was bad. The Grey Wolves were dangerous enough, but it would have been better if the group had been based in Turkey with only tenuous links with Cyprus. Then, presumably, they would have written in Turkish. But this message looked as though it had been written by someone with a good knowledge of English. Someone educated in English. A Cypriot.

'Ankara got it this morning, they say. They told our Embassy who encoded it and sent it to the Foreign Office. They sent it here.' Then the Old Man said, 'At least it looks as though Joanna was alive when they sent it.'

He didn't say that Joanna was alive as they spoke, because Joshua was a professional and knew that the message meant nothing of the kind. It meant that Joanna had been alive at the time she told them her name.

Joshua suddenly wondered. She knew about his work, or at least she knew as much as she had to. Had she deliberately given a slightly wrong name, knowing that he would recognise her while not risking the extra danger?

He felt sure that was what had happened. She was his daughter and he was proud of her, and she would have thought of that.

Unexpectedly, the Wykehamist spoke. 'It's a particularly tricky one, this,' he said. 'We have absolutely no room for manoeuvre at all.'

The Old Man said, 'Joshua Doyle, Sir rupp.' He obviously hadn't remembered the name, and now it was too late to ask. 'From the Commonwealth Office.'

'Yesterday,' said Joshua.

The Wykehamist half closed his eyes. 'They say they want us to recognise the Republic of Northern Cyprus. What they call Kybris. As far as we are concerned, the inhabitants of northern Cyprus are British subjects, and are governed by the Government of Cyprus. The position is absurd. If we wish to know what is happening in, say, Famagusta or Kyrenia, we do not ask anybody who has any authority in those places. We don't even ask anyone who might be going there. We ask people who under no circumstances whatsoever could possibly go to Famagusta or Kyrenia, who would probably be shot if they even tried.'

He opened his pale eyes and looked at Joshua. 'These people in northern Cyprus are British subjects, with, for example, the rights of British subjects to come to Britain. But they regard themselves as citizens of a country we deny exists. When one of them produces papers proving this citizenship we pretend he hasn't done so, and give him new British documents.' He paused, then said, 'I gather that part of the standard anti-terrorist technique is to play for time by hinting at compromises.'

Both Joshua and the Old Man nodded.

'In this case that is impossible,' said the man from the Commonwealth Office.

Joshua said, 'With respect, how we play is up to us.'

'No.'

Joshua looked to the Old Man for support, but he was showing a sudden interest in his pipe.

'I will explain, and you will understand.' The Wykehamist examined his finger nails. 'One. The Turks are using Cyprus as we used Australia. To house their problem families. There are some sixty thousand of these people from the mainland. As we regard the population of Cyprus as British subjects, the only way we can avoid having these people not just in Kyrenia but in Kettering is to pretend they don't exist. Every time a man from my Department drives into northern Cyprus to give documents to the citizens of this non-existent country, he passes villages with smoke coming from the chimneys of the houses, and people from Anatolia pouring in and out of the doorways. But this can't be the case, because these houses belong to Greek Cypriots who have fled, and the villages are deserted. If the houses were really occupied, then these Turks would be British subjects, which would be absurd. Right?'

'Yes.'

'That is point one. Point two is that there are between twenty-five and thirty-five thousand Turkish troops in northern Cyprus. Three times as many soldiers as we have in Ulster. These are foreign troops occupying part of a member state of the British Commonwealth. Obviously, this is intolerable. So they don't exist either. Point three is that Turkey is an essential part of NATO, and a more valuable military ally than Greece. Let alone Cyprus, the island of Aphrodite.'

He flexed his fingers, making the joints crack. 'The last and possibly most important point of all is that the only solution to these problems is time. Time for the Turks to realise what it is costing

30

them, maintaining an army in Cyprus. Time for the Greeks in the south to forget about their family houses in the north, and concentrate on what they enjoy most, making money. Time for the resentment over our bases to die down, so they become part of the scenery. You must realise that nobody really *cares*. The mainland Greeks don't care. The mainland Turks don't care. The Cypriot Turks are far happier now than they were under the Greeks. They'd like the mainland Turks to go home, but they don't care enough to do anything about it. The Greek Cypriots do care, because they lost most. But every day that passes they care a little less . . .'

He leant forward and picked up the telex. 'We cannot compromise, or offer to compromise, because that implies that we might move. That we might act. And that we cannot do.'

Joshua said, 'We have to do something.' Then, pointedly, 'I don't think it is British Government policy to ignore terrorists who kidnap British citizens.'

'What they are suggesting is not simply unacceptable. It has a false premise. It implies that there is such a thing as the Government of North Cyprus for us to recognise. There is no such body. There is no such state.'

Joshua felt his body tensing, but he kept his voice level. 'What do you suggest we do, then?'

'We will deal through the authorised Government.'

'The Government of the Republic of Cyprus.'

'Yes.'

The man from the Commonwealth Office rose elegantly to his feet. 'I have no doubt at all they will do everything in their power to help,' he said. 'Apart from being very discreet. They are looking for British investment, and British tourists. Neither interest is helped by kidnapping British citizens.'

He turned to the Old Man. 'I must be off. I'm having lunch with my Minister, and there are a number of things I have to prepare before I meet him.'

Then he smiled at Joshua. 'I'm sure the Cyprus Government will be splendid. But I wouldn't put too much confidence in the Turks, if I were you. They don't like the Grey Wolves. Obviously. Especially since one of them tried to assassinate the Pope. It gives Turkey such a bad name. But on the other hand, what the Grey Wolves are demanding in this instance is, after all, Turkish Government policy . . .'

He smiled again, and left. He didn't seem to need the normal security escort.

31

The Old Man looked out of the window towards Big Ben.

'You are to come off this case,' he said, then went on without changing the timbre of his voice. 'You are perfectly entitled of course to make a formal protest. It is felt that inevitably you would be too personally involved. You might take unnecessary operational risks. That is the belief. You might endanger your own life and the security of the Department.'

He turned and started to stuff tobacco into his pipe, the usual shreds somehow escaping onto the floor.

'All we can do now is wait,' he said. 'For perhaps a day. Even two days. After that, if you ask my opinion, I think you need a break. I've been looking up your records, and you're long overdue for leave. The last time, if I recall, you had to cancel because your wife was ill. Right?'

Joshua, uncertain what was coming next, nodded. He would make his protest, too damned right he would make his protest, but he knew to let the Old Man finish.

'After that,' said the Old Man finding his matches, 'I would suggest a complete change. Go somewhere you don't know. Right away from the office. I dare say I could find someone to fix you up. We have our contacts, after all.'

He lit his pipe, and concentrated momentarily on getting it going to his satisfaction.

'Somewhere in the sun. Mediterranean, perhaps. Somewhere you would have no responsibilities, no need to report, no links with the office at all. What about Cyprus . . .?'

Chapter Five

Brookside Hospital was the sixth hospital in which Barbara had been a patient. It was fashionable, in that household names murmured about it when deciding where to send the problem embarrassments of their families. It was comfortable, discreet, and expensive. From Joshua's point of view its position on the Hampshire borders was near enough to his home to enable him to visit his wife every Sunday; and far enough away to free him of the guilt of not visiting her virtually daily. It was once a small Georgian country house in 400 acres of land. Now, new white and glass wings srpouted from the original building, and the estate had been trimmed to a manageable twenty-two acres. The brook after which the house had been named ran through the land that had been sold off when the estate was sold to the American company who founded the hospital. The brook had never been economic.

Joshua arrived just before three. The day was fine, and the hospital gleamed in the early summer sun. There was the usual smell, a smell that Joshua disliked, a smell of excessive cleanliness, almost as though nature had been scrubbed away and sterilised.

As he pushed his way through the revolving doors he was still uncertain what, if anything, he should tell Barbara. Not the truth, that was out of the question. But should he invent some story about why he might not be able to visit her for a while? Or wouldn't she notice, locked in the timelessness of insanity?

The nurse on the reception desk smiled at him as he came in. Apart from the fact that he was a regular visitor, no trouble, and as such popular, the junior staff were instructed always to smile at visiting relatives.

'Good afternoon, Mr Doyle,' she said. 'Doctor Marshall would like to have a word with you before you visit your wife.'

She pressed an electric bell, and some sort of trainee – Joshua had never troubled to remember the ranks revealed by the uniforms – led him along the corridor to Marshall's office.

The trainee tapped on Marshall's door, smiled at Joshua, and ushered him in. Joshua had a fleeting suspicion that the trainees learnt deportment first, and only subsequently nursing.

Joshua had never liked Marshall. He placed the doctor in his late thirties, some ten years younger than himself, but already Marshall had acquired a polished charm that was both patronising and subtly offensive. Marshall spent just long enough finishing a note he was writing to establish that he was a very busy man, then looked up, smiled glacially, and indicated a chair.

Joshua sat.

'I thought it might be helpful if I had a word with you,' said Marshall. 'I don't see as much of you as I do of some relatives, so you might not be absolutely up to date about your wife's therapy.'

Marshall flipped through a folder. He clearly wasn't reading it. 'There is drug therapy, and we're trying that. Frankly, what drug works with a particular patient, and why, we can really only find that out by trial and error. With your wife, we're being more successful now than we were.'

Joshua thought, and that poor woman was crucified because you don't really know what you're bloody-well doing.

'The prognosis is not unencouraging.' Marshall looked up and smiled. 'I'm sure it would be helpful if you were able to see her more often.'

Before Joshua could speak, Marshall added, 'Though you've explained that you sometimes work irregular hours.' A pause, then, 'For this Government department.'

And we all know that every Government department works nine to five. If that.

There had always been this problem, ever since he had dropped out of the mainstream. His department was listed, if anybody knew where to look. It was allowed for, just, in government expenditure, but the costs were broken down under headings designed to mislead, not explain. The phone number he had given the hospital, if there was an emergency, would get an answering machine that spoke of temporary overloading of internal lines due to electrical work, requested a number to call, and promised to reply within five minutes. Within those five minutes the call would be traced and the identity of the caller established. His occupation had to remain a question, but a question that was not actually asked. His neighbours accepted, as far as he could tell without demur, that he worked for the police, not the uniformed police, more the Home Office, that sort of thing.

'We have managed, despite the difficulties, to establish a bond with your wife. Now, she trusts us.'

And you trust her, God forgive you. You believe her.

'I think you'd agree, she hasn't had an easy life.'

What the hell had she been saying? He felt too mentally exhausted to press the point. Anyway, what would be the use? They'd believe her, because, even in her wildest worlds of fantasy she always sounded more convincing than he did, when he was speaking the straight, literal, pedestrian truth. Not that he could often allow himself that luxury. It was part of the job, the obfuscation of truth.

'But I really do believe we are making progress.'

'But, frankly, it would make our work here easier if she felt that she could rely on . . .' Again there was the smile. 'On help and understanding from you.'

Joshua said nothing. He sat there, and took it. Even if he had been permitted to explain, it would have been a betrayal of his wife. And, of course, he was not permitted to explain.

But suppose he was, for some bizarre reason, allowed, just once, to recount the long, confused and confusing story. How, from what had seemed tiny, silly, inconsequential moments when her behaviour had threatened him and his work and all that lay behind him, from those incidents which he had hardly noticed up until the time when, walking round Regent's Park with the Old Man like something out of a fifties movie, it had been explained to him that Barbara blocked his way to the very top. Looking back, it had been done with superb tact: what he had suspected, that he was being groomed possibly even to take over, all that was now blocked by his wife. It had been put to him so well. The Office would help in any way it could. What had the Old Man really meant? That they would somehow arrange a divorce which they obviously knew Barbara would oppose every inch of the way? That they would find one of those small-part agents they kept for occasions like this, men of great charm and exceptional good looks, men who really understood very little of what they were supposed to do and nothing of the reasons why, that some such man would be produced from wherever he was being kept, and released with instructions to

35

seduce and compromise his wife? Is that what the Old Man had been offering?

Or had the real, dark offer been the ultimate offer?

There was no way in which, now, he would ever learn. But even if he told the psychiatrist across the desk everything that had happened, it was inconceivable that he would be believed.

'If, as you say,' said Marshall, 'it really is difficult for you to see your wife more often – and I think I have explained that she wants your company more than anything else, she talks a great deal about getting better really solely in order to be able to live with you again – if it really is impossible, couldn't your daughter come instead? It wouldn't be as therapeutically beneficial, of course, but it would persuade her that she isn't totally separated from her family . . .'

If you are too bloody selfish to make the effort, can't you sacrifice Joanna?

'She's abroad.' He wasn't going to explain. To be fair to Marshall, he could know nothing of the damage his patient had done. He had never seen Joanna crying helplessly because of what her mother had told her. He had no idea how long it had taken, how painful had been the process of bridging the gap between father and daughter that had been carved by lies. Paranoid lies. The doctor could not possibly understand that for years the father had been father, mother, and enemy. Even when, frightened, Joanna had first menstruated, it had been to the father that she had, finally, to turn, humiliated and resentful, because the school had only confused her, and the mother had not been there.

Marshall spoke on. Joshua was barely listening, because he recognised a man making a show of exposing his expertise. He saw it often enough among the government officials with whom he sometimes found himself working. At the end Marshall rose, extended a hand, and Joshua shook it.

'It may take time,' said the doctor. 'But as long as she needs us, we'll be here.'

If you can afford our charges.

Dismissed, he was escorted down towards his wife's room, a nurse walking half a pace ahead of him as though he did not know the way.

'She's been given a tranquilliser,' said the nurse in a lowered voice as though the message was somehow indecent. 'Doctor thought . . .'

36

He followed her down the corridor, past a well-dressed woman sitting in a chair, who smiled at him. Was she a patient or just another visitor, he wondered idly. It was sometimes difficult to tell. There had been one afternoon when he had been kept waiting and had chatted affably to a woman he later discovered had twice tried to kill her child. They'd talked about the National Health.

'She'll probably be in bed,' the nurse added. 'It's just that . . .'

It was going to be difficult, he knew that. He had thought what to say, he had stayed awake considering the pros and cons. In a way it was easier that they had decided to impose a security black-out for the moment. Otherwise, if it had just been a medical problem, he supposed he would have had to tell the hospital, and let them decide what, if anything, Barbara should know.

The nurse opened the door. 'A visitor!' she said. Joshua nodded, and went over and kissed his wife. She was propped up in bed, the sheet and blankets taut across her body. The nurse simpered and left.

'I know I'm ill,' said Barbara, 'but why do they have to treat me as a mental defective?'

'It's part of their training. Treat the patient as an idiot, and the relative as a threat.'

He sat in the leatherette chair by the bed, uncomfortably low.

'I saw Dr. Fluckberg today,' said Barbara. 'He asks me to call him Bruno.'

'So would I if I was called Fluckberg.'

'But I can't call him Bruno. I really can't! The only Bruno I've ever known was a toy kangeroo!'

'Then think of him as a marsupial.'

'With *that* accent?' She laughed. She looked ten years younger than she had on Sunday. 'Actually, he's very pleased with me. He said I was much better.'

'You are. You're better every time I see you.'

It wasn't true, but they all told him that she needed encouragement.

'But you don't see me very often, do you?'

Her voice had changed. It was suddenly hard, petulant.

'I saw you yesterday!'

'No you didn't.'

'Darling, today is Monday and I was here yesterday. You remember.'

She looked suspicious, but she didn't answer.

'Actually, I may have to miss next Sunday. Work.'

37

If only he could talk to her. If only he could share what was happening. But if he told her, would she understand? Would she even remember it later? Wouldn't he just risk upsetting her, pushing her back into that black world she was trying to leave, and all for nothing.

She said, 'It can't be much fun for you. All alone.'

'It won't be long now.'

'Me not there to cook, and look after the house, and do nice things to you in bed.' Then she stopped. 'I'm not really getting better,' she said. 'They'll let me out of here, I suppose. But I'll come back. Here or somewhere else.'

'No you won't.'

'I wish I didn't hate myself. It's funny, really. I try to think why I hate myself, and I don't really think I'm much worse than everybody else, but, you see, I hate myself. And silly Dr. Fluckberg writes it all down, everything I tell him, and when I ask him why I hate myself he just nods.'

She laughed. 'He nods like one of those dog things you used to see in the rear windows of cars.'

'The first marsupial canine.'

They were silent again, then Barbara said, 'How's Joanna?'

She asked as though she was asking about some other woman's daughter, a girl whose name she was pleased to remember.

He felt the shaft of pain again. 'She's in Cyprus.'

There was a pause, and then she said, 'I miss her.' Then another silence, and she said, 'Sometimes.'

He took her hand. She said, 'I'm so unhappy.'

'You're getting better. You're getting better all the time. It's just that it isn't something that happens in a hurry.'

He didn't believe what he was saying. The girl he had married, the girl he had lived with for all those years, he was never going to see her again. The woman whose hand he was holding was the real woman.

She said, 'Does that mean you're alone in the house?'

'Yes. Apart from Phyllis. But I hardly ever see her. I've usually gone to work before she arrives.'

'You ought to increase her wages.'

'I did. A couple of months ago.'

'Then she won't talk, will she?' Barbara looked at him, and her face was a mask of hatred. 'Then she won't tell everybody about what you do.'

38

He deliberately misunderstood. 'She hasn't the slightest idea what I do. She thinks I work for the Inland Revenue.'

'I'm not talking about your work. I'm talking about your women.'

She suddenly seemed to notice that he was holding her hand, and snatched it away. 'You think if you can keep me in here, then nobody will know, don't you? It must be very convenient, now you've got rid of Joanna as well! You can screw them all day and all night, can't you!'

There was a tear running down one side of her face.

'I will be going home,' she said.

'Of course.'

'They can't make me stay here.' There was now an edge to her voice. 'They can't make me stay here, not unless you commit me.'

'There's no question of that!' Then he wondered, did I say that too quickly? For there had been times, often, when he had thought, not that he would ask for her to be committed – drinking too much, talking so that it was dangerous, the sexual delusions, even the suicide attempts, always when he would find her before she was dead – none of that justified his asking for her to be committed. But if a doctor, an expert, a real expert, not like Marshall, if someone like that suggested it was the best thing to do . . .

'Nobody's thinking like that at all,' he said. 'It's simply to be sure that when you come home, you'll be absolutely well.'

Unlike all the other times, he thought, but he didn't say it.

'Do you love me?' she asked.

'Of course I do,' he said, and he didn't know if he was telling the truth or not.

Oh God, he thought, oh God make me love her like I used to do.

If only he could talk to her. If he could say that he was scared, that he was scared as he had never been scared before, because their daughter was in the hands of terrorists, and he knew what terrorists did, and he knew what might happen to her, and he knew how helpless he was. If he could explain the plans, such as they were. If he could tell her that he was going to Cyprus, and they knew he was coming but they didn't know who he was, and above all they didn't know that their daughter was one of the British subjects that were now the subject of all this activity. If he could say, don't worry if you don't see anything in the papers for the moment, because there are political complications and it's all being handled very secretively. If he could just say that he was going there because the Old

Man thought that he would be the best person on earth to have on the spot: if he could say that. He wouldn't have to explain that because of his expertise he knew how slight were the chances that anything that he or anybody else could do would make any difference.

He clasped her hand again, and waited for the blessed relief when the nurse brought the tea round, and he could have a cup and leave.

Chapter Six

The Airbus of Cyprus Airways banked, levelled out, landed with a discreet thump, taxied and stopped.

When Joshua stepped out the heat hit him, spitting up from the tarmac. Cyprus was normally hotter than Greece or Italy, even than Crete: he had checked, but he was still momentarily taken by surprise. As the passengers started to make their way towards the modest range of buildings that served Larnaca airport a tall, noticeably good-looking man in a short-sleeved white shirt and green slacks came across to him.

'Joshua Howell?' he asked.

Joshua nodded, for that was the name on his passport. Joshua Howell, place of birth Sheffield; residence United Kingdom; height 1.92 metres; date of birth near enough to his own; occupation insurance advisor.

'Nicos Tsardanis,' he said thrusting out a huge hand. 'Call me Nico. You were easy to spot!'

Joshua glanced round at his fellow passengers as they lurched towards the terminal under their hand luggage and their duty frees: a mixture of Cypriot businessmen, busy, balding in sparkling white shirts and pointed black shoes, and English tourists, tired family groups, some with over-excited children, a few couples with the tender uncertainty of the unmarried, one pair of newlyweds, confetti still in their hair.

'I suppose so, yes.'

He put down his suitcase and shook Nico's hand. It was a grip that could crush rocks.

'You got Cypriot money?'

'No.'

'They gotta place at the airport. I've put you in the Hotel Romantica. Damn awful name, but it's a quiet place and I guess mebbe you didn't want too many people round you. In Nicosia. How many bags you got?'

41

'Just one apart from this.'

Nico nodded, and led him into the terminal building. A ragged queue was beginning to form, but Nico took him by the arm and ushered him through a door marked Airport Personnel Only. Without looking up an official at a table took his passport and stamped it. Then out through another door to where luggage was being brought in on trolleys.

'You see your bag?'

'No. Yes! That one behind the backpack.'

Nico extracted the suitcase, tipping various others onto the floor, nodded to a porter who nodded back and, pushing Joshua ahead of him, went through a door marked No Exit into what proved to be the back door of the airport branch of the Bank of Cyprus. There Joshua changed his travellers cheques, a longish queue on the other side of a grille accepting this without question, and before any of the other passengers had even cleared Immigration, Joshua and Nico were driving away on the featureless road from the airport.

'You like the sun, eh? Better than England!'

The car was a Toyota, and very fast. Joshua recognised the extra mirror above the dashboard, fixed so that a passenger could check on whether they were being tailed without the driver having to take his eyes off the road. There was a map compartment beside the radio, with a lock on it. He wondered what weapon was hidden behind it.

'What are you with?' he asked, not expecting an accurate answer.

Nico caught his eye in the mirror, grinned broadly. 'Traffic police,' he said. Then the grin disappeared. 'You hear anything more before you leave London?' he asked.

'No.'

'Nor here. I don't get it. They tell you it was Grey Wolves?'

'Yes.'

'That's what I don't get. How are there Turks in southern Cyprus? All the bastards are in the north. How can there be Turks down here?'

'They'd only have to be here long enough to do the kidnapping.'

'Then how do they get here?'

'From the north?'

'It is impossible. You will see. It is impossible.'

With a scream of tyres they swerved past a donkey whose rider seemed to be asleep in the steeping sun. 'The Turks, sure they would let the terrorists into Cyprus. It's in their interest. And mebbe the

42

United Nations, they don't stop them. But then there are the Greek Cypriots.' Nico tapped his nose. 'We can smell Turks. I ask you, how did they get in?'

'By air?'

'Impossible.'

'By boat?'

Nico thought, then said, 'Mebbe by boat. It is difficult, but perhaps at night the bastards could come ashore. It is a long coast-line, and the Turks use caiques too. Mebbe they mistake a Turk boat for a Greek one. But OK, they come by boat. Where are they now?'

'You know your country. I don't.'

'In the mountains they could hide. But everybody knows a Sunswept bus! And in the mountains, they see a Turk, and soon everybody knows! I think it is all mebbe a hoax.'

Joshua said, 'They gave the names of the children.'

'So they make them up!'

'No.' His voice was quite expressionless. 'They didn't make them up. They were the names of real children. Missing children.'

He felt the pain again, physical pain across his chest. Concentrate. Concentrate on the problem, not the pain.

'Put yourself in their position. You are a Grey Wolf.'

Nico laughed bitterly. 'You never ask Greek to imagine he is Turk.'

'Just put yourself in that position. You know Cyprus. You've obviously planned this. Where would you take them? You've got one woman school-teacher, a lot of very frightened children, and a Greek Cypriot driver. Any of them could become hysterical any time.'

Then an idea occurred to him. 'Unless, of course, they didn't know what was happening.' Then the correction. 'No. The driver would know he wasn't supposed to hand over the bus. Let's assume for the moment that you're in charge of this bus; everybody in it is too scared to scream or break the windows or anything to warn anybody they were passing, then where would you go?'

Nico said, 'I know a lot of places.' He hesitated, then said, 'I was only a kid, but I was in EOKA.'

He was in EOKA. He had been a terrorist. Terrorist. Freedom fighter. Call it what you like, but on the other side.

Perhaps Nico sensed Joshua's reaction, for he added, 'I didn't kill anybody. British soldiers or anybody. I just used to take food up into the mountains for our people. I was only a kid.'

'But there are places to hide.'

'No shortage. We had places. The British surrounded them, and they still couldn't find them. But not a bus.' He laughed. 'We never tried to hide a damn orange and green bus!' He stopped laughing abruptly. 'And Turks, Turks wouldn't last ten minutes. Not now. Not after what they did in seventy-three.'

'So they must have taken the children into the north.'

'No. That's impossible.'

'Why?'

Nico alarmingly took both hands off the wheel to expound his arguments, only checking the car's direction at the last split second as he flung it through a village.

'The whole of the north, that's under Turkish bastards,' he said. 'Right west to east.' His hand sliced the air in front of him. 'The only exception, that's to the west beyond Kato Pyrgos. There's a village the bastards occupied, and that's cut off by Cyprus all round, except to the sea.'

Both hands indicated the sealing off of the village. The car was now accelerating out of the village, the speedometer registering over eighty.

'Everywhere else, the roads to the north, they're sealed off. There's check points. Cypriot, then UN, then Turks. Anyway, a bus, that would have to go through a major check point. Like the one in Nicosia. But it couldn't go through! Nobody would let it through! Not ever! Anybody who goes from the south to the north, like tourist on day trip, they have to hire a separate car the other side. Separate car, separate insurance, everything. No way they get a damn bus through.'

His hand chopped vigorously downwards, three times. 'Cypriot, UN, Turk. Mebbe the UN wouldn't check too good. Mebbe the Turks would let the bus through, because they'd be in on the kidnapping. But no way we'd let the damn thing go through!'

Joshua asked, 'What about things like farm tracks? Like the terrorists use in Ireland?'

'What damn farm tracks? This is Cyprus, not Ireland! If there's an old track that goes across the frontier, then it's mined! It's mined and there's machine guns covering it! From both sides! From their side so we don't try to go back to our land, from our side so they don't steal any more! People don't go near the frontier! Where any road goes anywhere near the Turk, we've got notices warning people! They say, you are now under Turkish observation! And that means keep moving, don't take photographs, because those bastards don't mess about! You don't even get the poor bloody peasant whose land it is near the frontier! Let alone an orange and green bus full of kids!'

Ahead of them a lumbering farm wagon was blocking half the road, and coming rapidly towards them was a taxi. The taxi driver, realising he could not possibly stop in time, switched on his headlights.

'What I don't get,' said Nico, accelerating, 'OK, you get the bus, you get the kids into the north, and you could hide them. Why? Because the Greeks have been thrown out of their villages –'

He swung the car onto the verge and passed the wagon on its inside, the taxi, lights on, hooter blaring, roaring past.

' – and now they're half empty.' He didn't even pause in his sentence. 'From the number of refugees we've got in the south, you could hide a fleet of damn buses in empty buildings in the north. But you couldn't – nobody could! – get them over the frontier! So they must be in the south. But they're not in the south! You couldn't hide *one* Turk, let alone a squad of Turks, a whole lot of kids, and a damn bus in the south!'

Joshua was suddenly aware that his hands were clammy. It was hot in the car, even with the windows open, but he suspected Nico's driving had more to do with his discomfort than the temperature outside.

He said, 'Could they have been got off the island altogether?'

Nico considered. 'Not through the airport, obviously. Not by private plane. Apart from our radar checks, there's all the stuff on the RAF bases. You couldn't get a swarm of bees in without them showing up on that stuff. So suppose they landed by sea. Suppose they had a fishing caique, Cyprus registered. That'd be possible. They land somewhere along the coast. Say west of Paphos. There's fewer people that side. You get the kids, you get them back to caique. Then what? All the way round the north coast, either to, say, Kyrenia, or even on to Turkey? It's possible, but it's crazy!'

Joshua said, 'The Turks wouldn't offer them sanctuary.'

'Those bastards would do anything,' said Nico bitterly.

As they approached the capital, the traffic grew thicker. From the shuttered shops a partial siesta was observed, but the degree of traffic said that the Greek talent for business was not allowed to slumber undisturbed.

They passed a house with the wall on one side missing. 'Bomb,' said Nico. 'Just ahead of where we are now was the front line in seventy-four, and one of their planes overshot.'

They turned off the main road into the city, running alongside the great Venetian wall that circled the old part of Nicosia. Most of the buildings seemed empty, abandoned cars rusted in the sun, the bullet holes rotting wider as the years passed. A few shops still traded among the surviving inhabitants. In one a Greek army cap was perched on the head of a dusty teddy bear that held a toy machine gun. Two old men with empty coffee cups on a table on the pavement watched in silence as they passed. A rust-red bicycle, its wheels, chain, handlebars long since removed, was fastened with a locked chain to a lightless street lamp. Sometimes the windows of the houses were boarded up, but more often they were missing altogether, and the brilliant sky could be seen through them, up where the roof used to be. The streets stank of sour defeat and aimlessness.

On a corner Nico drew up. 'Come,' he said.

They got out of the car, and Joshua followed him down a narrow street, the houses on each side burnt and empty. Half way down the street, blocking it, was a wall. It was not a towering, oppressive, obscene wall like the wall that divides Berlin: it was a ramshackle wall, a wall of oil drums, bricks, bursting sandbags sprouting weeds. Crudely painted on an overturned cart that was part of the wall was a map of Cyprus, a knife stuck into it, the northern third a blood-red wound. Above the wall, from a broomstick, the flag of Greece hung limp in the still air.

Nico shouted something in Greek, and from a doorway on one side of the street a soldier emerged. Nico shouted again, and with his rifle the soldier waved them forward. When they reached him, the soldier seemed to Joshua to look too young to fight, the helmet and the rifle too big for him. The soldier grinned. He had bad teeth and seemed to be trying to grow a moustache.

They went into the house, then up a flight of wooden stairs. 'Careful,' said the soldier to Joshua in English. 'Some is missing.' In a room on the first floor another soldier sat on an old cafe chair, his boots on the ledge of the gutted window, his rifle leaning against a wall. He rose to his feet when he saw Nico. The room reeked of urine.

Silently, Nico indicated the view from the window, the view over the absurd wall. The street was empty. The sign of a pharmacy dangled over an empty, looted shop. Then, the light blue, optimistic flag of the United Nations, a world encircled by an olive wreath, hope, freshness, life, sticking confidently out from the window above the shop. Beyond that, another wall as grotesque as the first, with the scarlet flag of Islam above it.

The second soldier spoke to Nico, and pointed. 'He says they've got a machine gun in there,' said Nico, then, quietly, 'The street at the end of this one, that was where I used to live.'

With a nod of his head he indicated the other direction. 'My school was just up there. The other end of the street. You see the church?'

Joshua leant forward, Nico's restraining hand preventing him from putting his head out beyond the protection of the window.

'That was Agios Iaonnis,' said Nico. 'You see they've taken the cross off the dome and put a bloody crescent there instead? Now it's a mosque. That was where my parents were married. Where I would have been married. It's bad enough them taking everything out of the churches to make them mosques, but why do they pretend they built them in the first place? When those bloody people were swinging down from the trees to look for nuts, we were building the Acropolis.'

They returned to the car. Joshua felt himself hunching his shoulders as he always did when he sensed a possibility of a shot in the back. He had never felt more strongly the sense that the great experiment was a failure, that one day, one day soon, God would run out of patience with his invention, and delete the planet Earth.

A few streets away it all changed. Shutters were coming up after the siesta, people shouted down alleyways and from windows, women bargained with traders over vegetables and fruit, clothing and shoes, fish and fabrics. The streets were narrow and mostly one-way, bicycles pushed against the prevailing stream of cars, Greek popular music reedily distorted from a hundred cafes and bars, newspaper vendors vying with men selling iced drinks for a crucial square yard on a corner, or a doorway in which a customer could stop just long enough to buy. It was a scene of the Levant, vulgar, ebullient, gaudy and exhilarating.

Joshua glanced at Nico beside him. As he shouted good-natured abuse at whoever happened to be in the path of the car, his horn adding to the cacophony around him, Nico was at home. This was his city, his island. Aphrodite wasn't only beautiful. She could be fun.

'Ledra Street,' said Nico, pointing. 'Your English papers called it Murder Mile during the liberation struggle.' He used the loaded emotive phrase unselfconsciously in front of the Englishman.

'Are we going down it?' Joshua asked, as Nico mounted a pavement in order to pass a stall selling oranges.

'Not any more,' said Nico, his expression changing. 'The other end is Turks.'

They cut through a web of narrow streets, then out into Nicosia's suburbs. Here the roads were almost deserted, slumbering gently in the sun. A man watering the flowers in his garden looked round as they passed, and a child on a bicycle wobbled to the side as he heard the car approaching. Many of the houses looked empty, but whether they were deserted or had owners who had not yet returned from work it was impossible to tell. Occasionally, unannounced, a house would be missing a wall, or its roof, or had simply been erased altogether. In the gentle domesticity of the setting the effect was strangely disturbing.

Nico turned down another interchangeable, well-groomed suburban road, and at the far end an unlit neon sign against the sky read HOTEL ROMANT. As they approached Joshua could see that the rest of the sign was twisted round, the result of a moment's casual shellfire.

'They'll treat you okay at this place,' said Nico cheerfully.

He stopped the car in the hotel's modest car park, and got out. 'If I were you,' he said, 'I'd take it easy tonight. There's nothing to do. If anything happens, I'll get in touch.'

'Thanks.'

He lifted the bags out of the boot of the Toyota. 'The hotel's convenient.'

'Convenient for what?'

'Everything. The British Consulate is a couple of blocks away. I've never found them any use, but mebbe they'll work better for you than they do for me.'

Nico nodded down the road. 'Just down there, that's the Ledra Palace. The main check point. UN Headquarters, everything. You'll see. It's convenient, this hotel. It's got a bar and the food isn't bad. It's okay. Convenient.'

He added, 'Beyond, three blocks, is frontier.'

Chapter Seven

Joshua lay on the bed, but sleep escaped him. He got out of bed and straightened the sheet for the third time. The temperature was dropping, he could feel it, and within an hour or two he might even need the thin bed-cover as well as the top sheet. But within an hour or two it would be broad daylight.

He had never felt so helpless. Somewhere beyond the hotel bedroom window was Joanna. He didn't know where. He didn't know what had happened to her, what was happening to her now. He didn't have the sensation that she was dead. He thought that if she had already been killed, somehow he would know. He had known that time in Rome that his contact had been murdered, and if he had sensed it for a man he had only seen twice, then surely he would feel it for his own daughter?

On the other hand, rationally, she could be dead. She could be lying somewhere with half her head blown away as he had seen those other two victims of the Grey Wolves. Considering that he was supposed to be based on London, he had travelled to a lot of places to see people who got killed.

She could have been raped. She could be being raped at that very moment he was thinking about her. If that happened, and he got her back, what should he do? How could a man, any man, help her? Who could he possibly find for her to replace her mother? Her mad mother?

She could be reacting the other way. What the trade called the Stockholm Syndrome. She could be doing a Patty Hearst and already, even this early, be starting to identify with her captors. She could be changing so that she would become one of them, identifying with whichever one became her terrorist lover rather than her policeman father.

That alternative was the most emasculating of all.

There was the pre-recorded sound of a muezzin calling the

49

faithful to prayer. He glanced at his watch. Three o'clock. Perhaps, he thought idly, there was a Japanese factory making nothing but time switches for the Moslem world. He walked onto the balcony, wrapping the top sheet round his naked body as he did so. He could see the minaret, clear in the moonlight. It was only just beyond the outside wall of the hotel; a hundred yards or so from his room. A hundred yards, two lines of barricades, and three armies away.

The sound from the mosque provoked a dog in the Turkish sector to start barking, short, not ill-humoured barks, more an announcement of the dog's existence than any declaration of intent. From a kennel outside the hotel another dog answered. The dogs could communicate across the frontier, but their owners could not. Joshua wondered, did the dogs of Cyprus find their way from one part to another? Not across the minefields, but through the check points. Did anybody, Turk, Greek, United Nations, trouble to stop a dog? Or did the dogs sense the menace, the enormity of the barricades and the men with weapons? Did they sense that to these men, dog owners though many of them no doubt were, the exact division of a street was something they were expected to die for if they had to? Did the dogs appreciate this, and turn back, just barking to make their point?

Cats would ignore the barricades. No doubt about that. Cats would never accept the curtailment of a traditional hunting area by a mere barricade.

Joshua tried to remember Kipling's line about cats. Something, something ways, and every single one of them is right. He couldn't remember it, and he got angry. The muezzin's call became an intolerable wailing, flat, unmelodious, meaningless. He couldn't shut the window to close it out because it was still too hot, and he felt angrier still. He came back into the room, and the phone rang.

Surprised, he picked it up. It was reception. There was a Mr Tsardanis in reception. Could he come up?

For a moment Joshua couldn't think who Tsardanis might be, then he recalled that Nico had either been Tsardanis or something very like it.

'Send him up,' he said.

Nico must have been on his way up as the girl in reception had been phoning, for there was a tap on the door and Nico entered before Joshua had put the phone down.

He was looking serious.

50

'I'm sorry, but I think it was worth waking you.'

'As it happens, I wasn't alseep.'

'Yeah. Well, I've just come back from Mari. That's a village east of Limassol on the road to Nicosia. All round there, they're building. Yesterday, one of the workmen lost his watch. He says it was a gold watch, but mebbe he's just saying that for the insurance. Anyway, he missed it when he got home from work, so he goes back to see if he can find it before it gets dark. And with the work they're doing, odds are if it's visible it won't be the next day because they're moving earth and that all the time. Right?'

'Right so far.'

'This workman, he drives a dumper truck. So he goes back to where he knows he was working with this truck, levelling off the ground, filling in holes, all that. And because he's looking carefully for his watch, he sees something he wouldn't normally have noticed. A finger sticking out of one of the heaps. So he tells the Limassol police, and they dig, and it's Costas Gavalas.'

Joshua said quietly, 'The driver.'

'Correct. The driver. He'd been shot through the head. Because it's a murder, they tell Nicosia. If it had looked like natural causes knowing them I doubt if they'd have broken sweat any. I got told.'

He exhaled heavily. 'I managed to do one thing right. I got him identified by the Limassol head of Sunswept. They were going to ask his widow.'

Joshua knew he had to ask. 'Have they found anybody else?'

'No. But they're looking.'

Nico walked over to the window, where the muezzin had fallen silent in the minaret. 'I looked down on that poor bastard, and I promise him I'd get a Turk for him.'

He turned. 'Then I came straight here.'

'Yes.'

'There's something else you ought to know. The driver said that the pile the body was in was from a tip they hadn't worked on since Monday morning. The body wasn't on the top, or they'd have seen him. It was only because the workman was looking for the watch – '

'Yes.'

'You see what that means. He was put there on the Sunday. He was already dead when they sent that note threatening to kill him.'

Nico said, 'So it looks to me like the girls will be dead by now, as well.'

Chapter Eight

When Miss Galsworth unlocked the door of the Consulate in the morning and opened it, she was taken aback to find an unknown man standing waiting in the doorway.

'Who is in charge here?' asked Joshua.

'Er . . . The Consul is on leave . . .' Miss Galsworth's life was an attempt to please one half of the human race without upsetting the other. 'I suppose Mr Earnshaw –'

Joshua nodded and pushed past Miss Galsworth, who retreated tactically behind a desk. The Consulate had always been rather small for its role, and the added work caused by the Turkish invasion had resulted in the near disappearance of anything except strictly functional space.

'Where is Mr Earnshaw?'

'Er . . . Have you an appointment?'

'No,' said Joshua patiently, 'As I was unaware of Mr Earnshaw's existence until a second or two ago, no, I haven't got an appointment. Just answer my question. Where is he?'

Miss Galsworth bristled. 'You can't see Mr Earnshaw without an appointment. Not now, certainly. He's very busy.'

When the Consulate opened, that was when Mr Earnshaw went through the mail over a cup of coffee. It was certainly not the time to disturb him.

Joshua took out his wallet, and carefully extracted a card from a concealed pocket in the back of it. The card was a Grade One Ministry of Defence Security Card, and listed, very briefly, what Joshua was entitled to do in furtherance of his duties, which seemed to be almost anything, and also what he would expect by way of assistance from whoever he chose to show it to. It carried his photograph, his signature, and two thumb prints. All Grade One cards were numbered, because very few indeed were issued.

Miss Galsworth reached out to take the card, but Joshua shook

52

his head, and instead took an envelope from the desk, put the card in it, and sealed it.

'If you'd be kind enough to give this to Mr Earnshaw,' he said, and smiled.

Uncertainly, Miss Galsworth took the envelope, and risked a fleeting smile back. She then hurried down a hallway and tapped on a door at the end.

In his office Mr Earnshaw looked up. He was in his late thirties, prematurely balding, and overweight.

'What the devil do you think you're doing?' he demanded.

'I was just – ' began Miss Galsworth, alarmed.

'Not you! Him!'

Mr Earnshaw stabbed a finger at Joshua, who, unnoticed, had followed Miss Galsworth in.

'Give Mr Earnshaw the envelope,' said Joshua, 'then if you wouldn't mind leaving us.'

'You'll stay here!'

Confused, Miss Galsworth put the envelope on the desk, and, scowling, Mr Earnshaw opened it. He looked at the card suspiciously, then up at Joshua.

'Have you seen one of those before?' Joshua asked.

'Certainly not!' He made it sound as though the card was pornographic. 'Have you got a passport?'

Joshua put his passport on the desk. The man examined it, checking the photographs against each other and against Joshua's face, then cried, 'They're in two different names!'

'That's right,' said Joshua.

'Now look here, Mr Howell or Mr Doyle or whatever you call yourself, you don't impress me!' He thrust the documents away from him. 'You get out of my office, and if you want to see me, make an appointment!'

Joshua slowly picked up the passport, and then the Security Card, which he replaced in his wallet.

He turned to Miss Galsworth. 'Please leave us,' he said, quietly.

Wide-eyed, Miss Galsworth backed towards the door. Joshua lowered himself into the chair for Earnshaw's visitors, and waited. Mr Earnshaw finally nodded permission to Miss Galsworth, and she tiptoed out. As she closed the door she heard Mr Earnshaw say, 'I don't know who you are or what you want, but I'll give you five minutes.'

Miss Galsworth, very conscious that there might be difficulties, posted herself outside the office, ready to intervene the moment she was needed.

Through the door, she couldn't hear the first part of the conversation. She didn't hear Joshua ask, 'Tell me, Mr Earnshaw, how do you feel about the Falkland Islands?'

Nor did she hear Mr Earnshaw reply, 'What the hell are you talking about? Are you insane? Why should I be interested in the Falkland Islands?'

She didn't even hear Joshua say softly, 'Because if you don't move your fat arse off that chair and do exactly what I tell you, the Falkland Islands are where you will spend the rest of your career.'

However, she did hear the crash as Joshua slammed his hand down on Earnshaw's desk. She heard his bellowed, 'Move!' She heard the clang as Mr Earnshaw jumped out of his chair, cutting his forehead on his desk light.

Chapter Nine

Nico was sitting on Joshua's bed, waiting for him, when he got back to the Hotel Romantica.

He said, 'I got half the damn police force looking for you. Where you been?'

Then, without waiting for Joshua's answer, he held out a large manilla envelope. 'Tell me what you make of this.'

As Joshua extracted the print from inside the envelope, Nico said, 'It came on the wire about one hour, one hour and a half ago. London said they sent it here the moment they got it. God knows though how long the damn Turks have been sitting on it.'

Joshua put the print down on the bedroom table. It was a photo taken from the look of it with some sort of instamatic camera, using a flash. There were two girls and the shoulder of a third. The girls were standing against a whitewashed wall, presumably an inside wall because there was what looked like a strip of curtaining at the edge of the picture. They were holding a newspaper to show the front page, and their faces were unreadable. Their mouths seemed to be laughing, but not their eyes.

He didn't recognise the girls. Neither of them was Joanna.

'What's the paper?'

Nico said, 'The Turks say it's something called *Gunaydin*.'

'Date?'

'Two days ago. But the damn thing is a weekly. It could have been bought the day before that. That's what they say. If you trust the bastards.'

'Where is it distributed?'

'Theoretically, only in the north.'

His eyes still on the picture, Joshua asked, 'Is there anything to stop anybody taking a copy of the paper out of Cyprus and getting the picture taken somewhere quite else?'

'Not a thing. Fly the paper to Adana airport in Turkey, then to

Athens, say, then to Larnaca. You could do it and get back in a day.' Nico stabbed his finger on the face of the girl on the left. 'I tell you, they never left the south. It is impossible. But anyway, I think the picture is a trick. I think they're all dead.'

Nico thought Joanna was dead. He didn't know about Joanna, he wouldn't have said it had he realised he was speaking to her father, but he thought Joanna was dead.

Joshua sat down slowly on the edge of the bed. He had to concentrate. He had to work out what was the likeliest eventuality. No. He had to work out *all* the possibilities, then assess them, and act in the way that would be most effective in the widest number of them.

If Nico was right, if they were dead, then there was nothing he could do. There was nothing anybody could do. So that was a possibility that could be eliminated. At least for the moment, it could be eliminated. Until it was confirmed.

He forced himself to forget about Joanna as his daughter, the girl he had last seen at a bus terminal, last heard on the telephone. He must think of her as one of a group of seven, six girls and a teacher. A group of seven that had been a group of eight, but of which one was already known to be dead.

He said, 'The bus they were in. You say it is impossible for that bus to go into the north.'

'Sure. Quite impossible.'

'So wherever the children are, the bus is in the south.'

Nico resented the words. 'In Cyprus, yes.'

'So what is anybody doing to find it?'

'They're looking every place!'

'What I'm saying is, suppose the bus is, while we're talking, being repainted, the plates changed, the engine number changed, the chassis number changed –'

'Goddam it, you're right!' Nico was suddenly animated. 'We've been thinking that the terrorists would want to keep the bus! But mebbe they want to get rid of it! We've been thinking, because they're terrorists, they wouldn't know how to get rid of it!'

Joshua said quietly, 'Believe me, Nico, any terrorist has contacts with criminals. Not always the other way round, but –'

'Sure! Sure!' He reached out for the photoprint, then said, 'You want to keep this? I can get copies.'

'Yes.'

Neither of the girls was Joanna, but perhaps, when that photograph had been taken, at that moment Joanna had been in that

56

room. Perhaps that was her shoulder, the blurred out of focus shoulder that could have belonged to anybody. Perhaps that was the last impression he would ever have of her.

'Nico.'

'Yes?'

'How would I set about going to the north?'

Nico's face darkened. 'They're not there. They can't be.'

'I'm asking you a question. Do they let people in?'

'Sure they let people in. You just pay them, and they let you in. That's if you're a foreigner. If you used to live there like us, if it was your damn country, then they don't let you in. But you, you go in for the day.'

'Could you fix me documentation to stay longer?'

'No. Not without blowing you. If the Turks know you've got permission to go in for more than a day, then they'll get suspicious. To go longer than that, you have to go in from Turkey.'

Nico added cynically, 'It's part of the British Commonwealth, remember. So you need permission from the damn Turk to go there.'

'For the day an ordinary passport is enough?'

'Yeah. You go in after eight, and back by six. But you'll be wasting your time. They're not there.' Then an idea struck him. 'If you really want to go, and I'm telling you you're crazy, I'll fix you a press card. Then our people will let you back any time before midnight. You'll need a couple of identity photos. You can get those in Ledra Street.'

Joshua took out his wallet. Identity photos were things that JBH officers tended to carry with them. Nico grinned admiringly as he took two pictures, photographs adequate to be accepted on most documents, yet not revealing enough to be a great deal of help if they fell into the wrong hands; photographs which also had an invisible strip down them which could be detected if used in, for example, a passport.

'I'll get our people to check every damn garage in Cyprus,' declared Nico. 'And I'll drop the press card with Anna.'

'Who's Anna?'

'Anna on the desk. You haven't noticed Anna? You really must be jet-lagged! Any paper you want to represent?'

'The *Morning Advertiser*,' said Joshua, picking the trade paper of the brewing industry, a paper which sounded plausible, could be checked, and certainly wouldn't already have a representative in Cyprus.

'*Morning Advertiser*. Okay.'

With a wave of his hand, Nico was gone.

Think. Think about this case as he would about any other case. No emotion, at least, no more emotion than his usual quiet anger at the ways of terrorists. Think coldly and impersonally. Think of the terrorists and their victims. However many terrorists, seven British citizens. Forget that one of them is his daughter.

The picture. Start with the picture. Handed to Ankara. Handed in by somebody who has contacts with terrorists, but isn't a terrorist himself. Or herself. Or somebody that it is in everybody's interest is not thought of as a terrorist, like the links British Intelligence has with, say, the Provos. *Dear Annabelle, I am writing on behalf of a friend who thinks her boy friend may be gay/is in love with a married man in her office/has smelly periods/cannot tell her mother about the boy she is going out with/thinks she may be pregnant.* Assume Nico is right. Technically the photo could have been taken in the south, and could even be in Ankara the same day. Is that really likely?

Two questions so far unanswered. One. Again assuming Nico knows what he is talking about, how do Turks hide in the south? Two. How do you hide a bus in the south?

Hypothesis. Suppose they are not in the south. Suppose Nico is wrong, and that somehow they have been spirited away. Where?

Nico has to be right about the impossibility of taking them out by air. To get seven people, assuming they'd already killed that poor bloody driver by then, to get seven people away you'd need a plane that seated at least ten, including the pilot, and assuming the pilot was a terrorist. And in a place swarming with Intelligence stations no plane that size would have a hope in hell of overflying without being challenged.

He rose from the bed and looked again at the photograph. It told him absolutely nothing. He didn't remember having seen either of the girls before, though they must have been at Victoria Coach Station. Then he had an encouraging thought. If the terrorists had known that they were holding the daughter of a senior British Intelligence officer, surely they would have included her in the photograph. Therefore they didn't know. And Joanna would know enough not to get herself photographed, because, perhaps, the picture might appear in a newspaper, and somebody would recognise her, somebody who knew her father's work.

That made sense. Then the converse of the thought struck him.

Perhaps Joanna wasn't in the photograph because she was already dead when it was taken.

Think. Think calmly and impersonally. Back to the hypothesis that they have been got out of southern Cyprus. How?

Boat. The only sort of boat that wouldn't be noticed would be a fishing boat. A caique. Would other fishermen recognise a stranger? Could they get wherever they wanted to go in the hours of darkness? Were Turkish fishing boats different in appearance from Greek ones? How fast did they go? Could they hide seven passengers?

He felt a sudden surge of frustration at the paucity of help available to him. At JBH he would only have to pick up a phone and the answers to all the questions he would need answering would be on his desk, neatly typed out, in minutes. Here he hadn't even got a map!

Calm. Cold analysis. Just another case, and God knows, he'd been involved in plenty.

Boat. Boat to where? To mainland Turkey, the headquarters of the Grey Wolves, where they would have their safe houses, and where they handed in the first demand note and the later photograph? How long would it take to get from Cyprus to Turkey? And where in Turkey could they land unnoticed?

Suppose they had used a boat, but only taken it as far as northern Cyprus. That wouldn't take long. Obviously, every moment they had seven healthy people in a boat they were in danger of exposure, so the shorter the voyage the better. Could they have somehow tricked the girls into thinking that the boat trip was some part of the tour? No. They might be able to fool the girls, but they couldn't fool the teacher. She'd know, Miss Whatshername. Boobs. She'd know what had been planned, and what had not.

They'd have had to sail some distance from the coast. They couldn't risk the girls shouting for help: or one of them trying to swim ashore, for that matter. Ashore, or to a passing boat. He didn't know about the others, but Joanna could swim like a fish. So if they'd had to sail, say out of sight of the land, that would have taken longer. Not all that long, but longer.

He looked out of the window. The minaret with the recorded muezzin looked so close in the clear air that he felt he could lasso it. Something something catch the sultan's turret in a noose of light. Something like that. Why the hell should they go to the trouble of capturing the bus, risking driving it to wherever they have their fishing boat, then sailing the bloody thing round the island, when

59

all they have to do is simply drive the bus a few hundred yards into the north?

Because there were three armies to stop them. Three armies, walls, road blocks, and minefields.

It didn't make any sense, but the division of Aphrodite's island didn't make any sense either.

He sat down again on the bed. Think. Rationalise. For a start, put yourself in the position of the terrorists.

You are a Turkish terrorist. Turkish, or Turkish Cypriot? Check if there are any records of known Turkish Cypriot Grey Wolf associations. Where, ideally, would you like to hold your prisoners?

Not southern Cyprus. Anywhere but southern Cyprus, where you are recognised and hated. Turkey would be better, but there's still the problem of getting there. Also the Turkish police have an impressive record of success against the Grey Wolves. No, the ideal place would be in northern Cyprus. Sleepy, indolent, laid-back northern Cyprus. Safe between the golden legs of Aphrodite. In a village in northern Cyprus. Normally terrorists prefer towns, but his instinct told him that one of the towns, Kyrenia, say, or Famagusta, might be just the wrong size: small enough for someone to notice an irregularity, big enough for there to be authorities competent to act.

A village. One of those villages the man from the Commonwealth office had spoken about, virtually deserted because the Greeks had all fled. And whoever else was in the village now, they wouldn't talk because they agreed with the demands the terrorists were making. If the demands were accepted, then the houses they were living in would be theirs, recognised as theirs by all the world, by all those countries who still believed the houses, their only homes, belonged to unknown Greeks who had not seen them for a decade, and whose only claims to the houses lay in boring legal documents interred who knew where, written in a language they couldn't speak or read, the language of the race that had humiliated them for so long. The others in the village wouldn't speak because the terrorists' demands were their demands. Besides, they would be afraid.

He was thinking clearly now. If the terrorists could, somehow, get their prisoners into the north, their position would be extremely strong. Momentarily he compared them with the men he had opposed in Ireland. They too enjoyed, not necessarily the support, but the tacit acceptance of the people among whom they lived. Border areas were also areas that bordered on the edge of lawlessness. The position of the Grey Wolves was, in fact, stronger than that of the Provos or the INLA or the others: for although it was difficult enough to goad the Eire Government into effective, overt action, at least there was an acknowledged Government to goad. In northern Cyprus, for whatever reason, Her Majesty's Government pretended there was not.

Take it step by step. The universal aim of the terrorist is the destruction of authority. (He had lectured from time to time, at universities mostly, to people who simply could not grasp this basic tenet, who really believed the liberal illusion that one man's terrorist was another man's freedom fighter.)

The Grey Wolves wouldn't give a damn about who ruled northern Cyprus. They wanted the rule of law, anybody's law, to fail. To this end they would use the people. From the terrorists' point of view, to campaign from within northern Cyprus was ideal. Apart from its obvious tactical advantages over mainland Turkey, he couldn't really believe that the issue of Cyprus was all that important to the people of Turkey. He recalled the man from the Commonwealth Office languidly dismissing Greek concern over Cyprus; and the Greeks had a reputation for being a lot more politically conscious than the Turks. But for Turkish Cypriots, and for the mainland Turks now colonisers of the north, this was the most important political issue in their lives.

It was a perfect terrorist campaign. It was a campaign to discredit government by being seen to force it to act in a manner which was not only what its people wanted, but which was its own declared policy! The attack was in fact upon the Turkish Government, and to a lesser extent the British Government, and after that the idea of government itself. The people of Cyprus, they were pawns. But that had been their historical role for four thousand years.

Again he looked out of the window, to the other world a few hundred yards away. She was over there. Not only his experience told him so, but his instincts as well. Perhaps a roof he could see from his balcony was the roof over her – though he doubted it, because he favoured a barely populated village. He realised how little he knew of what he would find the other side of the island. But the first time he had been to Belfast, it had been the first time he had even been to Ireland, any part of it, and still he found the man he was looking for. Training, instinct, sheer know-how, they were important. Along with luck.

He would be a day tripper. He took out his wallet and carefully removed everything in it that might give a lead to his real identity. He glanced round the room and put the evidence under the drawer in the dressing table, so that anyone searching would have to remove the drawer completely to find it. Then he left the room, and in the foyer of the hotel bought copies of the *Cyprus Mail* and the previous day's *Daily Express*. From a stand by the reception he selected a sling bag with the words Sunny Cyprus embroidered onto it. All he needed, he felt, was a sun-bleached cloth hat, loved souvenir from another holiday, saying Marbella. As always, the prospect of action acted as a tonic, almost an aphrodisiac. And it helped remove the fear, the fear that if he failed, if Joanna became just another victim, another unnoticed headline in a shortly forgotten newspaper, then he would not want to live.

A mustachioed girl appeared from the hotel office. 'Meester Howell?' He looked round. Either this was not Anna, or Nico had bizarre tastes.

'Yes?'

'Meester for you on the phone. He say he have press card for you. Ask please at check point. He say you understand.'

'Yes. I understand.'

He was impressed by Nico. The man was a professional, to fix a press card within half an hour.

'To get to the north. Where do I go?'

The girl indicated. 'To the end of road, left, end of road, again left, and straight.'

She had obviously given the instructions many times before.

Joshua nodded, and stepped out of the hotel into the sultry day. He reached the end of the road, and waited as a white-painted UN troop carrier rolled noisily past. A sergeant in a blue beret, the top half of his body sticking above the high sides of the vehicle, shouted a greeting to a UN sentry standing by a gateway. Joshua didn't recognise the language. It sounded Scandinavian.

The streets were strangely deserted, like streets after a fire-fight; but nobody had fought here for a decade. A big road junction that must once have seen the morning and evening rush-hour, echoing to the cacophony of competing horns, was now quiet. A ragged bird picked at something on the tarmac, moved slowly away as Joshua approached. There was a row of shuttered shops, one with ZITO ENOSIS scrawled across the doorway. They were dusty and looked as though nobody had ever owned them, worked there, shopped there. On the other side of the street there was another row of shops, slightly smaller shops, and there was a dark hole where one shop had disappeared completely. All that was left of it was a bath hanging grotesquely out into the air where the first floor had once been. A cafe had a sign in front reading *Now Open For Cold Drinks*, but it had not been open for years.

Joshua had a sense of *déjà vu* which for a moment he couldn't place. It was not like the empty streets of Belfast or even of Lebanon, for in those cities, when the firing stopped, and the gunmen withdrew, and the curfew was imposed, however empty the streets might seem he had always been aware of the eyes watching him, hidden men waiting for their moment to reappear.

Then he recognised the time he had felt like this before. It was a long time ago. He had only been a child. They had taken him – he couldn't even remember who or why – they had taken him to Pinewood, and he had gone onto the set of a street where they had just finished making a film. He couldn't even remember the name of the film, though he had seen it twice after it had been released. This place in Nicosia was like that film set. It was not a street where there were simply no people at that moment. It was a street where it seemed there never had been people, not real people.

Ahead of him two soldiers stepped out into the road. They were wearing olive-green uniforms, and had dark steel helmets unlike the jaunty blue of the UN. A blue and white striped sentry box beside a barricade told the story: this was the crossing point, this was where the Republic of Cyprus effectively ceased to exist.

From a complex of sheds on the right of the road Nico emerged. He said something in Greek to the soldiers, who stepped back and waited. Grinning, Nico waved a small grey card.

'Make sure you write the truth, eh, Mister Journalist!' he said as he thrust the press card into Joshua's hand. 'You write what the bastards are doing!'

Then his grin disappeared. 'Be careful,' he said. 'I think is damn silly you go to the north, but if you must, be careful.'

'I'll be careful.'

'The Turks, they're not like you and me.'

Nico took his arm and led him into one of the brick sheds.

'You sign here,' he said. 'Write it good. If you don't come back we want to know your damn name.'

Joshua looked round, but Nico was not smiling.

They didn't like people going to the north, and they made it plain. Unsmiling, they watched him as he signed out, checked his passport, handed it back and waved him through. He passed another blue and white striped sentry box, walked round a barricade, past one last blue and white post with a Greek flag above it, and a steel-helmeted soldier cradling a machine gun.

On his left the Ledra Palace Hotel towered above him. The building was scarred and pitted, a grotesque commentary: from the ornate baroque balconies hung army underwear, and many of the windows were blocked with sandbags, but the building as a whole still had a sort of shabby elegance, Brighton fallen upon hard times. Two UN soldiers, armed, and with the word CANADA on their sleeves, chatted together in French and took no notice of him as he walked past. Otherwise the long, straight road was deserted, but the knowledge of where it was and why it was meant that tourists did not stop to take in the absurdity of the luxury hotel with machine gun posts on terraces where white-coated waiters had hurried carrying the ouzos and the gin-and-tonics and the beers and the little bowls of nuts. A couple of hundred yards ahead another barricade blocked the road, with more soldiers. But this time the sentry posts were painted olive-green, and the flag that flew above them was the scarlet of Islam.

Chapter Ten

At a modest little cubicle like the kiosk attached to a crazy-golf course Joshua gave his name and showed his passport. He was then directed down a suburban street to a suburban house where, in the front room, he paid a Cypriot pound and was given a typewritten permit to visit the north for the day. It was banal and absurd. The only immediate sign of the division of Aphrodite's island was that the street names had changed. Instead of names in Greek with English translations underneath, the streets now had strange, curt Turkish names. It was exactly the same lettering, and the blue background had by now faded to the same colour as the name plates on the other side, and it looked utterly permanent, as though it had always been like that.

He was already consciously thinking like a tourist, like Joshua Welgrove Howell on a day trip. He had long ago been trained in the techniques of assuming an identity, but basically it was a talent some people had, and others had not. He had known agents who actually took time to revert to their own personalities, time even to speak with their normal accents. There was always the danger that an agent might become the other character as sometimes actors became their roles. It was a danger because, if something went wrong, an actor had to act as his part, but an agent had to act like an agent. As he walked away down the shabby suburban street, a match, indeed a continuation of the street on the other side of the armies, his gait was the healthy, untrained lope of an early middle-aged insurance advisor, his expression that of a tourist with a vague and quite uninformed interest in the foreign country he was seeing.

He reached an intersection with a dual carriageway, and found a tourist advice centre. Within a quarter of an hour he had heard about the Greek Barbarism Museum in Irfan Bey Street, secured a map with the place names in Turkish, and hired a car. In his insurance advisor persona he would normally have rented something

65

modest, but the proprietor of the car-hire firm was out of what he called 'compacts' – from his accent Joshua assumed some time on the Eastern seaboard of the States – and for the same price Joshua drove away in a Mercedes. His first impression was that there was noticeably less traffic than over the frontier, but whether this was because of the district of Nicosia, or because one fifth of the island's population now occupied one third of its land, or because the Turks were poorer than the Greeks, he had no way of knowing. The anomaly was that the two halves of the city had so much in common, not that they were so different. They both even showed their British heritage by driving on the left.

He left the centre of the city, out through the great Venetian walls that the Moor Othello would have known. There was even less traffic now, just two ancient lorries carrying fruit, a couple of Turkish army jeeps, and a white Alfa that dawdled along behind him, seemingly looking for an address.

Joshua drew up and looked at the unfamiliar map, with place names that meant nothing twenty years before, names that were a statement of political intent and military achievement. If his suspicions were right, somewhere on that map a group of terrorists were holding a group of British citizens, and one of those citizens was his daughter. It called for a large-scale, methodical police operation. There were techniques and skills, procedures and checks. They did not always work, but they worked more often than not. It was a fact that most terrorist actions were aborted before they were attempted, and that most terrorist targets escaped. Even in cases of kidnapping, like this case, the odds were that the prisoners would escape and the terrorists would not. It was when society failed that terrorists made the headlines, but the odds were on the side of society.

But all this depended on coordinated action. It depended on the overt and covert arms of the State working together. It depended on the State being able to call on assistance from other states if it needed it. It depended on at least the passive support of the people for the State against the terrorists. He was an expert on every part of this.

Here, now, nothing applied. There was not, and could not be, any coordinated action. The demands of the terrorists, were they to become known, would be supported by virtually every citizen. They would even be supported by the effective authorities in the area.

Above all, he could not use his expertise to assist the State, because, as far as his own Government was concerned, there was no State.

A uniformed policeman strolled past, glanced inside his car, smiled at him. Encouraging tourism was clearly policy. Joshua thought bitterly that the one policeman, simply by knowledge he doesn't even suspect he had, could eliminate half the area of this map. These damned deserted villages. Which the hell were they? Was Ilgaz deserted? Or Karangac? Or Lapta? Or were they in fact the Turkish words for Petrol Station, or Picnic Area, or Historical Monument? At first acquaintance Turkish seemed a very foreign foreign language.

He pulled the other, Greek, map out of the Sunny Cyprus sling bag, and compared it. The two maps were on different scales, but at least the larger places were identifiable. Kyrenia had become Girna, and Famagusta was Gazi Magusa. But there were areas on the Turkish map that were virtually blank while being full of Greek place names on the other. The mountains ran west-east, a solid mass rising up to Troodos in the western part of the Greek area, then a long ridge parallel to the coast in the north. At least the maps agreed on that.

The bus had been heading north out of Limassol. The driver's body had been at Mari. From what Nico had said, they had not expected the body to be found, so it was reasonable to assume that they would have continued on the same road. That road led to Nicosia. The bus could not have got through the check point by the Ledra Palace Hotel. Nico had said so, and Joshua had secretly doubted him: but having seen the place for himself he realised Nico had been right.

He was achieving nothing, sitting there. Perhaps he would only get the most elementary feel for the country, but at least it would be something he lacked at the moment. He pulled out, and set off for Kyrenia. Or Cirne, as the signs called it.

Again there was the sense of the familiar that was unkown, the mixture of the former English presence in a Mediterranean island, with a predominately Greek ethos that had been consciously stamped out wherever it became unmistakable: the houses, the white concrete arched boxes that the Greeks have built all over the old Byzantine world, but now with rambling Turkish families on the verandahs; the signs still in the dusty blue of Greece, but with short, brutal Turkish words stencilled over the Greek; the Orthodox churches, now gutted and with the Crescent where the Cross

67

had been. Yet still there was also the sense of faded Empire. It was still possible to imagine that, presaged by a few motor cyclists or the police band, round the next corner would come a little cavalcade as H.E. the Governor, in his open car and his white-plumed hat, passed on his way to the opening of the Assembly, or the reception for the Deputy Under-Secretary of State, or the races. Nothing had changed but nothing was permanent. The Cyprus of *Bitter Lemons* slumbered in the sun beside the memory of the Cyprus of the Greek entrepreneurs under the alert eyes of a Turkish troop convoy moving south.

Joshua drove carefully, his eyes missing nothing. From time to time signs warned in Turkish, English, French and German – not Greek, for there were no longer any Greeks to warn – against turning off the road, or taking photographs. This was a country effectively under military rule.

A thought struck him, and he drew up at the side of the road. The Turkish map confirmed his recollection: the roads off the main road, the ones that were barred, led to most of the villages that were shown on the map. Of the land he could see from the car as it climbed up into the mountains above Kyrenia, most was closed to . . . to whom? Not to the Turkish army, clearly. But if they had filled the villages with Turkish Cypriots, or Turks from the mainland, how did they check them as they went, every day, to and from the fields, or into the towns? Or were those villages really deserted? And if so, was there sufficient of an army presence to become aware that in one of hundreds of empty villages, one in dozens of its houses was now occupied by strangers, by a group of terrorists with their captives? Would anybody actually check?

A white UN jeep rolled past him, heading back into Nicosia. The UN patrols presumably covered most of the country. But they were not concerned with civilians. They were there to prevent the armies from clashing, the Cypriots of north and south, the mass of Turkish troops that everyone knew were there, and the mainland Greeks in their civilian clothes that everyone knew were there as well, but whose existence was never admitted.

He started the car again, and drove north. In his mirror he saw, some way back, a white Alfa. Was it the same one that he had seen before? And if it were, did it mean anything? After all, there was nowhere much to go except along the main road to Kyrenia, and logically a car would probably follow another all the way there.

But his professional awareness made him accelerate away, and within a minute the car was out of sight.

He tried to assess his impressions. Was it true that the houses looked seedier? They were basically similar houses to the ones south of Nicosia, because they had been built by and for the same people: Cypriot Greeks. But had they been allowed to rot a little since 1974? Or was his impression the result of the fact that, after all, this area was where the fighting had taken place? Was the absence of traffic a comment on any basic difference between Turks and Greeks? Or was it simply because fewer people occupied the land?

By a side road he saw a new, different, sign coming up, again in the four languages. NO UN VEHICLES BEYOND THIS POINT. He had no doubt at all what it meant. Down that road was the area closed to everybody; that area which, if Nico was right and the terrorists were hiding with the connivance of the Turkish authorities, offered the safest possible hiding place.

He knew that. But would Joshua Howell, insurance advisor, know? He decided not, and turned off down a narrow, winding road running parallel to the mountains.

He reached a hill top, and below him spread a sun-burnt countryside. The road he was on branched after about half a mile at a hamlet, one road then leading up into the mountains, the other ending at a whitewashed village which, from the cluster of camouflaged huts surrounding it, had been completely taken over by the Turkish army, and no doubt provided the reason for the ban on the UN.

Then he thought, how could the UN be expected to keep the peace when areas of the country were closed to them – areas of the British Commonwealth, come to that?

In his mirror he caught sight of a cloud of dust behind him, and at the base of the cloud was a car. A white Alfa. It was still quite possible that the driver was simply going about his normal business. There were few enough roads, and Joshua realised that in normal circumstances – even in the north of the island – he would not have noticed the car at all. It would have been lost in the traffic. Except that here there wasn't any traffic to speak of, except military traffic.

Whatever was happening, there was no point in risking having to explain. He had no doubt he could shake off a pursuer, if the Alfa was indeed interested in him. He had done it often enough before, in London, in Athens, in New York, in Brisbane. He accelerated away, at a speed calculated to separate the two cars without the intention being apparent. Within seconds he had lost sight of the Alfa behind the brow of the hill.

At the junction he swung the car up a winding road with scrub on either side – even Joshua Howell, insurance advisor, would recognise an army camp when he saw one. The Mercedes accelerated well, but he realised that the other car was closing. This was not a peasant returning home – this was someone tailing him.

From time to time the scrub grew thicker, and Joshua, one eye on his driving mirror, knew exactly what he intended to do. All he needed was a point on the road where he was out of sight of the other car, and with some sort of a track leading into and behind scrub. Then he would swing into hiding, get out of the car, and, should by any chance something go wrong he would be found bashfully peeing. But it would be highly unlikely that the other car would do anything but shoot past without seeing him, and he would be able to rejoin the road and return the way he had come.

He was now doing nearly seventy miles an hour and stretching the distance between the two cars. The scrub was becoming gratifyingly thick, and he selected a corner where, with any luck at all, not only would his pursuer have lost sight of the car, but also of the dust cloud behind it.

Tyres screaming, he threw the car round the corner. He slammed on the brakes and managed to halt the car, broadside across the road. Blocking the way ahead was a road block.

A Turkish officer emerged, a soldier on either side of him. The soldiers carried M16s, and they were pointed at Joshua. Joshua didn't understand the Turkish words, but he got the message. Come out of the car, hands in the air, or we will shoot you.

Chapter Eleven

The Turks knew their job, and they didn't mess about. Nico had been right. He had to admit that. On the other hand, Joshua had no doubt that he could, fairly quickly, talk his way out of his difficulties. It was obviously unwise for a tourist to stray off the normal road, but the car was not a UN vehicle. There was no problem that the laughing admission of his own stupidity would not overcome. Given time.

They drove him, in his own car, back down the road he had taken, and along the other road towards the whitewashed village and the military encampment that circled it, then drew up outside a building that had once been some unknown, forgotten Greek peasant's home. He knew what to expect before they pushed him inside, because he recognised the blocked-off windows of the room at the back. He knew they would take his watch, because he had been on courses involving disorientation. Come to that, he had usually played the interrogator. But of course Joshua Howell, insurance advisor, wouldn't know about these things, and noisily demanded a receipt which he didn't get before the door of the little room slammed shut on him and left him groping around in the near darkness with the only spot of clear light the peep-hole in the door through which they could watch him. Otherwise there was just a faint glow from the bright world outside, filtering through heavy cloth blocking the window.

As his eyes grew accustomed to the near darkness he found the plank bed running along a wall, and lay down on it, waiting for something to happen.

It was hot in the room, claustrophobic, and from time to time he rose and shouted demands for his immediate release. Once he heard footsteps, and then the spot of light in the door disappeared as someone looked in, then the footsteps moved away. Two, three, shuffle, four. So there was a guard in the actual room next to his,

71

not outside the house. He listened, his ear pressed against the door, and he heard a chair leg grate on a stone floor. A guard sitting, in all probability the chair leaning back against a wall. There was no sound of conversation. He couldn't be certain, but the odds were one guard, not more. No other activity. The house was used as a prison, not an office. And a prison to hold people for only a short time. The window wasn't that secure, and there was no bucket, and no stink of urine or faeces.

'Now look here!' he shouted. 'I'm a British citizen!'

Then he returned to the plank bed, and lay down again. They had taken his wallet, and they'd taken his passport. They hadn't searched him properly, but he knew there was nothing on him that could make them suspicious. He was, after all, a professional.

It was just under an hour later, he estimated, that he heard the guard rise abruptly to his feet, and voices speaking unintelligibly in Turkish. Then a key turned in the lock, and he was pulled, blinking, into the main room of the house. An unsmiling man in a camouflage jacket beckoned him to sit on an old chair which still had two Greek letters on the wooden strut holding it together, last evidence of the *cafeneon* from which it had, long ago, been taken.

He sat, and narrowing his eyes looked round him. The door to the world outside was ajar, to cool the room, and through the doorway he could see a squad of infantry drilling. It was some sort of an army post, not a police one. So far so good. The man in the jacket leant against a wall, the guard moved out of the room, and from outside another man, in civilian clothes, entered. From the way the guard reacted there was no doubt that the civilian, whoever he was, was in charge. Expertly, Joshua assessed him. The outstanding feature was the shock of absolutely white hair over a brown, sun-burned face, hair which might give a totally misleading guide to his age. Not fifty or sixty, thought Joshua. More like forty-five. His eyes were again noticeably white, and as he spoke to the man in the jacket his teeth were dazzling. Dazzling and perfect. He wore a short-sleeved shirt and slacks, and his body looked hard, the muscles unusually clearly delineated. Perhaps six foot, twelve stone, and tough. But it was the brown skin and the white hair that made him unmistakable. That and the easy grace of his movements.

'I don't know what all this is about,' said Joshua, 'but I'll have you know I'm a British citizen!' Then, because Joshua Howell would behave like that, he said, louder and more slowly, 'Me British citizen. Understand? Me want back my watch, my wallet, my passport!'

The man in the jacket leant forward, hit him across the face, and said, quite quietly, 'Shut up.' It wasn't a hard blow, more a cuff. There was no viciousness in it, and no expression whatsoever on the man's face.

Joshua dropped into his indignant tourist role. 'You realise what you've done? I will report you!'

'Shut up,' the man repeated.

The other man, the leader, the one with the white hair, sat on the corner of the desk. Joshua recognised the technique. Intelligence, he thought. Not normal police, not army. Intelligence. An officer accustomed to using his rank would sit at the desk, thereby establishing his position. Only officers beyond the rank of whatever may sit behind this desk. Ergo, I am such an officer. You will accordingly stand when I tell you to, sit when I tell you to, talk when I tell you to, and address me as sir.

But a man who wanted to establish contact with a prisoner, and through contact establish domination, he would do what this man was doing: think of the desk, not as a bulwark of authority, but an obstacle to communication. A barrier between him and the control he would establish over his victim.

When he spoke it was with a gentle, almost sing-song voice. There was the underlying occasional rasp of the Arabic languages behind the odd vowel, but the general effect was soporific.

'Let me explain,' he said. 'Let us look at your position. It isn't very strong.'

He had almost no accent, apart from the vowels, and the English rhythms were excellent. Joshua wished he had had time to listen to some of the tapes at JBH on the identification of speech patterns. Anyone who spoke English this well must surely have spoken it all his life. But were Turkish Cypriots of his generation, who must have spent their childhood in a British colony, were they taught English at school? Did they speak it at home? Or was he dealing with someone from Ankara or Izmir, a Turk from Turkey, one of the men who really ran the place?

'You are a day tourist,' he went on. 'We welcome day tourists. They can see that what the Greeks say is a lie. We are not barbarians. But we impose a few regulations. We try to make them simple. We put up notices telling them where they cannot go. Right?'

'I saw a notice banning United Nations vehicles,' said Joshua. 'And it should be obvious to anybody that my hire car is not a United Nations vehicle!'

Even as he was speaking he knew that he might well have been able to talk his way past the man who hit people, but that the man with the white hair would find him simply amusing. If he was lucky.

'You are Joshua Howell.' He flicked through the pages of the passport. 'You only arrived in this island yesterday, but already you have decided to visit the north. One might wonder why you didn't come here directly. Through Turkey . . .'

He waited for an answer, but Joshua shrugged.

'You are an insurance salesman.'

Again he fell silent, then finally said, 'Yes?'

'Yes.'

'When you are not being a journalist.'

Damn. They'd found the press card. He'd put it under the car seat, because he didn't expect to need it except with the Greeks, to explain why he was returning late.

Joshua laughed. 'I said I wanted to see the north, and this chap said I would have to be back by six, and I said damn that, and he said he could fix me up with a press card. Then I could stay here until midnight.'

'What chap?'

'A chap I ran into. Don't know his name. Said he worked at the Ministry of Information, or something.'

'I am glad that now they are encouraging people to come to the north.'

It seemed time for another outburst of British indignation. 'More to the point, what the hell do you think you're doing? I mean, I'm being held here against my will –'

'Shut up.' The man in the jacket perhaps only knew two English words.

'What are you really doing here, Mr Howell?'

'I've told you! It's perfectly obvious what I'm doing here! I'm a tourist! A perfectly normal bloody tourist! And you say you want tourists!'

'Shut up.'

Joshua whirled round. 'Shut up yourself!'

There was a flicker of a smile on the face of the man with the white hair. 'I will tell you, Mr Howell. You were under observation from the first moment you came over into our country.'

'Why, for God's sake?'

'Because you are a spy.'

'Don't be damned stupid!'

'May I put the arguments?' The man with the white hair reached into his breast pocket and produced a packet of cigarettes. 'At the crossing point you were seen with another spy. A Greek spy.'

'What bloody Greek spy? I don't know any Greek spies!'

'The man who gave you the press card.'

'I've told you! He was from the Ministry of Information!'

'No. He is from Greek Cypriot Intelligence. He has various names. What did he tell you he was called?'

'I never asked. Nico. He said, call me Nico.' After all, thought Joshua, about one in three male Greeks seems to be called Nico.

'We saw you with him. So we had you watched. As a spy you will know how most people in a foreign country behave.'

'How often do I bloody well have to tell you? I'm not a spy!'

'You knew exactly what you wanted to do. Not like a tourist. Not like an insurance salesman. Not even like a journalist. Because journalists always make themselves known. In case anything goes wrong and they need help. You got a map. You didn't even stop to look at Nicosia.'

The man with the white hair smiled. 'It is a very beautiful city, particularly the old part that we occupy. Every tourist wants to see it.'

'I am going to see it on my way back.'

'Back from where?'

'Kyrenia.'

'Girne. So we will leave for the moment why you turned off that road. You rented a car. From the moment you drove away we were watching you. You were alone.'

Joshua forced a laugh. 'Is that illegal here?'

'No. Just that tourists always come here with their families. Or at least with somebody. Perhaps you are homosexual. Are you homosexual?'

'No.'

'Only sometimes homosexuals come into Turkish Cyprus. There used to be a lot of them during the British period.' He paused, then added, 'Buggering each other.'

'What the hell's that got to do with anything?' For a moment Joshua felt Joshua Howell merging wth Joshua Doyle.

'We were treated as a pisspot of Empire.' The man with white hair drew out a cigarette. Without any indication the man in the camouflage jacket hastily produced a lighter. As he had his cigarette lit the man said, 'Cyprus was used as a place where you sent people you didn't want in England.'

Joshua thought, Lawrence Durrell? But didn't say anything because Howell would not have heard of Lawrence Durrell.

'You come into northern Cyprus. Into Kybris. You hire a car and you drive off, then you stop and examine your map. Why?'

'To find the bloody way!'

'But that was no problem. It is impossible for a tourist to go anywhere off that road, because every side road is blocked. There is only one place you can go to on that road.'

'Kyrenia.' He thought, Joshua Howell wouldn't take this lying down.

'Girne. Which used to be called Kyrenia. Then you drive on, and turn off down a forbidden road. When you think you are being followed you do not drive like a tourist. Not even like a frightened tourist. You drive like a racing driver.'

'You're very flattering.'

'Like a spy.'

'Balls.'

'So the obvious assumption is that you are a Greek spy.'

'And why the hell should I be a Greek spy? I'm a British citizen! Look at my bloody passport!'

The man with the white hair sucked on his cigarette, then said, 'Tell me, Mr Howell, where are you staying?'

'In Nicosia.'

'Who booked you in?'

'The tourist agency.' Joshua Howell would certainly have booked through a tourist agency.

'What tourist agency?'

He said it without thinking, then it struck him like a sword into his stomach. 'Sunswept Holidays,' he said.

Sunswept Holidays who offered cheerful orange and green buses, murdered drivers, and kidnapped children. Sunswept Holidays, last known custodians of his daughter.

He made himself think differently, think like Joshua Howell. 'Why the hell are you holding me? Am I under arrest? If so, I want to know why!'

'It isn't necessarily a question of arresting you.' The man with white hair frowned at his cigarette. There seemed to be something wrong with it. 'You appear not to understand the position.'

He rose from the desk and stood so that his back was to the door. Joshua recognised the technique. The prisoner was obliged to turn his neck uncomfortably to watch, and even then could not really make out the expression on the interrogator's face, because it was in silhouette.

'You left the Greek part of the island. They will have a record of your doing so, if they haven't already lost it. They are very inefficient. You passed through the United Nations zone, but they have no record of you because they don't keep that sort of record. Then you came into northern Cyprus. Kybris. The Republic of Northern Cyprus. If there are any records of your doing so, they are in the hands of the authorities of the Republic. Let us suppose that you do not return. Let us suppose that you have friends who wonder what has happened to you. Though we know that you came here without your family, on holiday alone, and you say that you are not homosexual. So there is no boy friend who buggers you who might ask.'

Joshua recognised the professionalism. He knew what was happening, that he was being deliberately irritated so that he would over-react. But he still said, 'You seem very concerned about anal intercourse. Do you have a problem?'

It was out of character. It was wrong. Joshua Howell would not have said that. However, the man with the white hair didn't seem to notice the mistake.

'But you see, nobody will ask about you. Because there is nobody anybody could ask. You are a visitor to a non-existent country, administered by people who don't exist either. You don't have to take my word for it. You have the word of the British Government.'

Back to the role. Joshua Howell laughed, the laugh of a man who was just a little bit frightened. 'You're not telling me you'll keep me here for ever!'

'I am telling you I could.'

The man with white hair gave up his cigarette, and tossed it out of the door. Then he reached into his pocket for another.

'I could produce, without any difficulty, enough evidence to have you held here as a suspected spy for the Greeks,' he said. Then he put the cigarette in his mouth, and the man in the jacket lit it for him. 'I could have you held on suspicion. After we have interrogated them for long enough, most people give us enough evidence to confirm any suspicions we produce. Because of the fact that your government has no contact with our government, there is, quite literally, nobody to whom you could apply for help.'

A faint smile flickered across his face. 'Those phrases in the tourist guidebooks. At the police station. I want to speak to a

77

solicitor, the British consul, Amnesty International. They would not apply to you because we need not reveal that you exist. Unless we say that we are holding you, nobody could ever learn. That is if we decided to hold you as a suspected Greek spy. But I know you are not a Greek spy.'

Joshua tensed. This was not the normal routine. He had thrown away his strongest card.

'I know you are not a Greek spy,' he repeated. 'I know you are a spy, but not a Greek one. It might appear sheer coincidence, but to use an old English expression, it is a small world. You see, I know who you are.' He drew deeply on the cigarette. 'Chief Superintendent Doyle . . .'

Chapter Twelve

They gave him back his passport and his watch and his wallet. Even the press card. Nothing seemed to be missing. Nobody spoke until the man in the camouflage jacket had left. He was not ordered to leave: it was simply made clear, without a word from the man with white hair, that he was no longer wanted. So he left, and closed the door after him.

The man with white hair pulled out his cigarettes.

'I forget. Do you smoke?'

'I used to. I gave up.'

Then the man with white hair ran his hands over his pockets and said, 'Damn. I have no matches.'

He put his cigarettes back in his pocket, and asked, 'Do you remember me?'

'No. I'm sorry.'

'Perhaps you would if you saw me as I was fifteen years ago.' He tapped his hair. 'This was black then. And I had a moustache. People said I looked rather like Clark Gable. Charminster House.'

Charminster House. The place in Oxfordshire where they used to run the courses on interrogation and pressure and stress. How much a human being could take, and how to avoid showing that a prisoner had been taken beyond that point. Fringe stuff. They'd closed it, because it was now all centred round Ashford, so he must be talking about some time in the sixties. A long time ago.

Joshua thought, I have one advantage. He knows me, I don't know him, and that gives me the advantage since it is important to him that I recognise him.

'A long time ago,' said Joshua.

Then he remembered him. He'd always sat at the back of the room during the lectures. They'd all been ridiculously young, looking back on it, but somehow the man facing him now had, even then, seemed to be a little different from the rest of them. Harder. More sophisticated, and harder.

'My name's Mustapha Pamir. That hasn't changed.' It mattered to him that he was remembered, no doubt about it. 'We were on the same course. I was attached to the embassy.'

He could remember him clearly now. There had been a game, he couldn't remember the details, but Pamir had played it so that someone had been taken away, and they'd never played that game again.

'I was at the embassy. The statutory Turk. I'd been educated at Harrow, and all my superiors spoke English like street-corner grocers, but they were Greeks so they were my superiors.'

He drew on the cigarette. 'Now tell me why you are here.'

'I'm a tourist. Even people in our occupation have holidays.' See if he rose to it. See if he gave any indication what his work was. But all Pamir said was, 'Tourists don't travel on false papers.'

'You know how it is. One doesn't want too many stamps on passports.'

Pamir looked coldly at him. 'I don't owe you a damned thing,' he said. 'I don't owe you, or Britain, a damned thing.'

'No.'

'What I said was correct. If I choose, you go back to the Greeks now. If I don't choose, you might never go back. So now tell me why you are here.'

He had to decide. They'd hinted in London, and Nico had been sure of it: the Turks would back the Grey Wolves over this issue. There was no common interest between the two governments. But could there be between the two men?

Joshua said, slowly, 'If I wasn't just here as a tourist, I would be concerned about reports of some English schoolchildren who've been kidnapped.'

Pamir was good, no doubt about it. But Joshua recognised the tiny reaction. He would not have seen it if he had not been looking for it, but he saw it. Pamir knew about the children.

'Kidnapping?' said Pamir.

'A group of British schoolgirls,' said Joshua. 'All from one school. They've been taken by Grey Wolves.' He paused, then said, 'Turks.'

'These Grey Wolves. They've shown you their passports?' Pamir was stalling for time. 'Is that how you know their nationality?'

'They're Grey Wolves.'

'They said so?'

He risked it. 'You know damned well they said so.'

He was thinking. What do I know about him? Pamir used to sit at the back, and he never said anything. Nothing at the question time at the end of the lectures; but later he was one of those who took over. He was hard. In the games, the role-playing, it really mattered to him that he won. He'd have been no damned use if it hadn't, but all the same, it mattered to him more than it did to most of them. When was it? Say twenty odd years ago. They were all the young hopes, the high-flyers, the ones They were going to rely on in the future. Whoever the various Theys were. But even then Pamir had been different. He'd been better educated, for a start. He had the arrogance of knowing that if this failed, there was always something else to fall back upon. For most of them, that had not been the case.

But as a man. What could he recall about Pamir as a man? Suppose he is in his late forties now. He looked older, because of the white hair, but he must be around forty-seven, forty-eight. That meant that he was in his twenties at Charminster House. He would have to be reasonably senior to have got there at all. Would he have been married? They had not been encouraged to discuss their private lives, but even if he had not been married then, odds are he would have got married soon afterwards. For God's sake, when do Turks marry? So could he have teenage children by now? Could he be approached through children?

Pamir said, 'If you wish to operate against terrorists in our country there is no problem. You have only to ask our permission.'

It was a risk, a calculated risk. He had no entrée into the north, and Pamir could be just that entrée. That was one side of it. The other side was that if Nico was right, even if he was half right and there was potentially a stronger bond between Pamir and the Grey Wolves, because they were all Turks and committed to a Turkish state in Cyprus, than between the two of them, because they were both graduates of Charminster, then he could lose everything. He could lose the support of the Cyprus Government while failing to win anything from the Turks.

He would be taking away what hope there still was for the children. Unless it was too late, and Joanna was already dead.

He hedged, waiting for a lead. 'You know my position.'

Pamir looked round slowly at him, then walked to the door and opened it. The man with the camouflage jacket was leaning against the wall, and stood up straight when he saw Pamir. Silently Pamir produced a cigarette, and the other man lit it for him. Pamir nodded, then returned into the room closing the door after him.

Pamir said, 'So we understand each other, I owe you nothing.'

'So you said.'

'I am a Cypriot, but first I am a Turk. When the Ottoman Empire spread from Spain to India, my ancestors were among those who ruled those places. My family produced scholars, and soldiers, and administrators. We taught Islam, we conquered for Islam, and we governed for Islam. One branch of my family happened to settle here.' He shrugged his shoulders. 'And for one reason or another we have stayed here for three hundred years. This part of Cyprus is as much Turkish as Anatolia. Every man who denies us our national birthright is our enemy. You understand?'

Joshua said, 'You and I know too much to be nationalists.'

It was a risk, but he had to take it. Pamir had to be dragged into controversy. The interrogator must be made to argue with the prisoner.

'I am not talking about nationalism. I am talking about Islam.'

'The Grey Wolves aren't talking about Islam.'

Pamir looked coldly at him. 'No man can always choose his friends. He can only choose his enemies. The Grey Wolves want for this island what I want.'

'No, they don't. They want the collapse of government. Islamic government, or anybody else's.'

'For the moment they want what I want.'

'And for the future?'

'In the future, when we have an independent Turkish Cypriot Republic that is recognised by every other nation on earth, then we will have no further use for the Grey Wolves. Then the situation will be different.'

Pamir blew a smoke ring in the still, hot air. 'There is no problem. You have influence. You will promise to use that influence to get the British Government to recognise us. The British owe us a debt. Who was it who guarded the British when the Greek EOKA terroritsts were trying to kill them? It was the Turks. Turkish policemen, and Turkish guards. Everyone knows that. It is history. So you use your influence. You will get a statement made by your government. It will be a compromise. The British are famous for compromises. It will say that the British Government recognises the needs of the Turkish Cypriots. That you appreciate our national identity. That you will use your good offices to secure an agreement satisfactory to both sides, but in particular establishing a Turkish state on the island of Cyprus.'

82

Joshua said, 'You're talking to the wrong person. You ought to be talking to the Prime Minister.'

There was a crash as Pamir slammed his hand down on the desk. 'Don't try to be clever with me!' It was real anger, not an interrogator's act. 'We are not prepared to tolerate the Greeks any longer, and if they hide behind the English, then we will not tolerate you either!'

'I was only – ' Joshua began.

'Listen! Listen to me!' Pamir leant forward, his face now only inches from Joshua's. 'To create this state, we suffered! We suffered because we were loyal to our friends! You understand? We did not choose to come and live in just one part of the island! Most of the Turks in this place are peasants, and a peasant does not easily give up his home and his land! But we had had enough! We had had enough from the Greeks, and we were betrayed by the English!'

'We're talking about terrorists –'

Again Pamir banged his hand on the table. 'Terrorists! I know of terrorists! In the Turkish quarter of Nicosia the Greeks killed hundreds of us! Hundreds! I was on leave when I heard of how they killed the family of Dr. Nihat Ilhan. His wife, three children, another woman who was visiting, slaughtered! I thought of my own family, and I stayed at my own home.'

His voice dropped, and he rose from the table. 'I stayed to protect them. I thought, the Greeks know who I am. They know I am a man who was a policeman. I was not a man of politics. But I was a policeman and all my family were afraid.'

He turned to look at Joshua, but he seemed almost to be talking to himself. 'The Turks are not a cowardly people. Not even the Greeks say we are cowards. But we were afraid. Most of us in the village – the Turks – we left our village. I went with them because who else would protect them? I should have gone back to my duty, but I had also my family. We went into the forests below Troodos. We were hiding. We were in that forest for six months. In that time my father died. It is possible he would have died anyway. He was an old man, I was his youngest son, and he had a cough. But he did not die in a hospital, he died in a cave. You understand? My wife, she was not ill. She was a strong woman. But she could not live like an animal in the forest. One night she ran away. I have not seen her again. Twice since people have told me they have seen her, but I do not believe them. And my daughter . . .'

Pamir stopped, lowered his head, then turned again and looked at Joshua with strangely empty eyes. 'Why do I tell you this?'

He stiffened and said, 'My daughter, my only child, caught pneumonia in the winter of sixty-four. There was no medicine, there was no doctor. We were living in caves and in huts we had made from branches, there was snow on the ground because we were two thousand metres up, and we were eating berries and animals we could catch in the forest. On the ninth of December she died. We buried her. She was aged four years, three months, and seven days.'

The silence that followed was because there was nothing for either of the two men to say. Finally Pamir said, 'I do not think about it too much. It was a long time ago, but it cannot be anything but the point when my life turned.'

Now he was speaking quietly and calmly. 'I remember it consciously every time I see myself in a mirror. I went from thirteen stone to six and a half stone while I was in the forest, and my hair went white. I have put the weight back on again, but my hair is as it was when I met my brother and he did not recognise me. You must understand that for us it is not playing politics like it is for the Greeks. We demand our nation. You understand? We fought for it, and we will fight for it again if we have to. We will do what is necessary. I am telling you what you must do. You will use your influence.'

'I don't have that sort of influence,' said Joshua.

Pamir waved a finger. 'The days when the Turks of Cyprus did what they were told are over. If ever we are able to work again with the Greeks, they will find that. We have got off our backsides. I want you to use the influence of JBH. I know that if JBH wants something, then it happens.'

'I assure you,' said Joshua, 'it doesn't. It really doesn't.'

'I could threaten you. I could tell you that if I give the orders, you would never leave this room.'

'I don't doubt it. But it wouldn't give JBH any more power.'

Pamir said, 'I am not talking of a full commitment. I am talking of a change of emphasis. If the British Government make the sort of statement I am describing, the Greeks will notice. Then they will put their tails between their legs and come to heel.'

Joshua waited. Pamir examined his cigarette, then put it down on a saucer, and started to pick at his left index finger. He seemed to have a splinter in it. 'A declaration offering to help negotiations under those conditions,' he said. 'That is all I am asking. And I can promise you now that the Government of Northern Cyprus will accept an invitation to such a conference, and will propose a British chairman for it.'

He shrugged. 'No doubt the Greeks will suggest a Greek chairman, or alternating chairmen, or a Turkish vice-chairman. Anything to prevent a satisfactory settlement.'

He pulled a small dark shred of something from his finger, examined it, then picked up his cigarette. 'Well?'

'That isn't what the Grey Wolves are asking. They're demanding a surrender now.'

And you never admit the possibility of accepting the terrorist's first demand. Joshua knew that, and Pamir knew that Joshua knew it, and who was bluffing whom?

Pamir sucked his cigarette. 'So,' he said, 'that is why you must compromise. You will make the statement, and we will support you. It must not be the Grey Wolves who win freedom for northern Cyprus. It must be the people of northern Cyprus.'

There was silence, then somewhere outside there was a scream. It might have been a prisoner, but it was most likely a bird. Joshua was thinking, trying, desperately hard, to separate the expertise of his experience from the involvement of his life. To think of the way ahead as a problem, like the other problems, not as anything concerning him personally. To think of the hostages as seven British citizens, one full adult and six adolescents; not as Joanna and some others.

He said, 'What will you do with the Grey Wolves?'

Pamir said, 'They are terrorists.'

They would be killed. They would be used, and then they would be killed. There was an attractive simplicity in the idea.

Joshua had to say it. 'Perhaps it is already too late. Perhaps the children are already dead.'

'No.'

Joshua looked up sharply. 'How do you know?' he demanded.

Pamir laughed. It was the first time any expression except contempt or the one moment of anger had shown on his face. 'You think it is because I am working with them? No. It is because every single man, woman and child in northern Cyprus wants our country to be recognised. For that, every one of them is on the side of the Grey Wolves. On this one issue. I tell you, our Government could not come out against the Grey Wolves over this issue. The President himself could not. But that does not make our people terrorists. If the Grey Wolves killed children for nothing, then the people here would kill the Grey Wolves.'

'They wouldn't know.'

Pamir said confidently, 'They would know. If the Grey Wolves are hiding those children in northern Cyprus, then the people who live around them will know. They will not know who the Grey Wolves are. They will probably never even have heard of the Grey Wolves. But if the message has been spread around – and it will have been – that the strangers who have taken over those empty houses are fighters for the people of northern Cyprus, then nobody would interfere. They will not help the Grey Wolves, but they will not help the police either.'

'They might know there are people who say they want your national identity. They might even know they're holding hostages.'

(God knows, it happened often enough in Ireland. The house which was inhabited but nobody ever seemed to enter, or to leave. The house you passed by on the other side of the street, not looking at the windows with the closed curtains. The house you didn't ask questions about.)

Joshua went on, 'They might know that. They might even know the hostages are children. But they wouldn't know if those children were killed.'

It was hard, making himself think impersonally, but he was succeeding.

Pamir said, 'You don't know these people. They are peasants. They are a close community.'

'So?'

'So they protect the people they think are helping them. But if those people behave in a way that they disapprove of, then they will stop protecting them.'

'You mean, they would tell the police?'

'I mean they would stop protecting them. It is nothing to do with the police. These people know terrorism. Greek terrorism. EOKA. They have never been terrorists themselves.'

He stubbed out the cigarette. 'Unlike the Greeks. But they are Turks. They may have criticisms of the Turkish Government of Northern Cyprus – that it is too dependent on Ankara – but still they are Turks. They know how to look after themselves. If they do not want the Grey Wolves as neighbours then . . .'

Pamir shrugged. It looked suddenly, unexpectedly, Oriental. It was not the embarrassed shrug of an Englishman who had made a social gaffe or realised his companion couldn't pay his share of the bill. It was a Levantine shopkeeper shrug, totally at variance with the clipped, almost perfect, English accent.

Joshua said quietly, 'The Greeks say that the children can't be in the north. They say that if they were kidnapped in the south, despite the fact that the demand came through Ankara, it is impossible for the children to have been taken to the north.'

'Did they point out that there are no Turks in the south?'

'Yes.'

Pamir groped into his pocket and shook out another cigarette. 'They claim to be a logical people,' he said. 'And logically they are right. It is impossible for a group of Turks to operate in the south, let alone get across the frontier.'

He tapped his pockets, then remembered he was out of matches. 'All the same,' he said, 'I have no doubt of two things. One, the children are still alive. Two, somehow, yes, they are here. In Kybris.'

Chapter Thirteen

They drove him back to the frontier in the Mercedes. He was pushed into the back, none too gently, and a soldier sat beside him. The soldier kept his M16 lying across his lap, the muzzle pressed hard into Joshua's ribs, and a large brown hand spread over the trigger and the safety catch. Every jolt of the car dug the weapon into Joshua's body, and the soldier knew it, but Joshua made a pretence of not noticing. Pamir sat in the front passenger seat, his arm round the driver's seat. The driver drove fast and rather badly, and from time to time his eyes flickered up to watch Joshua in the mirror.

Joshua said, 'If we're going to keep the windows closed, we might at least use the air conditioning.'

He watched carefully. Neither the soldier nor the driver reacted. They couldn't understand English, that much was apparent. Perhaps that was why they had been chosen. Pamir glanced at the dashboard, adjusted something, and almost immediately there was a noticeable drop in the temperature inside the car.

Joshua leant back in the seat. 'What are you going to do with me?'

'Give you back to the Greeks,' said Pamir.

'And the girls?'

'I've told you what to do.' Then Pamir took out another cigarette, and lit it with the car's cigarette lighter. 'You do that, and we'll get the Grey Wolves. If we're lucky, we'll save the girls too. Everybody will be happy. Except the Grey Wolves and the Greeks.'

'And I've told you. I don't have that sort of power.'

Pamir shrugged. 'Then I can't help you.'

Most of the traffic seemed to be military, camouflaged Turkish trucks and the occasional white UN transport. Over-burdened donkeys plodded along the dirt sides of the road, their riders with scarves round their heads against the dust. There was a seedy calm about the heat of the day. Men lay in patches of shade before start-

88

ing work again later, after the siesta. Outside the occasional cafe men sat with long-empty coffee cups or lemonade bottles, playing backgammon. They did not look round when the army lorries roared past. Joshua noticed that even an armoured car failed to arouse interest. This was a society under military control, and resigned to the idea.

'I have to come back here again,' said Joshua. 'You say the children are still in Cyprus, and this side of the frontier. If I'm to look for them, then I have to come back here.'

'Through Turkey. You can come back through Turkey.'

'For God's sake,' said Joshua, feeling his irritation mounting. 'My contacts with London are from the other side. You yourself say I can't get London from here. I have to be able to cross the bloody frontier!'

'What is so different about you?' Pamir's voice had a new, guttural edge to it. 'I cannot cross the frontier, and I was born here! I cannot go back to where I have lived most of my life, because the Greeks would kill me! What is so different about you? What is it that makes it possible for the English to do things in Cyprus that the Cypriots cannot?'

I'm coming back, thought Joshua. I'm not telling you, but I'm coming back. Somehow.

He said, 'How do I get hold of you?'

Pamir laughed bitterly. 'No problem. You use whatever you use to contact JBH. They contact Ankara. And Ankara contacts me.'

'I meant, give me a telephone number.'

'You ignorant English idiot!' He was angry, genuinely angry. It was the second time that Joshua had seen the blade of anger beneath the facade. 'You think you can pick up a phone in the Greek sector and phone here? 'You think that? The lines are cut! Perhaps you try to phone through Turkey, but you will be very lucky if you succeed!'

It was the insanity of the divided island again. A man could stand on a rooftop and shout to another man in the next street: but he couldn't telephone him.

They passed a deserted shop where, faint, there was still a painted Union Jack on the wall. The fascia read: The Victory Caf, then the rest of the board had fallen away. Joshua thought, this was how we left the place. This was the child of our abdication. Shuttered shops, peeling paint, and telephone wires that stopped at places that had no names, no meanings, no justification.

Pamir said something in Turkish, and the driver laughed. The man beside Joshua jabbed the rifle painfully into Joshua's ribs.

Joshua said to Pamir, 'Would you tell your friend beside me that if he sticks his rifle into me again, he may manage to shoot me later but I'll have taken his eyes out first.'

Pamir grunted something, and the rifle was pulled away. Joshua felt the soldier glaring at him, but he ignored it and looked straight ahead at the road to Nicosia.

Pamir opened his window to throw out his cigarette stub, then closed it again. 'You leave everything to me,' he said. 'Either you get your Government to make the statement, or what happens will be what we decide to do.'

The terrorists were an embarrassment. More than a threat, they were an embarrassment. They were reducing the room for manoeuvre of both the Turkish Government in Ankara, and the Turkish authorities in northern Cyprus. Therefore, logically, they must be silenced. Not brought to trial, because that would give them the free publicity that all terrorists craved. They must be silenced. Killed. If that meant that a few English schoolgirls got caught up in the crossfire, so be it. After all, the British Government refused to co-operate in attempts to save the children. People got killed in terrorist actions all the time. Compared with an aircraft hijacking, a school bus was nothing. It would hardly make the front page, and then only for a couple of days at most. The hard news would be that the terrorists had paid the price for what they had done. The terrorists would be blamed, and the Turkish authorities would be praised. The fact that the British were not present when the Turks went in was certainly not the fault of the Turks. The Turks wanted to be helped. It was the British who refused help, because help would mean recognition.

Pity about the children, but principles are more important than people. Everybody knows that.

They passed the first building without a roof, where there had been fighting. Joshua glanced at his watch. It was only a quarter to two.

He decided to try again, make one last attempt to establish a bond with this man who had shared Charminster House with him all those years ago.

'Let me buy you lunch,' he said.

Pamir looked watchfully at him. 'You are being expelled from Kybris. You will not be allowed back in. You are bloody lucky to be allowed to leave. You went into a prohibited area using false papers. You are bloody lucky that I am letting you leave at all.'

Joshua thought, I've blown my cover, I've been identified, I've told them why I'm here, and I'm no further forward. He said. 'We both want the same thing.'

'You mean, you want an independent Republic of Northern Cyprus?' Pamir laughed.

'I mean I want the Grey Wolves caught.'

'I want them dead.'

'Okay. Dead.'

Pamir shrugged his shoulders again, the Byzantine shrug. 'Then do what I said. Get your Government to issue the statement. Get them to be honest for once.'

He turned round and smiled, a charming easy smile, the dazzling white teeth in the sun-tanned face. 'Then it will be like the old days.'

The Mercedes drew up outside the car-hire firm. 'From here you walk,' said Pamir. 'You check out at the frontier. When you are ready to do what we want, tell Ankara and we'll make arrangements.'

He gestured to the soldier beside Joshua, who opened the door and climbed out. The soldier clearly resented having been reprimanded in the car, and tried to slam the door on Joshua's hand as he followed him out into the street. Joshua was ready for him, and savagely swung the heavy door outwards, catching the soldier painfully on the elbow. It was a pointless thing to do, but it made him feel better. For a moment the soldier started to raise his rifle, then he swore, and stepped back lowering the weapon again.

Pamir must have seen the incident, but he said nothing.

'Do I get a repayment because I returned the car early?' said Joshua. He was still hoping that, somehow, human contact could be made, that they could find again the tenuous ties that had linked them all those years ago at Charminster House.

Pamir looked coldly at him, then strode away towards the office of the car-hire firm. The two Turkish soldiers glanced at each other, then, after a moment of hesitation, followed Pamir.

Unexpectedly, Pamir stopped and turned. 'Do what I tell you,' he said, his voice clear in the hot, still air. 'Then you will find we will be co-operative. We will keep our promises. We are not Greeks. Do what I said. It is important. This is our country we are talking about.'

Joshua thought, no, we're talking about my daughter, but he didn't speak. Instead he turned and walked towards the grubby little kiosk that marked the final statement of the existence of the Republic of Kybris.

Chapter Fourteen

The reception desk at the Hotel Romantica was deserted. Joshua glanced at his watch. Seventeen minutes past two. Christ, had so much happened in these few hours? On the desk there was an electric bell and the legend, Ring Bell for Service. He pressed it, but there didn't seem to be any sound. He banged on the desk. 'Hello. Is there anybody around?'

There was a pause, then a door behind the reception area opened, and a girl hurried forward. She was hastily buttoning up a housecoat, and as he looked up Joshua realised that underneath the coat she was naked. He also realised that she was unusually attractive. This, he thought, must be the Anna that Nico spoke about.

'I am sorry,' she said. 'Everyone is asleeping.'

'Yes. I was just wondering if it's possible to get anything to eat. But if the restaurant's closed –'

'It is close. But still I can find something good.' She smiled. He thought, she has a lovely smile. She reached under the counter, and as she did so the neck of the housecoat opened and he could see her breasts, full, rich breasts, the nipples dark against lighter skin than that above it, where she had been wearing a low cut dress in the hot sun.

She put a typed menu on the counter, then, her lips pursed, indicated with her finger.

'Is not more that . . . or that . . . or I think that.' Then, again, the smile. 'But is not very good, the bifstekki. Is made yesterday. So.'

'Anything. Anything you recommend, and a beer.' He was hot, and he had had a rifle jabbing in his ribs, and his only child was in danger, and he knew how conscious he was of the body half hidden by the housecoat. He said, 'You're Anna, aren't you?'

Her eyes widened. 'Yes. How do you know?'

'Nico –' For God's sake, what was his impossible name? 'Nico in the police –'

'Nico Tsardanis?'

92

'Yes.'

'There is many Nicos!'

'Yes. He said there was a very pretty girl called Anna here.'

She laughed, and he knew that he wanted her as he had not wanted a woman for years. 'I think he would like to be naughty man, Nico!'

'I don't blame him.' Then, hurriedly, he said, 'How can you get any food if the restaurant's shut?'

'Is not a problem. It is micro-waved.'

'But if it's shut – '

'In the room. Is service in the room.' She looked at the registration book, open on the counter. 'You are Mister Howell?'

'Yes'

'Room six.' Then she realised that his eyes were on her breasts, and her hand pulled the collar together.

In his room he sat on the edge of the bed, and started to encode a report to JBH. They had closed the window and the shutters, and he knew that it was the best way to keep the room cool in the heat, but it made him feel enclosed, a prisoner as he had been a few hours before. He rose, flung open the french windows and opened the shutters. The sun poured in, but at least the air stirred a little and specks of dust floated like gold in the sunbeams. Then he sat down on the bed again, and resumed his work with the one-time pad.

It was less than ten minutes later that there was a respectful tap on the door. He checked that any evidence of what he had been doing was out of sight, and called, 'Come in!'

She came in, a tray in her hands. She pushed the door open with her hip and looked round the room. 'I think you will like best a Cyprus *meze*,' she said. 'Is a little of many things. Special from Cyprus.'

Then she smiled again, and added, 'Too it is very hot today, and I choose only cold things for the *meze*.'

She put the tray down on the table, and he rose from the bed. There were prawns and fish and cheeses and a salad and several sorts of meats and sausages and a green vegetable he didn't recognise.

'It looks like exactly what I want,' he said.

She smiled again, a shy smile, then produced a bottle opener from a pocket in the housecoat and opened the beer that was also on the tray.

'I pour for you?'

'Please.'

Just stay. It doesn't matter what you do, just stay and let me look at you, and feel myself stirring for you.

Her lips pouted in concentration as she carefully poured the beer into a glass.

She said, 'Is correct with Cyprus *meze* to bring all the foods one after other. But I think is better to bring now all at once.' Then she said, 'Is correct, that? You say, one after other?'

'Normally you say one after *an*other, but what the hell. The idea is to be understood.'

'One after *an*other.'

'Yes.'

If they stopped talking, she'd probably leave. He said, 'You speak English very well.' It was an idiotic thing to say. She'd have been learning it in school only a few years ago. And the other Greeks he had spoken to seemed to speak it better. Not to mention Pamir. But it kept her in the room.

'No,' she said. 'I hope to learn to speak it very well, but when there was fighting many months I did not go to school.'

She hesitated, then said, 'Please. Katherina say you go to the north. Is true?'

'I was there, yes. Who's Katherina?'

'She is girl who also work in this hotel.'

'Oh, yes.' He remembered the woman who had told him how to find his way to the frontier. 'At the desk. With a –'

He checked himself. He had been about to say, with a moustache, but it seemed offensive. She might resent it, and leave him. But his hand had already risen to his upper lip.

Anna smiled, then lowered her eyes. 'I think you are to say she has hair. Yes?'

'Yes.'

'It is sometimes problem for Greek girls, the hair. I do not think it is nice.'

'I agree with you.'

She laughed. 'There is one joke. How can you tell always the Olympic Airlines aeroplane at the airport?'

'I don't know. How do you tell?'

'It is the aeroplane with hair under its wings!'

He laughed, and then she laughed. 'It is not right to tell you that joke,' she said. 'Now you will not like Greek women!'

'I like some Greek women very much indeed.'

She looked up at him, and then said, as though there was not the atmosphere in the room, 'Perhaps when you go to the north you go to my village.'

He wanted to reach inside the coat, but all he said was, 'What's the name of your village?'

'It is called Agios Khrysoumos, but now the Turks call it Dikmen.'

'I don't know where I'll be going.'

He suddenly remembered why he was there, and for a moment the sexuality left him as though he had been castrated.

'My father is dying,' she said. 'And always he says, how is it, my house. All the time he asks, and we cannot tell him.'

'I didn't see much. It looked to me as though the Turks were looking after most places okay.'

I didn't see much. Mostly the inside of a rather small prison, but no need to tell her about that.

'If he could see again his house, even if it has Turks, he would be happy. But that is not possible.'

'No.'

She brightened. 'Perhaps you could see it, and tell about it to me, and I could tell him.'

Then they'd meet again. He would have the perfect excuse for meeting her again.

'Yes. Why not? I could do that.'

'Perhaps you take photograph! That would be best! I have a camera, and I will pay for the film –'

Joshua remembered the camera in his case, the camera that looked like any ordinary Canon, but which wasn't. But better to use her camera.

'I'm not much of a photographer, but I'll try,' he said. It fitted. It gave him a reason for going wherever he wanted, looking for this damned house. Who was to say where it was? He could go into any village, any town he wanted. It was just the daft sort of thing Joshua Howell, insurance advisor, would do, wander about looking for the abandoned home of an old Greek who was dying.

It fitted. And it meant he could see her.

'You have a map?' she asked. 'I show you where is Agios Khrysoumos.'

The two maps, the Greek one and the Turkish one, the maps that showed the same places with utterly different names, the maps that represented the legal truth recognised by the world and the factual truth represented by thirty-five thousand Turkish troops, lay folded on top of each other at the foot of the bed. He carefully opened them out, beside each other.

Anna said, very quietly, 'I have never see map like this. Turkish map.'

'Where is your family's village?'

She pointed to a name to the east of Nicosia, just off the main road to Kyrenia. 'Is there.' She sat on the bed, and he sat beside her. 'You see? The road divide, and here is the square in the village, with the *cafeneon*, and here is the church –'

She stopped, and then said quietly, 'Now they take out all the holy things and it is a mosque.'

'You know that?'

'Every church they do that.'

Then she seemed to brighten. 'You can tell the house from my family. It is the most big house in the village. Here, after the church, it is on the right of the road. It is white with gates. It is the only house in the village with gates. You can see it, and you can take photographs. Then . . . then my father will be happy when he die.'

'I'll take a lot of photographs.'

She was silent, and he could hear an insect buzzing sleepily in the room. Then the sound faded away as it flew out through the window.

'You are very kind man,' she said.

'No.' Randy, he thought, but not particularly kind.

'I see people come to the hotel. Tourists. Often they go to the north. I do not like to ask them to look for my village. It is only village like every other.'

'It's different for you.'

'Twice I ask, but the tourists did not go to the village.' She had her face turned away from him, and he wondered if her eyes were filled with tears. 'I trust you. I think you will do what you say.'

'Yes.'

'For my father, it is the most important thing in his life.'

Their arms touched, hers surprisingly cool in the hot afternoon. Then she said, 'I am taking your time! You have not eat your lunch!'

'More to the point, I'm not drinking my beer.'

He raised the glass. 'To you,' he said. 'To you and your village.'

And your breasts and your bottom and your pussy, he thought.

Anna reached out and picked up a large prawn from a saucer. 'In Cyprus we eat prawn so.' She expertly peeled it, then carefully dipped the tail into an unexplained dish of white sauce. 'Is special sauce for prawn.'

96

She held it out to him, watching him. He slowly leant towards her and took the prawn in his mouth, then her fingers. It all seemed to be happening unnaturally slowly: slowly but inevitably. His hands took hers, and very gently he licked her fingers. Her eyes were looking into his, then, again slowly as in a dream, they closed. He led her hands down his chest, down to the hard presence of his penis. A tiny tremble ran through her, but she did not open her eyes. He released her, then reached out and unbuttoned the coat. Still she did not stir, her hands resting on him, unmoving. He kissed her breast and felt the nipple jutting out between his lips. As his hand slid between her thighs he felt what he had half guessed, half hoped for.

'I see what you mean,' he said, his voice muffled by her body. 'No hair. Like a little girl.'

He felt her undoing his zip, then in the afternoon silence she slipped from the bed and, kneeling, edged between his legs. First her tongue, then her lips caressed him. He lay back on the bed and nothing mattered any more. It was like the first time, all over again. No, it was better than the first time, for then they had been young and clumsy and over-eager. This was different, isolated, unique. From some recess of his mind he remembered Barbara, and she was irrelevant too. This was different. When he reached out and stroked her breasts, then as she moved and he could feel the roundness of her bottom, it was nothing to do with Barbara. The bottom he held was round and firm and young, and Barbara, despite all her dieting and self-conscious exercises, was now soft and drooping. Barbara, even when they had first slept together, she had never been like this. Never. She had never tasted like this, she had never had this dewy youth. The smoothness round the temple of Aphrodite was utterly different from the bush that Barbara offered him, thrust at him, demanding love he didn't feel. He had always known it could be like this but, in all his life before, it never had been.

He felt her moving away from him, and opening his eyes saw her drawing her robe around her and moving towards the window.

'Don't go!' he cried. 'For God's sake, don't go now!'

She smiled, her eyes sparkling. 'I am not going,' she said. 'I shut the window. I think perhaps we will make a noise . . . '

Chapter Fifteen

When he entered the British Consulate Miss Galsworth rose fluttering to her feet.

'Mr Earnshaw is busy, but he left instructions that if you wanted to see him –'

'No. I don't want to see Mr Earnshaw. But thank him all the same.' He produced the coded message. 'If you could just send that. There won't be an immediate reply, but I'll drop in tomorrow morning for whatever they've sent by then.'

Miss Galsworth looked at the incomprehensible paper. From time to time messages were sent in code, but normally only after long conversations between Mr Earnshaw and total strangers who arrived on appointments made without her foreknowledge, but known to Mr Earnshaw.

'I'll tell Mr –'

'Don't bother him.' Joshua smiled. 'I'm sure he's a busy man. He told me so himself. Just send it.'

Then, because Miss Galsworth looked still a virgin likely to remain a virgin, and because he was aware that his body was pulsing from Anna, he said, 'And I will bring you a bower of whatever they grow here to set off your complexion.'

Miss Galsworth suddenly found she didn't know what to do with her hands, and knocked an in-tray onto the floor.

The Consulate's effective hours seemed to be a compromise between English office routine and the life of the island, which was based round the hours when the heat moderated and the Cypriots did not succumb to a natural desire to sleep. The sound of music from the cafes of Nicosia was beginning to fill the air, but nearer to hand, from the gardens of the houses that had mostly been abandoned during the fighting, bull-frogs and cicadas heralded the coolness of the approaching evening.

In the Hotel Romantica there was no sign of Anna. Instead at the reception desk Katherina smiled at him from below her moustache.

'I have one message for you,' she said. 'Please for telephone this number.'

She held out a sheet of paper, and he took it. The number on it meant nothing.

'Who left it?'

'I dunno. I think is mebbe policeman. Is very clean shirt.'

Joshua went to his room, checked the instructions by his room telephone. The number seemed to be a Nicosia one, and he could dial directly. At least he could be reasonably certain that Katherina would not be listening in.

He phoned, and a male voice said, 'Oreste?'

'Joshua Howell. I had a message to phone.'

'Ah, yes. Where you been?' He recognised Nico's voice. 'I send a car for you. Be outside the hotel in five minutes. Okay?'

'Okay.'

The line went dead. Nico had a sense of theatre. A sense of theatre, thought Joshua; and he'd seen too many thrillers in the open-air cinemas of Cyprus.

The car arrived in less than five minutes, with an unsmiling driver who either spoke no English, or preferred to give the impression that he didn't. There was no sign of Nico, and when Joshua asked where they were going the driver stared ahead as though he were deaf. They twisted through a series of narrow streets towards the centre of the city – now its Grecian limits, where the absurdity of the wall amputated it from its other half, Siamese twins neither sharing a life, nor free from their siblings.

They slowed past a building that looked like a police station, then drew up outside a cafe next door. Seated at a table in the street, glowering over a tiny cup of coffee, was Nico.

He waved Joshua out to a seat beside him, and the car drove off. Then he clicked his fingers, and indicated a coffee for Joshua to a waiter inside the cafe.

'First I tell you what you glad to hear,' he said. 'I think we found the bus.'

Joshua waited, then asked quietly, 'The children?'

He knew the answer before Nico spoke. 'No. Not the kids.'

Nico looked down at the table, and slowly drew circles on the painted metal top with a forefinger. 'I gotta hold of the CID,' he said. 'I told them I wanted to know about this damn bus. They ask around, you know?'

'Yes.' It was the oldest, least spectacular, most reliable of police procedures. Ask around. Ask those who are a little bit frightened of you, a little bit in your debt. Then wait.

'One officer, he had this guy. The guy say he hear someone gotta bus. He hear because it wasn't like usual. The story he hear was that whoever got the bus, they get it for nothing. They can sell it all, don't pay nothing for it, but it must not be traceable. You understand?'

'Yes.'

'That's why he hear about it. There aren't many things come for nothing.'

'No.'

'So it was taken to a garage at the back of Alexander the Great Street. Right in the middle of Nicosia. That sounds crazy, except it isn't. You put a Sunswept bus, all damn orange and green, in a village where they don't go, and everybody notice. But in Nicosia they're used to seeing the buses. So nobody says nothing.'

'Yes. Who gave the bus to the garage?'

'That we don't know.'

'Then who runs the garage?'

Nico inclined his head towards the police station next door. 'In there. But we've got problems. The garage belongs to a man called Jacovides. He's a big fat slob, owns a coupla racehorses, got a hotel, a bar, and he's into smuggling. He's in there, talking about what he's going to do to us when he gets his lawyer.'

For a moment Nico grinned. 'But the phone in the interrogation room don't work, so he can't call his lawyer.'

'But if you've found the bus –'

'That's it. We haven't.'

He checked as a waiter appeared, carefully wiped the table clean of Nico's circles, and put down a coffee in front of Joshua. As the waiter retired into the cafe Nico said, *'Metrio.* They make it *metrio,* medium, the coffee. Because he sees you are a foreigner. Less trouble, *metrio.* With a Greek, he has to ask how he wants it. The bus.'

'Yes?'

'By the time we got to the garage there was a lot of bits. Mebbe in among them was the bits from the bus. In England, in the United States, okay, we bring in the forensic lab. Mebbe they find say blood. Hairs from the girls.'

Nico laughed, 'Here, our forensic people, we'd be lucky if they found the fucking wheels!'

'But Jacovides doesn't know . . .'

100

Nico grinned, a wide, slow grin, then reached out and grasped Joshua's arm. 'You got it right! He don't know. We talk about what we find, and he gets a little worried. Then, mebbe he makes a mistake.'

'It could take time.' He said it quietly, dispassionately, as though it was a stranger he was thinking about, not his daughter.

'Yeah.'

Then Nico gestured to Joshua to drink the coffee. 'You see. Mebbe he make a mistake.'

Joshua raised the little cup to his lips, the gritty lees spilling across his lower lip. He wiped his mouth with the back of his hand, and rose.

Inside the police station a respectful uniformed Sergeant indicated a door at the end of a short corridor, a door with a spy hole in it. First Nico peered through the hole, then Joshua. For a moment it occurred to him that only a matter of a few hours before it had been some other unknown observer who had blotted out the prisoner's privacy; and that it had been he who had been the prisoner.

A large man in a sweat-stained white shirt sat behind a table that was too small for him. On a bench against the wall, facing him, two men were being interrogated. One was very fat, nearly bald, and looked to be in his late fifties. He had been wearing a brown silk suit, but he had taken off his jacket and tie, and they now lay across his knees. The pointed, patent leather shoes looked too small to be comfortable. His mouth was smiling, a smile calculated to show assurance and control: but his eyes were not smiling.

A couple of feet away from him, on the end of the bench, there was another man, younger and wearing overalls. His hands were dirty, and twitched. His face was pock-marked, and dark eyebrows met across the narrow forehead. His eyes flickered between the policeman and the fat man, and while Joshua was watching he made no attempt to talk.

There was a fourth occupant in the interrogation cell, a boy of around twelve years of age. He was standing in a corner of the room, and Joshua had to press his eye hard against the spy hole to see him. The boy had a thin, sensitive face, and there seemed to be something wrong about the way he was standing. One shoulder was higher than the other, and the weight seemed clumsily distributed. By peering at an angle downwards Joshua managed to see that one foot was turned inwards. The boy was a cripple.

Into Joshua's ear Nico whispered, 'Take a look at that policeman. You ever see such a damn stupid face?'

The big man momentarily turned, and Joshua saw what Nico meant.

'He doesn't look a size nine hat, no.'

'That's Sergeant Michaelis. He's the brightest guy in the Force. That's his trick, looking dumb. He's so damn lazy he never gets promoted, but he's the best interrogator in the island!'

'If the fat one is Jacovides –'

'Yes.'

'Who are the others?'

Nico pushed Joshua aside, and peered into the interrogation room.

'I seen the guy in overalls. He's a mechanic for Jacovides. I forget his name. But he works a lot wherever Jacovides want him. The other, the skinny kid . . . No, I don't know him.'

The Sergeant, who had been standing unnoticed behind the two men, murmured something in Greek.

'He say they picked him up in the garage,' said Nico. 'He hanging around.'

Michaelis either sensed that they were being watched, or, more likely, had some way of telling when the Judas hole was being used. He rose slowly to his feet, wagged a finger at Jacovides, and made his heavy way to the door.

Joshua stepped back as Michaelis tapped to be let out, and the Sergeant opened the door with an ancient and massive key, then closed it again behind Michaelis.

'Well?' asked Nico.

Michaelis glanced at Joshua, and on receiving Nico's nod that he could speak, said, 'As I read it, sir, yes, Jacovides has got the bus. Or he had it. It's in bits now. He's surprised if we've found anything to link the bus to him, but I think he thinks I think I've got him.'

He spoke very slowly, the logic forming in the darkening air like the build up of storm clouds. He had an accent that momentarily Joshua didn't place.

Joshua said, 'Will he break?'

'Give me a week, yes.' Then, after a moment of ponderous assessment, 'Sir.'

'You haven't got a week.'

Nico said, 'Technically, you haven't even got now. We've nothing to hold him on.'

'Yes, sir.'

'The people who gave him the bus,' said Joshua. 'Have you got anything on them? Anything at all?'

102

Michaelis hesitated, then again speaking as though he was giving formal evidence, he said, 'He says he doesn't know what I'm talking about. So, of course, he doesn't know about a bus, and he doesn't know about anybody who gives buses away. Sir. But - do you speak Greek, sir?'

'No.'

'Well, sometimes in Greek people let slip implications that you can't translate. You can't use them in evidence, but they're there.' Then he added, 'If you can recognise them.'

'And the other two?'

'I've hardly got round to them yet, sir. I would have separated them, but I hadn't really got a charge and Jacovides was making a thing about one being his employee and him being responsible for the boy. And, anyway, we've only got one secure room. So I thought I'd separate them after I've finished with Jacovides. Once he's been released I don't see him worrying much about what happens to them. And he wasn't at the garage. He was at home. We only brought him in after we discovered who owned the garage.'

Joshua was still confused by Michaelis' accent. He said, 'Tell me. Where did you learn English?'

He was thinking of the terrorists' note, the note written in cold, impeccable English.

'At school, sir,' said Michaelis.

'In Cyprus?'

'No sir. London. Camden Town.'

Nico said, 'You think he knows where the bus came from?'

'Oh yes, sir,' said Michaelis confidently. 'They all do. Even the boy. But the longer I talk to them, in one way it makes it more difficult. Sooner or later Jacovides will start asking when I'm going to come up with some evidence.'

'The bus is untraceable?'

'With our facilities, yes, I should imagine so. Jacovides seems confident enough.'

Joshua glanced through the spy hole, then said, 'Tell me about the other two.'

'The mechanic, he works for Jacovides. He's got a conviction for petty larceny, that's all. The boy, I haven't seen him before but he seems rather bright.'

The uniformed Sergeant hrrumphed respectfully, then spoke in Greek.

Nico listened, then turned to Joshua. 'The Sergeant knows the kid. He's more or less been adopted by Jacovides. The real father's dead. The mother's an English woman who came out here on vacation. You know? The moonlight, the wine. Next thing, she's pregnant. So she marries the guy.'

The Sergeant added something. 'Yeah, okay,' said Nico, '*Andaxi*.' Then, to Joshua, 'He say there was a girl, then that boy in there. He's going to go to high school next term.'

Then, by way of explanation, 'The boy's family and the Sergeant's family, they come from the same village. In the north.'

'Does he speak English then?'

'Sure.'

Michaelis added, 'He speaks it perfectly. He's another who's hoping for the bright lights of London.'

'Camden Town,' said Joshua cynically.

'Probably.' Michaelis sucked his teeth noisily. 'My family spoke Greek amongst themselves, but I had English all the rest of the time. And every night when it was pissing down with rain outside in London, they used to talk about the sun and the oranges and the olives. So when I decided to join the Force, I reckoned I could either be a London policeman who spoke Greek, and spend my whole life investigating break-ins at grocery shops, or I could be a policeman in Cyprus who spoke English better than most.'

He caught Nico's expression, and added, 'Sir.'

There was a hammering on the door. Michaelis put his eye to the spy hole.

'Jacovides is demanding his legal rights,' he reported.

There was a moment's hesitation, then Joshua was aware that the three men were all looking at him. It was the unconscious recognition of his authority, a subtle whiff of the power that they recognised in him, and knew they lacked.

'I want to talk to the boy,' he said.

The three Cypriots exchanged glances.

'Mebbe in the interrogation room?' said Nico uncertainly.

'Not in there. Outside somewhere. And alone.'

'I . . .' Nico looked round, then, unnecessarily, lowered his voice. There was nobody within earshot who would report what he said. 'My car. You can borrow mebbe my car.'

'Fine.'

'Only I don't know. I don't know you. I don't know nothing. If Jacovides say he protects the kid –'

'The Toyota?'

'Yes. It's outside.'

Joshua nodded. He had taken over, there was no doubt about that now. In the narrow corridor he could feel them backing away, distancing themselves from him. His world was not quite their world, and they didn't trust him.

'What's the boy's name?'

'I don't know,' said Nico.

'Iannis something,' said Michaelis.

The Sergeant waited until after they had spoken, then said, 'Iannis Mouzas, sir.'

'Give me time to get into the car. Then release them, and when the boy comes out shove him into the car. Front seat, beside me. Understand?'

'Yes, but –' began Nico.

'I'll need the keys.'

Nico groped into his pocket and produced a large bunch of keys held together on a chain with a lurid plastic clip made in the shape of a crucifix.

'And don't give him a chance to think. Just push him in.' Joshua turned and strode out into the cooling evening, the lights beginning to come on in the houses round the station.

The Toyota was facing towards the centre of the city. Joshua glanced round. The road appeared to run from the old town out into the suburbs. He wished he knew the town or even had a map, but the important thing was to keep the momentum going. He unlocked the door, climbed in, and closed the windows. The engine started immediately, and to his relief no pre-recorded voice told him to check his doors, fasten his seat belt, or concern himself about petrol or oil. There was a battery of lights built into the roof, but presumably Nico had somehow disconnected the automatic advice centre that Japanese manufacturers tended to fit.

He drove off, and swung the car round in the deserted street so that it faced west into the last glowing traces of the sunset. Then he crawled along the street, back towards the police station.

He watched as Jacovides emerged from the station, gesticulating, followed by the mechanic. For a moment he thought there had been a slip-up, then the boy appeared in the doorway, Michaelis holding his arm.

Joshua swung the car across the road, and threw open the passenger door. Nico suddenly stepped out from the darkness behind Michaelis and the boy, and in a matter of seconds the boy was in the car, the door slammed shut, and Joshua, with a scream of tyres, accelerating away.

Joshua reached across, locked the car door. No doubt there was some central locking mechanism, but he hadn't had time to find it, and he couldn't risk a mistake.

'Seat belt on, Iannis,' he said.

'Who are you?' The boy was frightened.

'Just put your seat belt on.'

Iannis hesitated, his head turning from side to side. Joshua reached across, grabbed the belt, pulled it across the boy's thin body, slotted it into its socket. Then unexpectedly, brutally, he pulled the spare length of the belt and looped it round the hand-brake, pinioning the boy to the seat.

'If you don't try to release your hands,' said Joshua affably, 'then I won't have to tie them together.'

'What are you doing?' He started to wrestle, but the belt held him hard back into the curve of the seat. It would take him seconds to free himself.

'I said, don't try to release yourself.'

The boy gave a sort of hysterical laugh. 'What are you doing? Who are you?'

'I want to talk to you,' said Joshua. 'We're going to have a chat. Okay?'

'Is this a stick-up?' The dated schoolboy slang with the slight Cypriot accent made Joshua grimace momentarily until he remembered what he could not forget.

'No,' said Joshua. 'I'll see you're taken home. Once I've learnt what I want to know.'

He reached forward and pushed in the cigarette lighter.

'You asked me who I am. I'm not going to tell you. But I will tell you this. There's nobody on this island who knows who I really am.'

Then he remembered Pamir, and something made him say, 'Nobody in this country knows who I am. Now, let me tell you something. In the books it says that the most dangerous people are idealists. People who do appalling things because they believe that what they are doing ultimately leads to good. Like the Spanish Inquisition. Have you ever heard of the Spanish Inquisition?'

'Yes.'

'Good.' They obviously did a better job in Cyprus teaching the history of the West than they did in the West teaching the history of

Byzantium. 'Then there are the psychopaths. If you get a society like Nazi Germany, then the psychopaths can achieve power and run concentration camps. But the most dangerous people of all are the ordinary people who are subjected to extraordinary stresses. Do you understand?'

'Yes.'

He was watching Joshua, eyes wide, more uncertain than frightened. The cigarette lighter popped, and Joshua took it out of the dashboard. Carefully he put the glowing end against his thumbnail. There was a smell of burning, but before it could hurt he put the lighter back into its socket. It meant nothing, but it shocked, and now the boy was uncertain if he was trapped with a madman.

'That's my problem,' said Joshua. 'I happen to be in a very extraordinary position. There is nothing I will not do to get what I want.'

Joshua could sense the boy working out his chances of releasing himself and throwing himself out of the car. The important thing was to keep him frightened.

Without warning, Joshua hurled the car off the road, accelerating as the wheels juddered over the rough ground that stretched away into the darkening evening. Still accelerating, he threw the car round in a tailspin, then brought it back onto the road.

'The first question,' he said, as though nothing had happened, his voice quiet and relaxed, 'is how well do you know Jacovides?'

The boy was now wide-eyed, his hands inside the belt gripping the seat between his legs. 'I . . . He's looked after us since . . . since . . .'

'Since what?'

'Since daddy . . . disappeared.'

'Disappeared?'

'He . . . tried to go back home. To where we used to live. Then . . . we don't know.'

There were tears running down the boy's face. The last vestiges of confidence drained away. The humane thing would have been to put a fatherly arm round the narrow, shaking shoulders: but he could not do that because he must press home his advantage. What was one child's misery to the lives of half a dozen?

'Daddy used to . . . work for Jacky.' Then he said, 'I don't really remember him. Daddy.'

'Tell me about the bus.'

'I . . . I can't.'

'Why can't you?'

'I promised Jacky I would never tell anybody. It's a secret.'

'You can tell me. It's important.'

'I promised.'

Hating himself, Joshua slammed the brakes on. Tied in by the seat belt the boy still jerked forward abruptly. He gave a cry of pain as the belt cut into him unexpectedly. Then Joshua put his foot flat down on the accelerator. Nico had obviously had quite a lot done to the car. In a matter of seconds the speedometer was registering seventy, then eighty, then ninety. As it edged towards a hundred miles an hour Joshua swung the car off the road. A row of telegraph poles ran parallel to the road, a shallow ditch separating them from the tarmac. He hurled the car between the poles, slaloming from the field to the road and back again. Finally, with an expert heel-and-toe flick he spun the car until it was facing back towards Nicosia, gently ticking over in neutral.

'Now,' he said, very quietly. 'answer my questions. Who brought the bus to Jacovides?'

'I . . . I don't know.'

Joshua revved the engine ominously, reached forward to put the car into gear.

'I don't know! Honestly! I don't know their names! I've never seen them before!'

'When was this?'

'On Sunday.'

'When on Sunday?'

'After . . . after church.'

Check. Check, because the boy might be wrong. He might even be lying.

'How do you know it was Sunday?'

'We were at church. And . . . I went with Jacky – that's what we call Mr Jacovides – while mummy was . . . getting lunch. He had a phone call, and . . . I went with him.'

Suddenly Joshua realised. He said, 'Tell me, Iannis. Where do you live?'

'At Jacky's house.'

'With your mother?'

'Yes. And . . . and my sister. Jacky is . . .'

'Yes?'

'He says he is going to marry my sister. Only she's not old enough yet to get married.'

Having, thought Joshua grimly, first seduced your mother all

108

those years ago, when she found herself penniless and homeless. He said, 'The people who brought the bus. How many of them were there?'

'Two.'

'Men? Both of them?'

'Yes. Please don't drive the car like that again.'

'Not if you answer my questions. What nationality were they, these men?'

'Greek.'

Joshua said carefully, 'No. You mean Cypriot. Turkish Cypriots. Is that right?'

'No! Not Cypriots! They were Greeks!'

'How can you tell?'

'Their voices! The way they spoke! Honestly!'

At the back of his mind Joshua remembered the Wykehamist at JBH. Something about mainland Greeks finding the Cypriot accent funny. So presumably there was a difference. Would a young boy be able to recognise it? Check. Ask Nico. Ask anybody. Press on. The boy was still shaking from fear: still talking.

'What did they say to Mr Jacovides?' He was being friendly. Now Jacovides rated the 'mister'.

'Just that . . . here was the bus. They were laughing. Jacky had been expecting it. Then one of the men saw me – I'd been playing in one of the cars in the garage – and they got angry, and that was when Jacky made me promise never to tell anybody about the bus. It was a joke, you see.'

'A joke?'

'Yes. One of the men knew the man who owns Sunswept Holidays, and they were going to hide the bus for a joke.'

A joke. The driver's body would still have been warm.

Casually, Joshua asked, 'After that, what happened to the bus?'

'I . . . I don't know. I suppose they gave it back.'

'Why do you suppose that?'

'Well . . . When I went into the garage next time –'

'When was that?'

The boy was thinking. He remembered the day the bus came, because it had been after church, and church was on a Sunday, but he had to think about when he went to the garage again, because it was like any other day.

'I think it was Tuesday. Tuesday, in the evening.'

'And where was the bus?'

'I don't know. It wasn't in the garage.'

'Didn't you ask Mr Jacovides?'

'I forgot to.'

Joshua believed him. It wasn't important to the boy, and he simply forgot about it. Because he hadn't asked the question, Jacovides might escape. The lead stopped.

No, there had to be a way forward.

'Could you recognise these men again? The two Greeks?'

There was a moment of hesitation. 'I . . . I'm not sure. I think so.'

'How old were they?'

'Oh, they were old. Grown-ups.'

Ask a stupid question . . . No child could be expected to guess an adult's age. But keep him talking, that was what mattered.

'Did Mr Jacovides know them?'

Again, the boy seemed to think before he spoke. 'I don't know,' he said at last. 'I suppose so. Except that most of his friends, they come to our house, and I know who they are.' Then he said, 'Please, why are you asking me about this?'

'It's important. It's a secret, like the bus was a secret. But this is much more important than the bus. This isn't a joke. Do you understand?'

The boy looked at him. No, of course he didn't understand. How could he? It was harder to get information from a child than from an adult. Adults: you could classify adults. Through the centuries the police, the security forces, Intelligence, all had worked out how to get the information they needed from adults. There was a long, squalid history of interrogation. Back to the Inquisition. Back to the open trials of classical Greece. Whoever it was who interrogated Socrates. With adults, there were known techniques and predictable reactions. But not with children.

Joshua cast his mind back to what he had seen through the Judas hole. Jacovides looked like a typical Mediterranean entrepreneur: sharp, mercenary, devious, and not too scrupulously honest. But he did not look like a terrorist. Terrorists, in Joshua's experience, came in many shapes and sizes: but not in Jacovides'. The man in the overalls, the one he thought of as the mechanic, yes, he could be a terrorist. But it was much more likely that he was simply a mechanic who was a petty criminal on the side.

'Tell me about Mr Jacovides,' said Joshua. 'I'm hoping to meet him.'

'He . . . he's looked after us.'

110

'I know. That was nice of him.'

'Yes.'

'Has he always owned the garage?'

'Oh, he owns lots of things!'

'How did your father first meet him? Through working for him?'

'No. Jacky said they met in the fighting.'

Fighting? Fighting who? As though to resolve Joshua's momentary confusion, the boy added, 'Jacky went up into the mountains with General Grivas.'

It was difficult to think of the dapper, pink, overweight man in the brown silk suit as a shabby, hungry guerrilla, scrabbling through the brush as the British army edged uneasily round Troodos, its tactics half-hearted, its mission uncertain.

'Now listen to me,' said Joshua. 'I want you to help me.'

'You . . . You're not going to drive the car –'

'No. Those men who brought the bus to Mr Jacovides, I want to meet them.'

The boy nodded.

'I want to find out what happened to that bus.'

'Is . . . Is Jacky . . . I mean, he's been awfully good to us, he's helped us with everything, my school fees and everything.'

And he's screwed your mother until your sister grew old enough to interest him, thought Joshua. He said, 'I'm not interested in Mr Jacovides. I think he's involved in something, but he doesn't really know what it is. Do you understand?'

The boy asked, 'You mean, he's been played for a sucker?'

'More or less. But – and I tell you this as a secret, a real secret – Mr Jacovides could be in danger. If those men think we're on to him –'

'Are they part of a gang?'

'Yes.'

'But . . .' The boy hesitated. 'Who are you?'

Joshua smiled. 'You asked me that before. And I'm still not going to tell you. But I'll make you a promise. When this is over, I'll arrange to take you to England for a holiday. If you help me. Okay?'

'Are you a policeman?'

'Not really. But I know a lot of policemen.'

'Do you know Scotland Yard?'

'Yes.'

'Will you take me round there?'

'If you help me, I promise. But you've got to help me.'

'I won't split on Jacky.'

'Nobody's asking you to. What I want you to do is watch out for the two men who brought the bus to the garage. Right?'

'Yes.'

'And – this isn't letting down Mr Jacovides but if you hear him talking about that bus – perhaps on the phone – then I want you to tell me. It's important for Mr Jacovides, too.'

The boy seemed to think for a while, then nodded his head.

'My name is Joshua Howell.'

'Is that your real name? You said –'

'No, but it's the name I'm known by here. You know the Romantica Hotel?'

'Yes.'

'If you want me, leave a message there.'

He glanced up into the mirror, and reached down for the gear lever.

The boy's face went white. 'Are you going to – ?'

'Don't worry,' said Joshua. 'We're going back and one of those policemen can take you home.' The car moved off. 'Your poor mother must be wondering what the hell's happened to you.'

Chapter Sixteen

There was something missing. There was a conclusion he should have drawn, and it had escaped him.

He lay in the bed, naked under the sheet, and methodically went through it all again.

Assume that everything he had been told as fact was actually true: a rash assumption, possibly an idiotic assumption, but at least a starting point.

The men who had brought the bus to the garage were Greek. Would they then have been the same people as those who hijacked the bus in the first place, and murdered the driver? If not, why not?

But those two men, Greeks, could not have been whoever it was who had taken the kidnapped children into the north. Two reasons. There were virtually no Greeks in the north; and in any case they had been in the south before lunchtime that day after the bus had been reported as missing.

He reached out to his bedside table, and on the pad he had put there wrote, Check times Greek Orthodox service, then Check how many Greeks left in north.

He put down the pencil, and tucked his hands behind his head. Outside a bull frog *waap waaped* irritatingly.

How did whoever it was take over the bus? The driver presumably knew his job. He wouldn't have stopped the bus just for, say, a hitch-hiker. He certainly wouldn't have stopped it for anybody he thought might be Turkish.

Suppose that somehow the bus was taken over. They took out the driver and shot him, and drove off with the children. Did the children realise what was happening? If not, why not? And if they did, surely to God at least one of them would have had hysterics and been noticed by someone outside the bus?

Or they were taken off in another vehicle? What other vehicle? And why should the terrorists bother to transfer them?

Were they really in the north? Pamir assumed they were. But would Pamir know? And even if he did know, would he tell the truth?

Take the political situation in Cyprus. What would be in the interests of the Greeks, and what would be in the interests of the Turks?

The Greeks. If the children could be shown to have been taken by Turks, and then killed, this would surely produce a wave of hatred in Britain. The Turks would be exposed as barbarians, and the fact that the terrorists' demands coincided with the aims of both the Turkish Government and of the unrecognised Turkish government in Cyprus would enlist enormous support for the Greek Cypriot cause.

The Turks. They could make a lot of capital out of the fact that the children were kidnapped in the south. Whoever had taken them, one thing was certain. They had not been kidnapped by Turks, because there were no Turks in the south. But suppose Pamir was right. Suppose they were, somehow, in the north, in the State that didn't exist, in Kybris. If the terrorist demands effectively strengthened the case of the Turkish authorities, would the Turks really go out of their way to find them? And if the worst happened. He found himself considering, quite coldly, the possibilities, though he was aware of fighting off sleep. If the worst happened. If the children were to die. If they were already dead. Suppose they were in Kybris, and they were dead. What would be the interest of the Turkish authorities? No doubt about it: to make sure that they were never found. That nothing ever got out. That the last that was seen of them was in the south, on a Greek Cypriot road in a Greek Cypriot bus with a Greek Cypriot driver.

That was the worst that could happen, the nightmare.

There were six girls and a school mistress in that bus. Why has there not been a single sighting of them? Why, if they were being kidnapped, did not one of them somehow give anyone any indication that something horribly wrong was happening?

His thoughts were now coming out of sequence, and he could feel the exhaustion of the day catching up on him. Before sleep reached him he sat up and wrote on the pad: What was last sighting of bus? Check Pamir's position through JBH.

But the main dilemma remained. If everybody he spoke to was to be believed, somehow the terrorists had kidnapped children in the Greek area and taken them to the Turkish area through the Greek

114

Cypriot army, the United Nations forces, and the Turkish Cypriot army. Plus an assortment of Greek Intelligence who weren't supposed to be there, and a very large and very conspicuous part of the main Turkish army. They had been taken through check points manned by three lots of mutually suspicious troops, or else across minefields that, he had been assured, were impenetrable.

And either way, everybody assured him, what they believed to have happened could not have happened, because it was impossible.

He switched out the bedside light and prepared to sleep. For a moment he thought he heard Anna's footsteps outside his room, and he tensed, hoping they would stop. But they went on and a few seconds later he heard a lavatory flush, then the steps retraced their path, past his door.

He sighed audibly, turned onto his side, and fell asleep.

Chapter Seventeen

When Joshua arrived at the Consulate in the morning it was obvious that he was expected. Miss Galsworth stuttered when she wished him good morning, two unknown girls found reasons to come out of offices, cast hasty glances at him, and disappear into other offices, and Mr Earnshaw had let it be known that he was even more busy than usual.

There were two sets of messages for him, one of which had come in during the night and the other only a few minutes earlier. Joshua, after thanking Miss Galsworth, shut himself in the small room they had put aside for him, and settled down to decode them.

He started on the most recent message, which simply confirmed that Chota Peg was at stand-by awaiting instructions. The earlier message seemed more important and more ominous. It said that a Colonel Peacock, Source Apricot, of Bray House, Kyrenia, had reported a Turkish security cordon thrown round Bellapaise, normally a tourist attraction. It added that the Colonel was an able house-trained fox, which meant that he had security clearance, and was authorised to contact, but was not normally regarded as active.

Which in turn, in Joshua's experience, meant somebody who had been in Intelligence in the days when operators spent their time trying to steal each other's briefcases, and who happened to have been washed up in somewhere that might, just possibly, one day be of passing interest to the organisations of today. The fact that JBH had bothered to mention him also meant that for reasons they were not prepared to disclose even to one of their own senior agents, somebody – presumably the Old Man – thought that Colonel Peacock would be of interest to Joshua.

He glanced at his watch. Ten past nine. It was already getting hot, and the little room was oppressive. He lit a match from the box attached to his one-time pad, burnt the messages, the decoded messages, and the sheet from the pad, crumbled up the ashes, and emerged. As he left he smiled at Miss Galsworth and said, untruthfully, 'I haven't forgotten about the flowers, but the only ones I could find this early were all the wrong colours for you,' and strode off.

In the street, quite suddenly, he felt angry: angry and helpless. His daughter, who meant more to him than any other person on earth, more than the rest of the earth's population put together, was somewhere quite near to him. She was alive, and she was on this island. He had to believe that because otherwise he had nothing left to live for. And of all the people in all the countries of the planet, if he had to choose one man to find her, he would pick himself. He would pick himself because it was his job, defeating terrorists. It was his job, and he was exceptionally good at it. He could prove this. There were compliments that would never be recorded, citations that would never be published, decorations in other names, that indicated that it was not vanity that made him assess himself in this way: his peers in the world's Intelligence and anti-terrorist forces also recognised his skills.

Technically he was almost uniquely equipped for this assignment. Emotionally he was absolutely uniquely equipped because he alone would do anything, make any sacrifice, to get this one girl back. As he walked down the dusty, empty, meaningless street that had had its *raison d'être* stripped away by the casual bombardment of a few Turkish artillerymen who could not identify it on their maps, men who a few hours earlier had had no idea the street existed, there were prisoners being held all over the world. The families of these mostly forgotten victims tried to reach the leaders of their governments, or rouse interest in their press, or just stood helplessly outside embassies with photographs of the missing. But ultimately whether there would be reunions depended not on presidents or generals but on people like himself.

In this one case he would be willing to sacrifice all the other prisoners now being held for one prisoner. He would, if he had to, pay for her life with the lives of others. He would pay for her life with his own life. Yet he was helpless.

It was really the need to do something, anything, that decided him to go again into the north. From the hotel he picked up the two maps and his meaningless press card. When he came downstairs into the reception Anna was behind the desk. A flick of her eyes warned him that the manager was in his office, within earshot.

'Good morning, sir,' she said. 'You are perhaps going again into the Turkish occupied land?'

'Yes.'

'My family,' she said, as though she had never said it before to him, 'used always to live in Agios Khrysoumos. Now it is call Dikmen by the Turkishmen. If you go there, perhaps you could see if it is now nice? I have camera.'

'I'll try and remember.' Then, certain that the manager might be able to hear him, but could not see him, he winked at her.

As he reached the door an idea struck him. 'Tell me, miss,' he said, 'how would I find an address in the north?'

'We have one old telephone book,' she replied, reaching under the counter. 'But now is all the people gone.'

'This one's English.'

'Perhaps he stay.' She obviously disapproved of expatriates who had clung on to their houses. 'What is the name?'

He came back to the desk, and she put an old, fading telephone directory in front of him. He took it from her – there was no reason why she should learn who he was looking up – and at the bottom of a page found Peacock, Col. H.P. de L., Bray House, Kyprianou Road, Kyrenia.

He closed the book. 'You know Kyrenia?' he asked.

'Of course.'

'Do you know Kyprianou Road?'

She thought for a moment, then nodded vigorously. 'Is a new road. You come in on the left from Nicosia, and is soonest when you are to Kyrenia. On the left.' She produced a camera from under the counter. 'You may keep it please while you are here.'

'First on the left. Thanks.'

He winked at her again, picked up the camera, then walked out of the hotel and headed towards the check point.

As he approached the seedy little crossing point he considered the possible problems. The Greeks clearly disliked people visiting the north. Would they object to his going through on consecutive days on what was supposed to be a day pass? He could get through. He had only to get Nico to vouch for him; but Nico must not be seen with him again, not by whoever it was who was presumably perched somewhere down the road, beyond the Ledra Palace Hotel, perhaps from the top of a minaret, perhaps from the spire of a desecrated church, watching every movement on the Greek side through binoculars. Even to get Nico on the phone would make him stand out, someone the Greek sentries would follow with their eyes, and he wanted to be the man nobody noticed, the man that later nobody could be sure had, or had not, been present.

More difficult than the Greeks were the Turks. He was crossing over at a different time of day, so the odds were that the sentries and the official in the little kiosk would not be the same as before. But would the bureaucrats be different? Would the men and women in the hot little bungalow who took the money and issued the passes, would they have regular nine to five jobs, day after day? And if they had, would they have noticed him among the other tourists?

Would Pamir have notified the people in the bungalow? And if he had, would they remember? Or would Pamir assume that having warned him, he would not come back again, except through Turkey?

He found a corner from which he could see the Greek Cypriot post, but was out of sight of any watcher in the Turkish area. After a few minutes a white United Nations Land Rover was waved through and almost immediately after it a car with CD plates, which, Joshua noted, was carefully checked before being allowed through.

Then what he was hoping for approached. A taxi drew up and an English family descended, man, wife, and two children aged approximately seven and five.

There was a protracted and noisy row between the man and the taxi driver over first the fare, and then the driver's refusal to go any further. The wife tried to translate using execrable French, and the five year old started to cry.

Joshua dropped in behind them as they signed themselves out at the Greek post, then followed in their bad-tempered wake as they went past the hotel, through the United Nations strip, to the Turkish check point.

The formality of signing in at the kiosk presented no problem, but Joshua carefully stood aside to allow the family to go first. The wife said, very loudly and pointedly, 'At least some people are English and don't try to shove themselves ahead,' and smiled at Joshua in a conspiracy of shared superiority.

The family, all four of them, were carrying bags of groceries, as though they expected food to be unobtainable in the north. At the bungalow office the husband protested loudly about the bags being searched, and from time to time cuffed the five year old who was now wailing incessantly.

Unnoticed, Joshua signed, paid, and left.

There were several car-hire firms along the wide streets of what had once been part of the administrative and commercial heart of Nicosia. He selected a different firm, because there was no point in getting known unnecessarily.

The firm seemed to be in a moment of crisis. The owner was shouting in Turkish at a girl who was in tears, the phone was ringing unanswered, an Irish soldier with the United Nations was involved with another girl in a dispute over the exchange rate of various foreign currencies, and Joshua was able to hire a Volkswagen without anybody even looking him in the face for more than a passing instant.

He drove away, and again the absurdity of the divided city struck him. He edged along the shabby wall that split the city like the scab on a wound, then through a massive Venetian gateway with a Turkish soldier standing atop it silhouetted against the brilliant sky, and turned towards the hills that separated him from the sea.

At one stage there was no traffic at all, and nobody to be seen except a woman with a baby on her back weeding between a sparse crop in a field beside the road. It could have been anywhere in the great arc of land that stretched from Sicily to India: any time over two thousand years.

The road wound up, then crested down towards the coast. Kyrenia spread out below him, the Dome hotel at its geographical and financial centre.

Kyprianou Road must have been the last development before the Turkish invasion and the subsequent curtailing of building. The Greek street plate, if it had one, had been removed and not replaced. The road began as a wide tarmac surface, and one could see where it had been planned to sweep along the hillside with large, separate buildings each combining traditional English privacy with a commanding view over the Mediterranean. But only half a dozen or so houses had been completed. There were the concrete skeletons of another four, with rusting steel rods thrusting up to where the roofs would have been, and lizards scuttling in the unfinished basements. At that point the road stopped abruptly and became for some hundred yards a wide track, the scars left by some long-ago withdrawn crawler tractors still clear in the baked earth. Then that in its turn stopped, and Kyprianou Road became a winding goat path between the thorn bushes.

The third house, and the first to appear inhabited, was Bray House. It would have looked more natural outside Farnham or Guildford than on the steep hillside above Kyrenia, the close-mown little lawn defying the sun through regular, and expensive, watering with a rotating sprinkler, the hibiscus trimmed back to resemble as closely as possible a domesticated rhododendron, a vine sprawling up a wall and masquerading as a rambler rose. The house itself, though presumably built in the early seventies, had the styling of a twenties road-house, with every material pretending to be something it wasn't. It had oaken beams made of rusting iron, overlapping Kentish tiles made of plastic, brickwork of concrete, and metal-framed Elizabethan windows with bottle glass panes. The roof galloped through nations and centuries in a matter of a few square yards. There was a Norman turret, a French conical tower shrunk from the Loire, a water tank built as a Cycladic dovecote, and a ventilator as a minaret.

Before his front door in khaki shirt and Bermuda shorts stood Colonel Peacock, a watering can in one hand a gin and tonic in the other.

Joshua drew up in the road and walked down the short drive to the house. As he approached, Colonel Peacock watched him silently. He appeared to be in his seventies, a lean, wiry figure, an almost bald head, and startling blue eyes.

'Colonel Peacock,' said Joshua. The Colonel looked at him, neither confirming nor denying the identification. Joshua glanced round the garden. 'Working in the garden, I see. I admit it, I'm hopeless at things horticultural. I couldn't tell an apple tree from an apricot.'

The Colonel seemed to ignore his identification. 'Come on in,' he said. 'Too damned hot to stand out here if you've nothing better to do than talk.'

Joshua followed Peacock into the house, finding himself in an unexpectedly large and cool entrance hall that occupied most of the ground floor.

'Sit down, sit down,' said the Colonel, vaguely indicating a large sofa covered in white linen. 'A drink? I'm drinking gin and tonic, but there again I've been up since dawn and I doubt if you have. I have some cold fresh lime juice.'

'That would be fine,' said Joshua, sitting on the sofa.

Colonel Peacock disappeared into what was presumably the kitchen, and reappeared with a tray, and on it a jug of lime juice, an ice bucket, and a glass.

'Ice?'

'Please.'

Peacock wandered behind sofa, and reached over Joshua's shoulder to put the glass down on a table beside him.

'Used to be a chap who sold orange juice from some sort of old

Turkish thing that came up like a swan's neck over his shoulder. Used to lean forward to pour it out. Haven't seen him for years, though.'

Something pressed against Joshua's neck, something cold and hard. 'Don't make a move or I'll blow your bloody head off.'

The pressure went away. Peacock was an expert. He knew that with a gun pressed against his body a trained man could usually twist himself out of the line of fire in the time it took to press the trigger.

'Got any identification papers on you?' demanded Peacock.

'Passport. That sort of thing.'

'Security papers?'

'Not here, no.'

'Put your hands on the table. Slowly. That's good. Just stay like that.'

Peacock came carefully round the sofa into Joshua's sight. He was holding a Webley .45, and as he walked round to face Joshua it remained pointed very accurately at the centre of his body.

'Who are you from?'

'JBH.'

'Name of its chief?'

'Membury.'

'Since my time. What was the name of his predecessor?'

'Elsworth.'

'Any physical peculiarities?'

'Yes. He had an artificial hand. Lost the real one in Albania.'

'Which hand?'

'The false one was the left. He always wore gloves.'

Peacock nodded, and grinned affably, then put the revolver on the table. 'No offence, old man. Can't be too careful.'

'No.'

The Colonel sat down facing Joshua. 'Haven't seen anybody for ages,' he said. 'The wife died, you know.'

'I'm sorry.' It seemed the thing to say.

'Best thing, really,' said Peacock. 'Cheers.'

He raised his glass and drank noisily. 'Used to be in AAB myself.'

'AAB?' whatever AAB was, Joshua had not heard of it.

'Alexandria Accidents Bureau. Odd outfit. We'd have these people we couldn't get at, you see. In places like Turkey or Syria. Talking of wartime.'

'Yes.'

'So we'd find these British squaddies who'd committed crimes. Rape, mostly. Or murder. Absolute scum of the earth. After they'd been sentenced to death we'd trot along and say, look, if you do absolutely what we tell you, no need to get hanged.'

'Oh.'

'Or shot. Varied, depending on what they'd done and where they were. So we'd rig them out with new identities, and they'd go off into these neutral countries and cope with our problem. Their families were told they were dead, of course. Killed in action. Anyway, eventually we'd shunt them off to some country that didn't look too closely at proofs of who people were and Bob's your uncle. Chance to start again.'

'After the war.'

Peacock looked surprised. 'Oh no, we ran the Bureau for quite a while later than that. What are you doing here?'

Joshua said carefully, 'You sent in a report about a police cordon at Bellapaise.'

'That's right. Glad they picked it up. What's it got to do with you?'

There was no reason why Colonel Peacock should learn more than was absolutely necessary. Joshua was not absolutely certain the Colonel was not a raving lunatic. He said, 'There may be a case developing here.'

Peacock grinned. 'And I've got to prove I ought to know about it. Quite right. You want to see what's happening?'

'That's the idea.'

'All I know is that there's a police barricade across the road to Bellapaise. Nothing odd about that. Well, not too odd. They keep putting up barricades left right and centre. But I saw Kemal Ozal there.'

Joshua's head jerked up sharply. '*The* Kemal Ozal? You're sure?'

'Oh yes. Know him well. Deputy head of the Jandarma. So I wandered over to him and asked him what he was doing in Cyprus. He said he was on holiday. So I said, do you normally spend your holidays manning roadblocks? And he laughed, and said old habits die hard. Then he sort of smiled and said that if I let it be known he was in the island he'd make sure *I* wouldn't be in it much longer. Bluffing, of course. He knows me too well to try that sort of thing on me.'

Peacock finished his gin and tonic, then added thoughtfully, 'The other thing was, there was an ambulance just down the road. Not a normal ambulance. A military one. And there aren't any Turkish troops stationed in Bellapaise. Plenty of them wander through it, but not actually stationed there.'

123

An ambulance. They had said they would kill.

'Tell you what,' said the Colonel. 'We could go and take a look see.'

'Could we get through?'

'Won't know unless we try!'

Peacock rose to his feet and tucked the Webley into the belt round his shorts.

'Won't they stop you, wearing that?' asked Joshua. It seemed just the sort of idiotic gesture that would provoke the Turks.

'Oh, they know all about this,' Peacock explained. He pulled the revolver out and broke it. 'Quite harmless. Firing pin's been filed away. They all know about it.'

He slammed it closed and put it back into his belt. 'The point is, it stops them looking for the other ones I've got in here.'

Then he strode out into the sun, Joshua following.

'Better take my car,' said Peacock. 'They know it, you see. Elderly English lunatic with limited licence to go where most people can't.'

Peacock's car was hidden behind the house, a pre-war Daimler. It had a crest mounted on its roof. Peacock noticed Joshua glancing at it. 'Damned useful,' he said. 'People think I'm the Governor-General or something. Gets me into almost anything. Actually it came with the car. Used to belong to the Lord Mayor of Bournemouth.'

From a glove locker in the car Peacock produced a small Union Jack on a metal pole, and started to fix it onto a mounting on the radiator cap. He looked round at Joshua.

'Before we go,' he said, 'I want an answer to a question.'

Joshua waited.

'Yes or no will do. Are you here in connection with a kidnapping?'

'Yes,' said Joshua quietly, then, 'How do you know about it?' The officials in the British Embassy in Nicosia didn't know, but Colonel Peacock did.

'Learnt from the Turks. Good chap, Johnny Turk. Absolute barbarians, of course, but straight once they know you. Bit like the Afghans. Can't stand Greeks myself. That's one of the reasons I get on with the Turks, I suppose. But they tell me most things, sooner or later.'

He seemed to have fixed the flag to his satisfaction, and climbed into the car, patting the seat behind him. As Joshua got in he had a momentary sense of *déjà vu*. Then he remembered what it was: the last time he had consciously got into a car with a running board. There was a photograph of it at home. Outside the church, when he had married Barbara.

The car turned majestically round in an enormous circle, and Peacock headed west towards the main road and then the road that went off towards Bellapaise.

'Make the best of it,' Peacock was saying. 'One thing's for certain. The Turks aren't moving out of here. Not unless there's another war and they lose it, and who's going to beat them? Certainly not the Greeks. There's a bottle of duty free under the seat if you feel like a nip.'

'No thanks.' He was still thinking of Barbara.

'And I keep a spare automatic where your feet are. Under the carpet. Had the floor built up to hide it. Interesting. Nobody ever finds it. They bloody nearly stripped the car once in Iran, and they still didn't find it. Mind you, I don't expect to need it. Not here. Only once had to use it in all the time I've had the car. Nice to know it's there, though. Let me do the talking, right?'

'Yes.'

'Don't anticipate any problems, but you never know.'

Colonel Peacock abruptly turned off onto the minor road that led to Bellapaise. In four languages a notice warned against stopping or taking photographs.

'What do you know about Bellapaise?' Peacock asked.

'Not much.'

'One of the most beautiful place on earth. Knocks the Taj into a cocked hat. It's a question of the difference between death and dying.'

Joshua looked round. He hadn't the least idea what Peacock was talking about.

'The Taj is a tomb,' said Peacock by way of explanation. 'A celebration of death. Basically sterile. Mind you, it was improved a lot when us Brits put that water in front of it. Must have looked ghastly surrounded by Indians saying *baksheesh sahib*. But be that as it may – '

Peacock stopped talking to concentrate on swerving round a donkey heavy-laden with kindling, then said, 'It is basically dead. Now, Bellapaise is in a sort of permanent twilight. Ruined, you see, but it looks a lot better than it must have done before it started to fall down. Most evocative place I've ever seen.'

Joshua realised to his astonishment that Peacock's eyes were full of tears.

'Like this island. Aphrodite's island. You know that, of course.'

'Yes.'

125

'Trouble with Cyprus is nobody ever took it seriously. Like Aphrodite. So you get an abbey like Bellapaise. And they just let it fall down. But what they don't realise, you see, is that in Aphrodite's island that was what was meant to happen. It was meant to be perfect. It was doomed before it was completed. Tragedy. That's what this island was made for. If you're too hot just open the window. Only keep it shut because of the dust.'

'I'm fine.'

'So everything that Aphrodite touched, somehow it never quite came off. Whatever she did – and she only meant well – people got hurt and resented her. Same with Cyprus. Always means well. Always gets screwed. And the absolute quintessence of the whole bloody island is Bellapaise. You'll see.'

Peacock wiped his eyes with the back of his hand, sniffed noisily, and then relapsed into silence.

At a corner where the road dropped away dramatically towards the sea, Peacock slowed, frowning.

'This was where they had the road block,' he explained. 'Better get out and have a look see.' The car drew up, the engine ticking over.

He climbed out of the car, ignoring another notice warning passers-by not to stop, and clambered a few yards up the hillside. Joshua, very conscious of the necessity for him not being denied access to Kybris, stayed in the car.

'Yesterday they had a machine gun position where I'm standing,' shouted the Colonel. 'No sign of it now.'

He slid down the slope with an agility remarkable for a man of his age, and got back into the car. 'No cartridge cases,' he said. 'Wonder what they were up to.'

Then he set off again, the car reaching the outskirts of a village, houses hugging the narrow road.

'Bellapaise,' said the Colonel. 'That house over there is where Laurence Durrell used to live. Good writer, everyone says, if you like high-brow smut.'

Abruptly the road ended, and facing them was the abbey. It was, Joshua had to agree with Peacock, an extraordinarily evocative sight. The thin tracery of elegant Venetian arches and windows towered bare and roofless against the blazing sky, walls reached up to nothing, flowers, scarlet and purple and gold, thrust between flagstones, competing for the attention of the butterflies. It was a place at once empty and haunted, a ruined masterpiece of its time, and timeless.

The Colonel bounded out of the car, and strode purposefully over towards a group of old men sitting round a listing table outside a cafe. He was obviously known, for a stranger was summoned from down the street and introduced to him. Then a hookah was produced from inside the cafe, and Colonel Peacock settled down, carefully lit it and started smoking.

Joshua got the impression that he had been forgotten, but an almost imperceptible gesture from Peacock indicated that he was to remain in the car. A group of small, dark children started to gather round the Daimler, then, getting more adventurous, began to clamber over it, grinning hugely at Joshua. Peacock could see what was happening, but didn't seem to mind as filthy prints from hands and feet began to mark the paintwork. One child unfastened the Union Jack from the radiator cap, and holding it stood to attention, then saluted Joshua. Joshua solemnly returned the salute, whereupon the whole party erupted into hysterical laughter. One of the old men shouted something in Turkish, and immediately order was restored. A new piece of wire was found, and the flag carefully reaffixed to the car.

To Joshua's relief, Colonel Peacock rose, handed over the hookah to his neighbour, and came across to the car. The children respectfully parted before him. He opened the door.

'Come on over,' he said. 'Don't try to say anything. Do you speak Turkish?'

'Not a word.'

Peacock nodded. 'No need to make a point of it, though. Try and look as though you're getting the drift. I think we're on to something.' Then he spoke sharply to the children, who scattered.

At the cafe table half a dozen pairs of very old eyes watched Joshua as he sat and a coffee was put before him. After a long, silent assessment they continued their conversation in Turkish as though he were not there. At one point Peacock said something which roused interest in Joshua, and the silent scrutiny was resumed. Then some very sticky sweets were produced on a saucer, and this seemed to be the signal for the end of the conversation. Everybody rose, and Peacock and Joshua returned to the car. By now the children were nowhere in sight.

As they got into the car Peacock said, 'Don't for God's sake smile. You've just had very bad news.'

They drove away down the street, back towards Kyrenia. As they left the village Peacock said, 'How much of that did you gather?'

'Nothing.'

'Well, the old chap with the red dyed beard, he's a hadji, been to Mecca, he's the head of the village. Quite illiterate, but very holy. There's two things, really. One is that they're very ashamed it's happened, and don't want to talk about it. That's why I said that you were the son of Lord Harding.'

'Who?'

'Lord Harding. The last Governor we had here. They had a regard for him so I said you were his son. And the other thing is that they've been ordered not to talk about it, even amongst themselves.'

'Talk about what?'

Peacock looked surprised at the question. 'About the murder, of course. The English girl who's been murdered.'

Chapter Eighteen

'Nothing we can do. Just wait,' said Peacock.

The setting could not have been more idyllically beautiful. In an hour the sun would be too hot, the sky too bright, the sea below them would hurt the eyes with its glitter; but at that moment it was perfect. There was just sufficient breeze to rustle the leaves in the olive tree beside the little building, and sufficient shade for them to sit outside the cafe and watch.

There was nothing to be done until the Turkish soldier on guard was changed. Peacock had said so, and if Peacock knew his Turkish military habits – which he seemed to – then the guard would be changed at midday. The new guard would, with any luck, not have been specifically warned that the two Englishmen sipping, in Joshua's case fresh lemon juice, and in Peacock's gin and tonic, must not be allowed to enter. In all probability he would not even have any clear idea why he had been ordered there. The morgue was not normally a place that rated an armed guard.

The building had once been a Methodist chapel. It was a modest place, and had never sought to challenge the authority of the Church of England's St. Andrew's Church in Helena Palaeologos Street, let alone the Orthodox churches that had dominated the religious life of the town. Now even the cross over the chapel had been removed. But it had not been replaced by a crescent, and the interior still had the odd pew stacked against the walls, and lacked the austere purity of Islam. Instead of the other pews and the pulpit and the font there were structures that looked like large filing cabinets. Instead of the board that had once announced the hymns there was a baize notice-board with memoranda in Turkish. Hidden in what had been the vestry there was now an operating table. On that table some time the previous day Dr. Baykal had examined the body that had been found at Bellapaise. He had then agreed, after some protest, that his report should not be presented through the usual

129

channels, but should instead be handed to Turkish Intelligence. He had also promised not to discuss the matter with anyone, even with his wife. He had been given no explanation why this was being asked of him.

Across the road, Joshua and Colonel Peacock waited and watched. Two tables away sat Mustapha Guley, watching Colonel Peacock. Guley had agreed that for £30 Cypriot he would mislay his caretaker's key to the mortuary for long enough for them to enter the building and see whatever it was they wanted to see. He did not ask any questions, partly because he was a rather stupid man who rarely questioned anything, partly because he had, occasionally, met men who were prepared to pay him to be allowed to look at naked, dead women. Guley did not like to think about these things, and normally avoided doing so. But he had the key in his pocket, and on receiving a signal from Peacock he would rise and leave the key on the cafe table. He had been given £5 in advance, and he knew and trusted Colonel Peacock. He could only assume that it was the Colonel's friend who was the pervert, because the Colonel had never shown any interest in the bodies in the morgue before.

It's seven to one it isn't Joanna. It doesn't even have to be one of the kidnapped group. Over and over again Joshua tried to rationalise the nightmare, but fear was not a rational thing. He was a man used to having access to power, almost unlimited access to power. He would let it be known that he had to see something, to be somewhere, to know something, and without his even having to ask it was arranged. He said come, and people came, go and they went, sometimes kill, and people were killed. But now he had less power than a Turkish caretaker.

Seven to one. Unless they had somehow found out who Joanna's father was. Then, suppose that, then what would they do? It could be that she would be the one they would murder first. It would be the ultimate gesture of defiance, look, we can kill the children of the best protected people of your land. Or, perhaps she would be the very last one they would kill, because while she was alive they would still have the ultimate threat. It was one thing to murder the child of a civil servant, or a shopkeeper, or a bank clerk. To be holding, to be able to kill the child of a senior officer in JBH, that was different.

If they knew who she was. If they understood. If whoever was supposed to be in the morgue was one of the group and not some tourist who happened to have died in Bellapaise. If there was anybody there at all.

130

Colonel Peacock could have been reading his mind.

'Only reason I think we're on to something,' he said, 'was the way that old village chief told me. Understand? He did it out of friendship, you see. Knew he shouldn't be telling people, and after all he's a Cypriot and still not used to being told what to do by people from the mainland. But he saw I was interested and told me. That's the only reason. Apart from your being the son of Lord Harding, of course.'

For a moment it seemed that Peacock believed in the ancestry he had created for Joshua. 'Remarkable man, Harding. Not like some of the other disasters they sent out here. You two have a lot in common.'

'But why should she be here?' Joshua found it difficult to speak, and his tongue seemed to hang in his mouth.

'Told you. Take her to the morgue in Kyrenia. The chappie with the cow heard them say that. And there's only one morgue in Kyrenia.'

Peacock thumped on the table, and indicated that he wanted another gin and tonic.

She was there. She, or one of the others, she was in that building across the sun-parched road. He knew it.

'Well, you learn something new every day,' said Peacock cheerfully. 'Look!'

Across the road a Turkish soldier strolled towards the entrance to the morgue. It wasn't so much the changing of a guard as a casual replacement. The soldier who had been there since before the two Englishmen had first seen him chatted affably with the newcomer, then slung his rifle over his shoulder and wandered towards the cafe.

Joshua tensed, but the soldier ignored him and Peacock, and disappeared into the cafe. There was a pause, then he emerged, eating an ice cream.

Joshua exhaled. 'Only twenty past eleven,' said Peacock. 'Must be somebody's birthday.'

They watched until the soldier reached the end of the street and turned away out of sight, then Peacock nodded to Guley. The caretaker, with elaborate furtiveness, rose and slid a large key onto the table like an uncertain nouveau riche leaving a tip. Then he strolled away. Joshua thought, it's remarkable he doesn't whistle to indicate his innocence, and ensure that everybody notices what is happening.

Peacock, on the other hand, showed that he had been properly trained. He rose, and from the doorway of the cafe settled the bill. He dropped some coins on the table, wandered past where the caretaker had been, picking up the key as he did so with just the right amount of causal reaction to indicate that he had left it there in the first place, and wandered across the street.

He was engaged in friendly conversation with the new guard when Joshua joined him.

'He says he's not allowed to let people in,' Peacock said. 'But I've explained that I've got permission from the authorities who've given me the key.'

He nodded affably to the soldier, then unlocked the door. The soldier grinned happily, and held it open for them as Peacock and Joshua entered.

There were four cabinets, each with four drawers.

'We should have asked the caretaker where they put the body,' said Joshua. Then he suddenly thought what he might find, and wished he believed in God, so that he could pray.

'I did ask, actually,' said Peacock. 'The man seemed a bit uncertain. My guess is he wasn't allowed to watch, but he didn't like to say so. Well, better work top to bottom, left to right. The important thing is that our friend on the door doesn't start getting ideas.' He turned and spoke in Turkish. The soldier grinned and rested his rifle against the wall.

The first cabinet proved to be completely empty. In the bottom drawer of the second one there was the body of an old man, his hands folded across his chest, his face utterly peaceful. There was the body of a baby in the second drawer of the third cabinet, and a young man with a horribly smashed face in the bottom drawer.

'Know about this one,' said Peacock. 'Damned motorcyclist. It was in the papers.'

The top drawer of the last cabinet was locked. The two men exchanged glances, and checked the last three drawers which all proved empty. If there was another body it was in the locked drawer. For a fleeting moment Joshua wanted only to leave, to ignore the locked cabinet, simply not to know.

'You try to get it open,' said Peacock. 'I should imagine you're in better practice than I am. Years since I did any breaking and entering. I'll go and divert chummy.'

Peacock strolled over to the door and got into animated conversation with the soldier. Whatever it was about it made the Turk laugh, and when, seemingly casual, Peacock stepped out of the morgue the soldier followed him.

Joshua looked round. There was nothing immediately to hand to force the lock. Surely to God nobody normally locked bodies up in morgues! There must be a key somewhere, a key that was hardly ever used. The only likely place for such a key was a desk standing against the wall where the altar used to be. He checked that it was out of sight of the sentry, then went across to it. It had two drawers, neither locked, and in the first one there was a bunch of five keys. Four of them were old and rusty, the fifth newer and smaller.

He returned to the cabinet. The soldier still had his back to the building, and was chatting with Colonel Peacock. Joshua tried the fifth key in the lock. It fitted.

He closed his eyes, then turned the key. He felt the lock click open silently. Only one chance in seven. Not even that. The drawer could be empty. But he didn't really believe it.

He pulled the drawer towards him. For a moment it stuck, then it came right out, its full length.

He opened his eyes. The bullet had been fired into the back of the neck and most of the forehead had been blown away. At a guess they had used something like a heavy calibre revolver. An Astra .357 Magnum in all probability. There was little of the top half of the face that was still identifiable.

Swaying, he closed the drawer. He fought back the vomit that rose into his mouth, and walked unsteadily to the door.

Peacock turned. 'Was anybody at home? he asked.

'Yes.'

'Recognise her?'

'I can never remember her name,' Joshua said. 'But her nickname was Boobs.'

Chapter Nineteen

'From the look of you,' said Colonel Peacock. 'You need a drink.'

He rose, and there was the sound of ice being shaken in the kitchen. 'A G & T is my prescription.'

Joshua spoke, consciously keeping his voice quiet and level. 'Tell me exactly what you learnt from those men in Bellapaise. When they found the body, how long it had been there, everything.'

'Right.'

Peacock came back into his drawing room, and held out a large, frosted gin and tonic. 'Put a slice of lime in. Better than bloody lemon, I always think. About the body.'

'Yes.'

Peacock sat, and then leant back in his chair. 'Right. Remember that they weren't supposed to be talking. So there are bits missing in the story. But yesterday apparently one of the boys who looks after the goats found the body.'

'When?'

'Coming to that. The boys go out for the goats at first light. So say four o'clock, five, something like that. You're not drinking.'

'Sorry.' Joshua sipped the gin and tonic. Peacock was right. He needed it.

'Anyway, he told his father, who told the hadji. Now some time after that one of them told the Turkish police in Kyrenia. My guess is that it would have been one of them whom who worked in Kyrenia. I don't see them going to tell the police specially, because the odds are that whoever told them would get arrested. Bearer of bad tidings, that sort of thing.'

'Yes.'

'That's where it starts to get a bit odd. According to the chaps in the cafe. Instead of the police, in came the bloody army. And they took one look and sealed off the village.'

'How long had the body been there?'

Peacock shrugged. 'No way of telling. In a village like that they mostly go to bed at about nine. But you get the odd cowman or love-sick swain wandering around after that. Apparently the body was put slap in the middle of the abbey ruins. The point is, you see, anybody going to take a look at the ruins, tourists, would be bound to find it. But no reason why the villagers should. They don't go in the abbey much. Like Londoners don't go into St. Pauls.'

'So the idea was that it would be a foreigner who'd find the body?'

'Can't tell, old man. Anyway, they seemed a bit hazy about where exactly the body was. And I couldn't really press them.'

'No.'

It fitted. The terrorists would by now be wanting recognition. They would be wanting the world to know about them and their demands, and they were being frustrated by the secrecy. Poor Boobs. She died because in a police state nobody need know they even existed.

'How was it the body was found by this boy, not by a tourist?'

'Sheer fluke. One of the goats broke loose. Or something like that. As I say, they weren't very keen to talk about it.'

'Yes.'

'Where the hell did I put my drink?' Peacock peered around him. 'Must have finished it. By God, I'm going senile if I don't remember finishing a drink.'

He rose to his feet and set off back into the kitchen. 'Then Kemal Ozal turned up. Not that the villagers knew who he was, of course.' Peacock was shouting now to make himself heard from the kitchen, above the sound of ice being vigorously shaken. 'But I recognised him from the description. And he said they were not to talk about it to anybody. Well, old villagers like gossip. So they talked, but not much.'

Peacock came back into the room with a new drink. 'The other thing they all agreed on was that they had never seen the girl before. And they haven't much else to do, except watch the passing world. They'd have noticed her. We don't get tourists like the old days, of course. Doubt if anybody would notice one particular tourist in the old days.'

Joshua said, 'So the odds are the girl was put there some time during the late evening or the night.'

'Suppose so, yes.'

'By someone who knew that tourists would be likely to find her the following day.'

Peacock mused silently, then said, 'I think you're being a bit too logical. It could be like that, yes. But they could just have put her there anyway.'

'Could she have actually been killed there?'

'No idea. Presumably the police would know, but . . .'

Once again there was the barrier, the barrier between the world of power he was used to using and the impotent world of the ordinary citizen. Normally he would go to the police. No, the police would be summoned and come to him. Anonymously. Now, he couldn't even ask.

'Ah.' Peacock reached under the table. 'Here's my drink. Thought I hadn't finished it.' He carefully tipped the remains of his first drink into the second. 'Can I offer you a bite of luncheon?'

'No thanks.' Not that he had any plans. Boobs was dead, but Joanna was alive. Or as far as he knew she was alive. That was all.

He tried to consider what might happen next. What would the Turkish authorities do? They had kept the news blackout. They had told the villagers to keep quiet about it. In any case, how many tourists to Bellapaise would be able to speak enough Turkish to gather what had happened? The villagers only spoke in front of Peacock because they knew him of old, trusted and liked him. They certainly wouldn't go out of their way to try to explain events to a total stranger in fractured English: particularly when they had been ordered not to by men of whom they were afraid.

He realised that Colonel Peacock had been talking. 'Sorry,' Joshua said. 'I was miles away.'

'I was saying,' said Peacock in a very clipped and formal way, 'that I hope you will agree that I have been both cooperative and reliable.'

'I couldn't have done a damned thing without you.'

'Exactly.'

Peacock finished his drink, and then said, 'And in return I think I am entitled to the answers to a few questions.'

'You're not entitled to anything,' said Joshua. 'You know the rules. But try me.'

There was a momentary flicker of a smile on Peacock's face. 'Fair enough. Question one. Why have JBH gone to the trouble of sending you here? From what I've picked up it isn't a big enough operation to involve JBH.'

'I never said that JBH were involved.'

'You said you were from JBH!'

'That's not the same thing.'

Peacock considered this for a moment, then nodded. 'Got you. Question two. Do you understand that I haven't the slightest intention of letting you know who my sources are?'

'I never thought otherwise.'

'Nobody pays me, at least not regularly, and if I care to make a bit on the side, that's none of anybody else's business!'

'So long as it doesn't conflict with our interests, of course.'

'I'm a patriot! Just because I happen to live here! –'

The idea of Colonel Peacock being anything else was too absurd to consider. He was one of those men who stood to immediate attention on hearing the National Anthem played half a mile away. On the other hand, Joshua had little doubt that the 'bit on the side' he made, while being in no way contrary to British interest, would certainly be illegal.

'I'm sure you're a patriot,' said Joshua consolingly.

'Question three.' For some reason Peacock had become aggressive. 'If JBH didn't send you, what the hell are you doing here?'

Joshua was tempted to say that he was minding his own business, but he needed Peacock's cooperation. He said, 'How much I can tell you depends on how much you already know. The old need-to-know principle.'

Peacock snorted. 'You won't find anybody in this part of the island who's much better informed than I am!' Then, presumably referring to some long-forgotten incident that haunted his waking hours and had adversely affected his career, he added, 'Despite a tendency to disobey orders when obedience would have literally endangered the whole damn show!'

Joshua had no idea what Peacock was talking about, but there was no reason why Peacock should learn this. Kidnapping had been established, so he said, 'How much do you know about the kidnapping?'

Colonel Peacock's eyes narrowed and he hunched his shoulders. For a moment he looked like somebody playing a mandarin in Aladdin.

'How much do *you* know? That's the question!'

Joshua rose to his feet. 'Don't start playing silly buggers with me,' he said. 'And thanks for the drink.' He started to move towards the door.

It worked. It wasn't the sudden fear of authority that had its effect on Peacock; it was the sudden fear of loneliness.

'No need to take that attitude, old man!' Peacock cried. 'Only covering my tracks! Be reasonable! Of course I'll tell you what I know!'

Joshua stopped and waited.

'What I've heard,' said Peacock, 'is that some people have been kidnapped. Kidnapped on the other side. What I can't make out is why the Turks are interested. There's no way they could be brought into the north. Not unless they were taken out of the south, say to Egypt, then to Turkey, then into the north. But why would anybody bother to do that?'

'But they are interested?'

'Absolute panic stations, old man! Absolute panic stations!'

'Have you heard who these people are who've been kidnapped?'

'Only that they're female. When they were talking about them in Turkish they used the female gender.'

Quite suddenly, Joshua realised. He knew how it had happened. He had no evidence, let alone proof, but he knew how it had been done. He could account for the kidnapping of the bus in the south where there were no Turks and the hiding of the children in the north where there were no Greeks. He even knew how they had been got across the frontier, through posts manned by three armies, without anybody noticing.

Peacock was still talking, but Joshua was no longer listening. He knew. The danger was even worse than he had feared, but at least he knew what had happened.

Peacock stopped talking, his head on one side and clearly expecting an answer to something.

Joshua asked, 'Have you heard what nationality these people who've been kidnapped are?'

'For God's sake!' exploded Peacock. 'I've just told you! They're supposed to be Brits! I don't see how they can be, but that's what my source says! But I've just told you! Don't you damned well listen to what people are saying?'

'I was – '

'I don't like being ignored! I'm not used to it, and I don't like it!'

'No. Tell me. If I want to get in touch with you from the south, is there any way?'

'Of course there isn't!' Peacock was still angry.

'But when you have to get intelligence back – '

Perhaps he had a radio transmitter. If he hadn't, it shouldn't be difficult to get him one. But would he know how to use modern equipment?

Peacock's eyes swivelled round, he hunched his shoulders again and lowered his voice.

'I have a method,' he said. 'But if the Turks got to hear about it . . .' He indicated with a forefinger that he would have his throat cut. Then he added hastily. 'Not literally, of course. But they could get me out of the house, you see.'

'Yes.'

'Bit complicated. I'd only half paid for it – well, actually, just put down the deposit – in '74 when the Turks took over. So the Greek who owned the land and was building it for me, technically I dare say it could be argued it's really his house. So long as I'm here, keeping an eye on what's going on, there shouldn't be any problem. I'm telling you this in confidence, of course.'

'I understand.'

'But if the Turks wanted to make life difficult for me – '

'Yes.'

'So I go to a lot of trouble to keep my nose clean. But there's a little wimp called Merritt. He has the job of seeing Turkish Cypriots who want to go to England, and getting them the appropriate papers. Which means he comes over here from time to time. In actual fact, he comes a lot more often then he has to.'

'Why?'

'Boy friend. Waiter. Nasty little shit. But, not to put too fine a point on it, I'm in a position to lean on Merritt.'

'Yes.'

'So, *inter alia*, he takes stuff I get and gives it to a contact I have in Nicosia.'

'And who does the contact work for?' Joshua reflected that he had not been told of any JBH contacts in the south except for Nico.

'I don't ask,' said Peacock abruptly. 'At a guess, CIA most of the time. Everybody else does, so I don't see why he should be the exception. KGB occasionally. But when I tell him, then exclusively for us.'

It all sounded very insecure and amateur. Surely Peacock couldn't have slipped so far since . . . Then an idea struck Joshua.

'Would I be right in thinking that your contact pays you for information? Then sells it again himself?' he asked.

'I gave you that.' Peacock obviously resented Joshua's question. 'If London paid me a proper pension, then I wouldn't have to sell stuff. But I'm still a patriot. No business of mine if, say, the Ruskies learn about what the Turks are up to here, or NSA pick up a few names. But I'd never let England down. Never!'

'And would I also be right in thinking that you have something on your contact in the south?'

It was the way he would work. Everything would have a price except patriotism: and the only way to ensure that understandings were kept would be blackmail.

Colonel Peacock grinned. 'You're not a fool,' he said. 'I don't like you, but you're not a fool. Another drink?'

'No thanks.'

'I think I might just manage one more myself.' He turned towards the kitchen. Joshua wondered if he detected a momentary instability in the Colonel's steps. He'd claimed he'd been up since dawn. Had he had his first gin and tonic watching the sun rise over the mountains?

From the kitchen Peacock said in a loud voice, 'You didn't answer my question. I answered all yours, and you didn't answer mine. Sure you don't want another?'

'Quite sure.'

'Up to you. You can lead a horse to water. Or you can lead a whore to water but you can't make her drunk, as an old CO of mine used to say. Bloody silly remark, really. Doesn't mean anything, but I've always remembered it.'

Peacock emerged from the kitchen. 'My question. My question, which you didn't answer was, what the hell are you doing here?'

For a moment Joshua hesitated. So much of his life consisted of answering questions, making decisions, usually without enough time or enough evidence. And of all questions, the one that arose most often was, should I trust you?

The Colonel stood there, if not drunk certainly on the way to being drunk. What effect would drink have on him? On one side of the decision to be made was the absurdity of the figure, the unrecognised, washed-up grotesque with the rumpled Bermuda shorts and the revolver struck into the belt; on the other was the unstated recognition that somewhere in the years long gone this had been a hero, a leader of men in some forgotten, nameless war. To balance the fact that Colonel Peacock was a joke was the fact that Joshua needed him.

Joshua said, 'There was a busload of English schoolgirls kidnapped. One of them was my daughter.'

Peacock looked at him in total silence, carnation-blue eyes narrowed. 'My God,' he said at last, very quietly, 'My God, you're a cold fish!'

Peacock sipped his drink, his eyes still fixed on Joshua. 'If it had been my daughter, there's nothing I wouldn't do to save her. Nothing. But obviously your daughter means absolutely damn all to you. Well, all I can say is I don't like you and I didn't like you from the moment I saw you. I'll help you. But I just feel damned sorry for any girl who has you for a father.'

Chapter Twenty

If there was a public library, he couldn't find it. In any case, he thought, presumably it would be impossible to take books out across the frontier.

Though how could they check? Or would a book somehow become contraband, crossing into the other part of this absurd island?

He found a small junk shop some streets in from the harbour. It sold a miscellany of rubbish, but at the back there were several hundred books. About half of them were in Greek, and presumably had been abandoned by the previous owner when he fled the shop. (They were arranged by authors, and the man who ran the shop clearly didn't speak Greek, or know the Greek alphabet.) Among the other books there were a few of the kind that Joshua was looking for; guidebooks and local histories. Cyprus had been rich in retired English who had published, at their own expense, works on the island. In addition to *The Island Guide*, *See Cyprus*, Thurston, standard guidebooks, there were *Walks in the Cypriot Mountains*; *Pathways of Aphrodite, with Six Original Photographs by the Author*; *Venetian Memories*; *In the Footsteps of the Crusaders*; *Richard Coeur de Lion in Famagusta*; *Untrodden Byways round Troodos*; *Pythagoras and Paphos*; *Six Essays on the Cypriot Experience*; and, most valuable of all to Joshua, an incomplete but extensive set of maps of a large area around Kyrenia, which had been prepared in the nineteen-twenties in anticipation of some road construction that had never taken place.

The shop-owner did not speak English, but Joshua indicated that the books he had put to one side were the ones he wanted. Unsmiling, the shopkeeper wrapped them in a newspaper, tied a piece of string round it, put the parcel in a paper bag, and held up two fingers to indicate two pounds. Joshua paid, and walked out into the street. He was aware of something niggling at the back of his mind, and then he realised what it was. The newspaper in which his books had been wrapped was the newspaper that the two girls had been holding in the photograph; the photograph that was sent to prove that the children had really been taken.

He passed an open-air kebab stall, and the smell made him realise that he was hungry. In the little Venetian harbour there were a number of restaurants and bars, mostly with more tables than customers, and welcoming notices and menus in a variety of mis-spelt languages. Joshua selected a restaurant where there was a largish table on which he could spread out his books and maps half hidden behind a trellis. The owner of the restaurant combined a face of infinite tragedy with the professional heartiness of a stand-up comic. But either he or some hidden employee was a talented cook, and over roast goat, salad, and a bottle of unfamiliar dark red Turkish wine, Joshua tried to learn what he could from what he had just bought.

Now that he had solved the question of how the children had been taken into the north he was beginning to know what other questions he had to answer.

The Turkish authorities could have helped. They would not know what he was looking for because he still wasn't certain what it was, but they would know what he could eliminate. The Greek names on the maps with their English names in brackets beneath, both now presumably supplanted by Turkish names; the local people would know if they represented living villages or dead memories. They would know buildings that could be used because they could be approached unnoticed, where stocks of food and weapons could have been laid in earlier without arousing interest, where there was water, where there was a hiding place from which a look-out could warn of approaching strangers.

The Turkish authorities could have helped, but he was not able to ask for that help. The Turkish authorities did not exist.

Carefully, methodically, he started to work out the possibilities. He began at Bellapaise, because that was where poor Boobs had been found. It did not mean that the terrorists were hiding somewhere in the village: indeed, it would indicate exactly the opposite, because they would know better than to leave what JBH called 'litter' so close to home. But it would mean that Bellapaise was a place they could reach. They could reach it carrying a body in a car, or a pick-up, or a lorry, or hidden under the burden of a mule. They could reach Bellapaise, drop the body, and return, with the reason-

143

able expectation that nobody would notice them. He did not believe, now he had had time to think about it, that Boobs had been killed in the abbey. It would be unneccessarily risky to take a healthy young Englishwoman aiive to the middle of a village for her execution. No. They had killed her wherever they were holding their victims.

Would the girls know what had happened to their teacher? Would she have been shot in from of them? Or would the terrorists be working on the Stockholm Syndrome, the gradual identification of prisoners with their captors? There had been cases, never published because no normal reader would believe them, but they had happened, of prisoners who had so identified themselves with the terrorists that they had taken part in the murder of fellow prisoners. But that took time. It could not yet be happening here. Please.

He looked at the maps. They were somewhere on those maps. He was sure of it, now he had worked out what had happened. They were there, and Joanna was one of them.

Start at Bellapaise. The road into the village had been rough. It was mostly craggy mountains round Bellapaise, with a smattering of hamlets along the roads and at the ends of paths. Or so his old map said. Normally he would methodically check every location, either personally or using police. Here, he couldn't. He was liable to be arrested at best, shot at worst, if he strayed too far off the roads, and the forces of the State were not at his disposal.

He studied the maps again, then was pleased to find that the *Pathways of Aphrodite*, which a Mrs Heather Armitage had traced in 1936, taking her Six Original Photographs en route, included two in the immediate area of Bellapaise. One photograph seemed to have been taken from something like the top of the church in Bellapaise, and it was easy to check the identity of the scattering of houses in the photograph with the place names of hamlets on the map.

He decided to ignore the land between the main road to Kyrenia and Bellapaise. Bellapaise was a tourist attraction, Kyrenia a minor naval base. (A hundred yards from where he was sitting there was a sign warning visitors against walking further round the historic walls of the port.) The terrorists would wish to get distance between themselves and military forces, and also away from a route used by tourists. In addition, he had noticed some sort of army post on the hillside overlooking the road to Bellapaise.

No, they would have gone either north or south of Bellapaise, or else through and beyond it to the east. They would have to get into the village and out again during the period of darkness. Check exactly how long that was. From the map and the impression he'd got, there wasn't much of a road into Bellapaise except the one from above Kyrenia. So they would be unlikely to have used a car. If they had the body on a mule, then surely to God they couldn't have started more than a mile and a half, two at most, from Bellapaise.

He turned to another of Mrs Armitage's excellent photographs. A village of half a dozen whitewashed houses, a flock of goats, a pig, and an old woman looking at Mrs Armitage.

A finger stabbed the photograph.

'The goat on the left is a KGB agent,' said a voice behind him. 'Hello, Chief Superintendent. What are you doing here? Not that you'll tell me.'

Joshua looked up. For a moment he thought that he might try to bluff his way out, then dismissed the idea.

'Hello, Weinstein,' he said.

'Can I join you?'

Without waiting for an answer, Weinstein pulled up a chair from another table, and sat down. 'You know, of all the people on earth I wasn't expecting to run into here, you'd come second on the list. After the Queen but ahead of the Pope. Not that you'll tell me, like I said. But what *are* you doing here?'

'I'm on holiday.'

Weinstein grinned. He was, thought Joshua, one of the most physically unattractive men he had ever known. His features were an ill-assorted, unrelated jumble, the nose too big for the eyes, too small for the mouth. One ear stuck out nearly at right angles, the other was half-missing where it had been bitten off in a fight. Coupled with the thinning hair of middle age, ranging from fawn to khaki, was the acne of adolescence. It was strange that a man so ugly should choose to have his face, albeit touched up, on the page every time he wrote for his paper: and he wrote, in the opinion of JBH, far too often. His voice, so well known and apparently attractive to millions of television viewers, mixed the flat vowels of the Midlands, where he had spent most of his youth, with the whine of Australia, where he had spent the rest. Weinstein leaned back in his chair, his hands behind his head, and Joshua was reminded that Weinstein also had problems of personal hygiene.

On the other hand, Weinstein had qualities that Joshua admired. He was extremely intelligent, he was dogged, he was courageous, and he was an idealist. It was those qualities that had made him, arguably, the most respected campaigning journalist in Fleet Street.

Not that he spent much time anywhere near that street, or indeed in England. He had an undoubted flair for languages, all, according to JBH sources, spoken with a foreign accent that no native of a society could ever quite place. Every major Intelligence service had a file on Weinstein, and if the ones that Joshua had seen were typical, they were all wrong. For example, the French had him down as an Israeli agent for Mossad, the Italians believed he was English but that his parents were Germans, and the CIA told Joshua that he was, they were almost certain, working for the GRU, unless, they added darkly, he was really working for M16.

'I like that,' said Weinstein. 'You're aware that if the Turks knew that a senior JBH operator was at loose in their non-existent country, you could easily start World War III?'

'What's JBH?' It was a game, but they had to play it.

'I've no idea. It was a name I invented for a piece I wrote.' A piece that had been the first time ever that JBH's existence had been revealed. Weinstein went on, 'I'll tell you why *I'm* here. One . . .' He ticked the reasons off with his dirty fingers and bitten nails. 'One, like you I'm on holiday. Two, something's going on. I don't know what, but I'll find out. You know Colonel Oztec is on holiday here too?'

Oztec was the head of the Turkish secret police who dealt with problems that it was felt the rest of the secret police might find distressing.

'No. I didn't know.'

Over the years Joshua had found that it paid to be honest with Weinstein. Honest within reason.

'Suite seventeen at the Dome Hotel. Arrived two days ago. So far nobody's complained about any blood in the swimming pool. Three, there's been a series of checks on visiting Turks from the mainland. Checks like being held up at gunpoint in your hotel bedroom at two in the morning. Four, there's an airborne unit on standby outside Adana airport. Five, a man was killed at Bellapaise a couple of nights ago. A foreigner.'

It wasn't a man, thought Joshua. It was Boobs. But he didn't say anything.

'And six,' said Weinstein, grinning hugely, 'you're here.' Then he added, 'To be honest, that's a bonus. I didn't know you'd be here.'

It was Weinstein's way of telling him there hadn't been a leak. It was all part of a very complicated, unstated relationship between the two men, and a small favour would be expected in return.

146

Joshua started to fold away the maps. There was no point in giving Weinstein any leads he hadn't picked up already. 'Tell me,' he said, 'What's this about a man being murdered?'

'I've only just heard. A foreigner. I just happened to overhear some conversation.'

'I didn't realise you spoke Turkish.'

'I speak it very badly. It's a simple language, but I never had a lot of reason to learn it.'

That fitted. Peacock spoke it more or less fluently, and realised they were talking about a woman. Weinstein only spoke a little, and missed that point.

'I'm surprised that you should be interested in a casual crime like that.'

'If it were a casual crime,' said Weinstein, 'I wouldn't be. I'm going to have a brandy. Can I offer you one?'

'Why not?'

Weinstein either knew something, or he would find something out. He was quite remarkably good at ferreting out information that people like Joshua were paid to keep secret. One day, probably, he would go a step too far and find out one thing too many, and that would be the end. But he knew the rules, and he backed his judgement, and in the meantime he made a great deal of money. Once, several years ago, Weinstein had confided in Joshua that he had already bought what he had called his bolt hole by the sea, and he had a new identity, complete with documentation to go with it. He had avoided saying in which country – or even which continent – this bolt hole was located, and when Joshua had made enquiries through JBH they had come up with a blank. But Joshua had no doubt that the bolt hole existed.

'This island is weird,' said Weinstein, trying to catch a waiter's eye. 'Everywhere I go I keep seeing people I thought were dead. In that I thought of them at all.'

'What sort of people?'

'Oh, agents from the distant past, old, unreliable informants I used to use, *passé* couriers – it's a sort of espionage time warp.' The proprietor had noticed his gesture, and hurried to the table. 'It doesn't matter what brandy you order, it's all the same.'

Then he spoke rapidly and more fluently than Joshua expected in Turkish to the proprietor, who nodded and scurried away. Weinstein turned back to Joshua. 'Everybody who has ever really let me down in the past seems to have got washed up here. Haven't you noticed?'

'I've only just arrived.'

Just arrived, and in those few hours two people were dead. A sudden memory of Anna, because she was part of it too, but at the core of his mind there was the fear, the fear of what had happened to Joanna, what might be happening at that moment.

'Remember Iliana Marinescova?'

Joshua remembered her. She'd been the mistress of the Rumanian Foreign Minister, and a dancer, and a wildly unreliable CIA agent. She'd left Bucharest, and somebody had seen her in Bari, then she'd been reported in Hong Kong. But it had all been a long time ago.

'Just.'

'She's here,' said Weinstein. 'Looking slightly older than God. I saw her a couple of days ago, at nine o'clock in the morning, wheeling a mattress on a bicycle! Would you believe?'

It was a strange idea. Iliana Marinecova, hostess of the legendary party when she had entered in a dress made entirely of carnations which the male guests were expected to pick for buttonholes, pushing a bicycle in Kyrenia.

'Everybody with a really long track record of proven failure seems to wind up here.' Weinstein pushed Joshua's plate to one side as the proprietor arrived with the brandies on a tray. 'I'm expecting any time to run into Queen Anne's gynaecologist.'

The proprietor cleared the table, said something to Weinstein, and left.

'He was saying he can't get staff,' said Weinstein. 'Which is a load of crap. What he can't get is tourists.'

He raised his glass. 'Cheers. Do you mind if I follow you about a bit?'

'Yes.'

'Where are you staying?'

'The other side. In Nicosia.'

Weinstein raised an eyebrow. 'And they let you come through any time you like?'

'No. I'm a day tripper.' Joshua was beginning to feel under pressure. 'I told you. I'm on holiday.'

'We're all on holiday, all the time. Life is just one big Butlins.'

Weinstein examined his brandy, sniffed it. 'Not too bad. A thought. If for any reason you want to stay overnight in the north, without bothering the authorities, I happen to be spending my holiday in a sort of chalet thing that could put up an extra visitor or two.'

It was an interesting offer, subtly put. Weinstein would expect something in exchange. But it could be that he would be a better prospect than the unreliable Peacock.

'Just a suggestion,' said Weinstein. 'I'll give you the address.'

He took a paper napkin from a holder, and wrote on it. 'They call the place the Jolly Bungalows. It's somebody's idea of colloquial English. It's proper name is Jordani's, after the Greek who got chased out in seventy-four. But the point is, I'm the only tenant. As I say, there's no tourists. If you try to check in normally, not through an agency in the UK or somewhere, you'll get the whole of the Turkish secret police descending on you. But my chalet has three beds and isn't overlooked.' Weinstein grinned. 'You won't be compromised.'

Joshua took the napkin and folded it away in his jacket pocket. 'I might even take you up,' he said.

He drank the brandy and rose to his feet. 'Thanks for the drink.'

'My pleasure.'

Joshua tucked the maps and books under his arm. Weinstein had seen them, and he hadn't asked about them because he knew enough not to, but he would have drawn his conclusions and there was no point in trying to fool him. Not yet, anyway.

There was a man standing in a doorway, very obviously watching his hire car, when he reached it. Joshua ignored him, and as he drove off he could see in the mirror the man step out into the street and walk away. From the lack of haste there seemed nothing urgent about it; a routine check on cars used by foreigners rather than surveillance of him personally.

He couldn't think of anything useful he could do. He had left half the wine, but he still felt sleepy. Round him the town had largely closed down for the siesta. He could not go back to Bellapaise because he did not want to be noticed. He could not get hold of the authorities, because he was forbidden to. He would have contacted Pamir again, but he had no way of doing so. He felt frustrated and helpless and lonely.

The sight of three heavily armed Turkish soldiers coming towards him down the nearly empty street decided him. He turned the car round and wound through the narrow streets back onto the main road south over the mountains. South towards the frontier and the check points; south towards the British Consulate to check with London; south towards the smooth, tawny, hungry body of Anna.

Chapter Twenty One

The machine chattered on, and then fell silent. He carefully decoded the message and tried to assess its significance. The message was simple enough: THERE HAS BEEN NO REPEAT NO REPORT FROM ANY TURKISH SOURCE OF ANY DEATH OF BRITISH SUBJECT IN BELLAPAISE STOP FURTHER NO REPEAT NO REPORTS OF ANY OTHER DEVELOPMENTS IN CASE STOP.

What the message meant was that for reasons of their own the Turks had stopped playing.

He left the office, and found himself facing Miss Galsworth, who had taken up a position across the corridor in the Consulate.

'There were some Cypriots came in,' she explained breathily. 'I was afraid they might walk through and . . . interrupt you.'

'Thanks.'

Damn, he'd forgotten about the flowers again. Obviously she wasn't really expecting any, but it would be something she would remember for the rest of her unexciting life. He said, 'I haven't forgotten the flowers.'

She said, 'Flowers?' to indicate that she had no idea what he was talking about, but she was a bad actress and her delight shone through.

'If there's a message for me,' said Joshua, 'and I've asked for any update, it'll have the prefix HBJ. Like Hello Billy Junior.'

'Hello Billy Junior,' she said, eyes wide, as though the words had some enormous mystical significance.

'That's right. And it'll end JBH. Same letters, but the other way round. Okay?'

'Yes.'

'It'll be in a one-time code, so don't try to decode it because your stuff isn't valid. But please, get it to me as soon as you can. Please.'

'Yes.'

'If I'm not at the Romantica, don't leave the message. For God's sake don't leave the actual message.'

He had worries enough without the bloody hotel knowing

150

he got code messages through the Consulate.

'No. Of course not.'

'Just say that there's a personal telegram for me at the Consulate, and I ought to get it as soon as possible. Something confidential. Like, my mother has died or something. Don't tell them, just give them that impression.'

'Yes!'

He realised she would walk barefoot over blazing coals to bring him a message. He was taking advantage of her, cheating her, but he didn't really have any choice. It was part of the job.

'It's good to know there's one person I can trust,' he said, and smiled.

As he walked back to the hotel he tried to make sense of the information from London. The Turks had first failed to report the murder of Boobs, then, when directly questioned, had denied any knowledge of it. Why?'

Start at the beginning. They had never admitted that the kidnapped children were in Turkish territory. The only person who had said he thought they were there was Pamir, and that had been a personal assessment. At the time it had seemed almost impossible for them to be anywhere but in the south, but now that he had worked out how it could have been done it all fitted together. Suppose the Turks still thought the kidnapping did not affect them?

No, that was nonsense. Not only did they have the body of poor Boobs in a drawer in a mortuary, they had imposed a security clamp-down about how she got there. Suppose Turkish Counter-Intelligence believed, but the Turkish authorities in the north did not. Indeed, did those authorities know? Had anybody thought to tell them? Because of the unique position of their administration, all the information that reached them had earlier been filtered through Ankara. In any other place on earth he would only have had to ask. He could have asked directly, or he could have asked through London. But in Cyprus he couldn't ask, because there was nobody to ask in the first place. There were people, but because of the game of let's pretend they could not be reached because they didn't exist.

Who benefited? Why should the authorities – whether in north Cyprus or in Ankara – why should they deny what they knew to be the truth? But was there any certainty that they had known who Boobs was? From that body, with half the skull blown away, she could have been almost anybody. It was ironic that it was her breasts that had enabled him to identify her. No, they must have known she

151

wasn't, for example, a local peasant girl. They would have checked her clothing and found it was bought in Britain. But people went to and fro between Cyprus and Britain all the time. Assume that the Turks were not being devious, just incompetent. Why was that cabinet the only one that had been locked? The ideas were coming in a disorderly rush.

Again, who benefited? Suppose they had decided to use the terrorists' demands. That would be logical, because they were what the authorities wanted anyway. Would they really cooperate with Grey Wolves? Perhaps the people in Cyprus might, because they hadn't encountered them before. But would they in Ankara?

In the meantime, there was a check to be made. While JBH in London had been talking to God knows who in Turkey, he had got the name of Berrisford's Irish major serving with the UN. He was a Major Liam Cooney, and the only address was care of the Ledra Palace Hotel. When Joshua had asked how JBH were in a position to lean on the Major, there had been a delay – because this sort of information would not be directly on the computer – then back had come the message he had been expecting: Four Seven Four Finance. Cooney had been caught with his fingers in the till. Message to continue. Further. Mess accounts 1st Seventh Leinster Rifles JBH has signed confession in exchange for repayment without detection and commitment to service.

It all seemed a very simple, clearcut case.

Joshua reached the Hotel Romantica. There was nobody at the reception desk. He had work to do, and in a way he was grateful that Anna was not there. He felt his penis stiffening at the thought of her, and he knew that if he saw her he would find a reason to postpone doing what he had to do.

He took his key from the pigeon hole, and in his room, after locking the door, he opened his suitcase. The cases used by JBH varied considerably, to avoid any danger of an agent being recognised by his luggage. But they all had the same ingenious double lining in the lid, invented, legend had it, by a clockmaker who had been a refugee from Nazi Germany. To open it required a combination of pressure and a reverse twist of one of the case's two locks, and nobody who had not been shown the technique had ever succeeded in solving it. Even tearing the case apart revealed nothing, unless the compartment was in use – simply a well made case with an inner lining.

From the compartment he selected the identification papers of a Metropolitan Police Inspector attached to Interpol in Paris. Then

152

he closed everything up, and went downstairs. There was still no sign of Anna.

At the Ledra Palace a gum-chewing French Canadian Corporal escorted him in, past piles of bedding, army filing cabinets, and the general detritus of passing armies – for the change-overs not just in units but in nationalities seemed to produce a remarkable amount of equipment that was not sufficiently standardised to be of any use to the incoming force.

To Joshua's surprise Major Cooney was not only known, he was actually living in the hotel. By now the French Canadian had been replaced by a Swede, who led him to the third floor and tapped on a door. There was a pause, then a voice said, 'Yes, for Christ's sake, I'm off fockin' duty!' in a thick Cork accent. The door opened, and Cooney glowered at Joshua.

Cooney must have been six foot six in height, and had the physique of a weight lifter. Joshua silently showed him the identification papers, and Cooney examined first the papers, then Joshua.

'You'd better be coming in,' he said.

The Swede flapped his hand in what was perhaps meant as a salute, and stomped off down the corridor as Joshua entered Cooney's room.

The room had once been one of the more expensive in the hotel. It was twin-bedded with a bathroom en suite, and a pleasant view over the old town. Now the pale lemon walls had ominous brown stains on them, one of the beds was propped against a wall, the glass of the windows had been knocked out and half the resulting space was blocked with sandbags. A light machine gun rested on the floor, and Cooney's dress uniform was on a hanger suspended from a nail driven into the bathroom door. There was a sour smell of whisky.

Cooney was in his underclothes. He sat down heavily on an unmade bed, and started to hunt for his cigarettes.

'I was asleep,' he said. 'I was up all fockin' night.'

He found the cigarettes, which had fallen on the floor under the bed, extracted one. 'What can I do for you?'

Joshua said, 'I'm from JBH.'

Cooney slowly looked up, then lit the cigarette, his eyes always on Joshua. There was a long silence.

'Jesus,' he said at last, 'You don't leave a man alone, do you?'

Joshua looked round, then pulled a chair towards him and sat down. Outside someone was shouting orders in a language he didn't recognise.

'I'm not asking a lot. All I want to know is about the movement of UN vehicles on one particular day.'

'What day?'

'Last Sunday.'

Cooney thought for a moment. then said, 'I'm in armoured cars. There'll be our records in our office. But you'll be wanting to know about all of them?'

'Yes.'

Cooney nodded. 'I can find you that. There's regular patrols, then if there's any trouble we always report in where we've been and when.'

'And UN vehicles frequently cross from the south into the north? And vice versa?'

'All the time. We can cross. Nobody else can, of course, but we can. Unless one side or the other's getting stroppy. Then sometimes we get stuck. It's orders, you see.' Cooney expertly blew a smoke ring in the still hot air. 'If I had my way, the moment either of them stepped out of line, then we'd go in and sort the fockin' bastards out. But that's not orders.'

'Who keeps records of when a UN vehicle crosses the frontier?'

'I've told you. We all do.'

'But would they keep a record at the actual crossing point?'

Cooney didn't seem to have thought of this. He said, 'I suppose they must, yes. The infantry. But we don't see those.'

'Where would those records be kept?'

'I dunno. In here somewhere.'

'That's the second thing I want from you. I want you to check the records of whoever is responsible for the vehicles against the infantry records of vehicles crossing the frontier. Okay?'

Cooney looked sourly at him, but said nothing.

Joshua rose to his feet. 'Then I'll try to use my influence to save you being bothered too much in future.'

'Where can I find you?'

'I'm at the Hotel Romantica. Just up the road.'

'I know that all right. And your name's Howell.'

Joshua smiled. 'More or less.' Then he stopped smiling, and said, 'It shouldn't take you long, should it.'

'How long have I got?'

'Well,' said Joshua, glancing at his watch, 'If you get dressed now . . .'

He left. As he closed the door he heard Cooney saying 'Jesus!'

154

Chapter Twenty Two

He took off his jacket and threw it on a chair. It was almost too hot to think, but he knew he had to pose the right questions, then find their answers. For the first time since he had arrived in Cyprus, he felt that he was moving towards knowing the truth.

The truth. He sat bleakly on his bed, and kicked off his shoes. If the truth was that it was too late, Joanna was dead, would he want to know the truth?

He unfastened his belt, pulled off his trousers, and tossed them on top of the jacket. Then he lay down on the bed, his hands behind his head.

The UN vehicle. That was just a question of waiting. Cooney would find the answers because he had no alternative. Bellapaise. Find someone here in the south who lived there. There must be people, plenty of them.

The body in the morgue. Boobs. Poor Boobs. If he had access to a path lab he could get them to examine the body. Find out any evidence of how it was taken to the abbey.

He felt his head swimming, then concentrated again. Body. If it had been taken in a car boot, then there should be traces that would indicate the fact. On a mule. On a mule under a load of. . . Of what? What are they carrying on mules at this time of year? But if it had been a mule, there should be hair or something.

Mules. Mules smell. He hadn't noticed any smell. He should have thought of it.

A vague dream-picture formed in his head, Boobs with her breasts, one either side of the mule, and then he fell asleep.

He woke to know there was somebody in the room. There had been a stage in his training when he would instinctively have thrown himself across the room at the intruder, and in the time it took whoever it was to react, one of a series of murderous blows would have landed, and the danger would have been over. Then there had

155

been the ex-Olympic fencer at Ashford who had looked at his class and murmured, 'Gentleman, let me be frank. The last thing we want is a lot of pre-conditioned homicides. The Green Berets spend all their time trying to untrain their people. So shall we forget what we have been taught to do and imagine that we are being threatened by an elderly madman in the Athenaeum . . .?'

Joshua imperceptibly prepared himself. He could throw his body in any direction, he could turn, he could twist, he could kill. Then he felt the weight of a body sitting on the bed beside his legs. A hand very gently, almost imperceptible, reached inside his underpants and held his penis, then slipped it out. He felt it stiffening even before the tip of the tongue touched it. First the tongue, then the lips.

He kept his eyes closed, and did not alter the slow rhythm of his breathing. He was asleep and he was more awake than he had ever been in his life, every part of him concentrated in what she was doing. Her fingers ran along him while her lips still held him, then he felt her fingers reach between his legs and stroke, round and up, round and up. She was breathing more rapidly than he was and he longed to reach out and search her body, but that was not part of the game they were playing. For a moment she seemed to leave him, then he felt soft pressure and realised that she was enfolding his penis between her breasts. Again a pause, and again the hot mois-ture of her lips. Slowly she took more and more of him into her mouth and it was impossible that she didn't realise he was awake, because no man could sleep through that agony and that ecstasy. Her lips slid up him and for a moment there was just her tongue like a fluttering butterfly, then even that ceased. He was about to cry out when he felt the weight on the bed shifting and he realised that she was moving until she was sitting astride him. She lowered her-self, very slowly, onto him, then gripping him rose up and down, up and down, tightening, rocking, loosening, then tightening again. Her hand took his and led it to her, and the game was over as his fingers were pressed against her. She gave a little moan, and he opened his eyes to see her above him, but she didn't see him because her head was turning from side to side and her eyes were tight closed. He could stand it no longer and he reached behind her, seizing her bottom, and rose, impaling her, her legs wound round him like a mantis round a stalk.

As he crushed her down on the bed she gave a cry and a frenzy seized them both. Now there was no control, no pretence, no

156

restraint. In a roar the avalanche came, a storm, wave after wave crashing on the defenceless coast, blackness and lightning, the unendurable, the ecstatic, and then the incredible release.

They lay beside each other in the timeless afternoon, and he felt a peace he had not known since he had come to the island, a peace he had forgotten could exist ever since the first phone call that had told him the unthinkable. He felt nothing except blissful satiation. There were no thoughts in his mind, just a vague sense of tender gratitude to the smooth soft body beside him. The late afternoon was cooling rapidly, and a gentle breeze had come up. He was aware of nothing except sensuality, and because of that he was happy as he had not been happy for years. There was no tension because reality was not in the room. All that was in the room was his body and her body, and what they had done.

When the phone rang for a moment even that was somehow part of the erotic reverie, a musical accompaniment. Then he realised and the dream shattered like a mirror dropped onto the floor.

He sat up and reached across her to pick up the receiver.

'Yes?' Now his mind was fully alert, and the dream was over and the nightmare that was real had replaced it.

'Mr Doyle?'

Doyle. Someone was calling him by his own name. There had been a mistake somewhere. He said 'Yes' again in a way that could be denied immediately.

'What on earth is going on?' demanded a tetchy male voice. 'I ask for you at the number I have, and they tell me you're on holiday. Then they give me a number in Cyprus and the hotel says they've never heard of you. I describe you and the girl says you're staying under the name of Howell. It really is very unsatisfactory.'

He knew who it was, but he said, 'Who am I speaking to?'

'This is Dr. Marshall at Brookside Hospital. More to the point, is that Mr Doyle?'

He breathed heavily and said, 'Yes.'

'I hope somebody knows what is going on. I can't say that I think this is quite the best time for you to be taking a holiday. Particularly without leaving a contact number with the hospital.'

Then, with heavy sarcasm, Marshall asked, 'I suppose I am right in thinking you are still accepting responsibility for your wife? We haven't been given any other name.'

'No. I'm responsible.'

'Good. That's one thing clear. She has discharged herself. As I

157

told you, she was perfectly entitled to do so at any time. I think you will recall that I also gave you my professional opinion that it would be disastrous if this were to happen.'

'I remember.'

Anna's eyes were open, and she looked sleepily up at him. Then she reached out, and started to run a finger very gently over his stomach.

'When Mrs Doyle announced that she proposed to leave, we didn't become unduly concerned. She has said she was going to leave a great many times before.'

'Yes.'

'I had my secretary phone your home, but there was no reply. I then had her leave a message at the number you had given as your place of work. I don't know exactly what your position is there. We tried to leave a message with your secretary, but apparently you don't have a secretary.'

'Not as such, no.' What was worrying you, thought Joshua, was how could a man who doesn't rise to a secretary manage to pay the fees of the Brookside Hospital. But he said, 'I'm away a lot of the time. It's rather informal.'

'I assumed,' said the cold voice on the line, 'and it seemed a reasonable assumption, that at least you would be at home. In England. We'd had no notification that you intended to take a holiday abroad.'

'It cropped up suddenly,' he said, and then the idiocy of the idea struck him. A sudden holiday. A cancellation in a package tour. But he could not make Marshall understand because making him understand would be a breach of the Official Secrets Act, for Christ's sake. He said hastily, 'It isn't really a holiday. Also work.'

'That was not what your office said. But if you say so . . .'

There was a long silence, and he felt Anna sliding off the bed, kneeling before him, her hands gently folding round his penis.

'Hello! Hello! Are you still there?' Marshall demanded.

'Yes. I'm here.' I'm here, and so are you, as real, as un-understanding, as irrelevant as if you were in the room.

'As you're not at home, as you've decided to go on holiday, it's fortunate that there is someone to look after your wife.'

Now he was puzzled. 'Look after her?'

'The woman you're living with.'

'I'm not living with anybody.' As he spoke Anna was trying to push him back, giggling, her tongue reaching out for him.

158

'Your personal relationships are nothing to do with me,' said Marshall. 'Except in as much as they affect the health of my patient. I am referring to . . .'

There was a pause while, presumably, Marshall found his place in some notes. 'I'm referring to a Phyllis Delworth. Your wife confided to a nurse about her, and she told me because she thought it might be relevant in understanding her psychoses.'

Joshua said wearily, 'Phyllis is my cleaner.'

'That was not the impression the nurse got.'

'She comes in four times a week, usually after I've gone to work. I hardly ever see her.' For God's sake, why was he bothering to explain? But he found himself blundering on. 'She comes in at nine-thirty and she's supposed to work until twelve.'

And she's extremely plain. There had, once, been a morning when he had been in bed after working all night, and they'd both known that he had only got to make the gesture and she would have joined him. But he hadn't made the gesture, and in any case Barbara knew nothing about it. Why was he even thinking of it now? Except that Anna was licking him and Marshall was droning on.

'Are you saying that when your wife went home there was nobody there?' demanded Marshall.

'Nobody.' Then he thought and said hastily, 'Unless she left in the morning. If she left in the morning, then yes, Phyllis ought to have been there.'

'Why do you say, ought to?' Marshall spoke as though he had caught him out in a lie.

'Because she tends to slope off early.'

'How do you know that? How do you know that if you are not there?'

'Because the bloody work hasn't been done!'

It was absurd. Why should he be defending himself over something of which he was entirely innocent? He said, 'I had told my wife I would be going abroad.'

'When was this?'

'The last time I saw her. The day before I left.' Then he remembered that he hadn't told her. He had intended to, but somehow there hadn't been the chance. Not that it mattered. The knowledge would somehow have been twisted inside Barbara's brain, and in any case Marshall wouldn't have believed him.

'I have notified her doctor,' said Marshall. 'I don't know if he has been to see her, but I strongly urged him to.'

'Thank you.'

Anna slid round behind him, wrapping her legs round his body. She tried to wriggle round so that he could penetrate her, but with one arm he held her back.

'Is there anything I can do?' he asked the doctor.

'Simply, I presume you will be coming home!' The answer was crisp and clear, there was the silent sound of a casebook being snapped shut as an interview was terminated. Until next time. We will be in touch.

Joshua said, 'I can't come home. Not yet.'

There was a silence, then Marshall said, the dislike he felt unmistakable over the thousands of miles, 'I don't think you understand. Your wife is a very ill woman. If you think that having a holiday is more important than her safety, then all I have to say is that I disagree with your priorities.'

'I know. It isn't quite like that.'

'Whatever it is *like*,' It wasn't dislike in the voice now, it was utter contempt. 'To put it bluntly, we cannot consider ourselves responsible for what happens. Have I made myself clear?'

'Yes. Yes, you've made yourself clear. But I want you to do one more thing.'

'We have done everything – '

'I want you, the moment you get off this phone, to ring whoever you know to get a nurse to move into my home with my wife. I – '

The interruption was icy. 'This is a private nursing home, not an agency! We're not in the business of – '

'You will get somebody in there, to look after my wife, twenty-four hours a day, until I get back! Do you understand?'

'I am certainly not used to being – '

'You say she's ill.'

'Very ill.'

'Then you, as a doctor, you have a responsibility! If she's been at your nursing home all this time, and you've subjected her to all that treatment – '

'I don't like your attitude, Mr Doyle! I am not – '

'And if, after all that treatment and all that time – and all that money, I might add – the best you can do is let her loose, admitting that she is very ill, knowing that I am several thousand miles away and cannot help, then I think apart from the Medical Council – '

'This is not a matter for the Medical Council!' Joshua could hear the sudden alarm in Marshall's voice.

160

'I was saying the apart from the Medical Council, I am not without a certain amount of power.'

Thank God, thought Joshua, he just thinks of me as some fairly senior civil servant. Ministry of Health. Who knows?

Marshall was beginning to splutter. 'This is all quite absurd! Apart from anything else, how am I supposed to engage a nurse? Who's going to pay for her?'

'I'll pay,' said Joshua. 'Don't worry your mercenary mind about that. And if you doubt my ability to pay, or my integrity, then you have my business number. Ring that number – have you a pen?'

'Yes, but – '

'Ring that number and ask for Clearance. Got that? Clearance.'

'Yes.'

'Say who you are, and say that I have told you to phone them. Right?'

'Yes.'

'They should put your mind at rest.' And a brisk surveillance on your every move for a few days, he thought. Plus a phone tap.

There was the sound of Marshall breathing heavily, then he said, 'I don't like being bullied, Doyle. But for the sake of my patient I will engage a nurse.'

'Fine.'

'But if your wife somehow survives despite this total lack of attention, something which seems not to concern you, I would ask you, next time you decide to send her to a hospital, that you do not send her to this one!'

The line went dead. He sat on the edge of the bed and he felt tears coming into his eyes. Tears of rage, tears of despair, tears of pity. His wife was alone and mad and piteous, his only child was in desperate danger, and he was helpless.

'God,' he said quietly. 'God, what a bloody mess.'

Anna rose and stood before him, her hands gentle on his shoulders. 'Is not good?' she asked. 'Is everything not good?'

'No.' He closed his eyes. 'Everything is not good.'

He felt her push her body towards him and for a moment the smooth secret part of her brushed his lips.

She whispered, 'Perhaps we make love again?'

He opened his eyes and looked at her, and she was beautiful. He reached out and pulled her down onto the bed.

'Why not?' he said. 'What the hell else is there to live for?'

161

Chapter Twenty Three

She had left while he was asleep, and when he woke up, towards six, he realised that it must be many months since he had slept as deeply. His body had the heavy, sensuous smell of woman, and he got up and turned on the shower. Through the shuttered windows he could hear the distant sounds of the city rising from its siesta and preparing for the evening, the clatter of shops being opened, the cries of street vendors, the games of children, radios being turned on. The temperature was gently perfect, the air like silk.

When he went downstairs the mustachioed girl was behind the reception desk. He was uncertain whether he detected a knowing sideways leer as he pushed over his key.

'Any messages?' he asked. If Cooney was as apprehensive as Joshua thought, then he might already have acted, but the girl shook her head.

He turned down the empty streets towards the frontier. A dog emerged from an over-grown garden, snarled, wagged its tail, and then lost interest, watching him go past without further reaction. The dog looked dirty but fed, and he wondered who in that area looked after it. It was not an attractive enough animal to have become the pet of any of the soldiers, and there were no civilians any more.

He walked into the Greek command post and produced the card he had used to get into the Ledra Palace. 'I'm not crossing,' he said. 'Just calling on someone in the hotel.'

'Business?'

'Yes.'

The Greek on duty, a hard-looking man in his early thirties, examined him thoughtfully.

'I wouldn't stay too long if I were you,' he said in nearly faultless English. 'The Turks have brought up a tank. Perhaps two, we're not sure.'

'Why?'

The Greek shrugged. 'Probably just to make us worry about why they've done it. But they might decide to provoke an incident. You can never trust the bastards.'

He pushed the card back. 'I won't sign you out because if you pass here theoretically you're going into Turkish occupied territory and it's too late for that.'

'I won't be long.'

He walked past the blue and white painted barrier towards the other world a few hundred yards away. Nobody stopped him as he walked into the Ledra Palace. Professionally, he recognised the symptoms: an army grown slack because it had not had to prove itself for too long.

Eventually a Swedish Lieutenant appeared, who escorted him to Cooney's room. Cooney was sitting on his bed, and apart from the fact that he was now wearing trousers it looked as though nothing at all had happened since Joshua had left him several hours earlier.

'It doesn't make sense,' said Cooney by way of greeting. 'It doesn't make fockin' sense. That's why I haven't been over to see you.'

He was anxious to keep in with JBH, no doubt about that.

'What's the problem?'

Cooney stood up and from inside the wardrobe produced a number of folders.

'I'm not supposed to take these away,' he said. 'They're not that secret, there's nothing here anybody wants, but they're still classified I suppose. Anyway, you can see for yourself.'

He spread them out on the bed.

'These are the analyses of troop movements from unit reports,' he said. 'If you feed them back you can follow what any one vehicle was doing at any one time.'

'Yes,'

'Most of it's what you'd expect. Regular patrols. You get the odd variation.'

He indicated a place on one of the sheets. 'This was my own section, so I know what happened. You can see we diverted to Yeri. In fact we'd got this message that there'd been a fire-fight there. Well, we knew bloody well there was nothing because there's no Turks in the south any more to fight, but we went there anyway. Turned out it was an idiot peasant who'd gone off his head and was blazin' away wi' a shotgun. But you can see . . .'

He found another page he was looking for. 'Here's the original report. From the police. If they'd been any good they'd have gone and sorted it out themselves, but I suppose they were still thinking they might find themselves up against a whole lot of Turkish paratroops. Anyway, that meant that we should have crossed the border at thirteen hundred hours, more or less, but we didn't get to the check point until fourteen-twenty. Here's the infantry confirmation. Nobody can move in this island without somebody making a report about it.'

'You said something didn't make sense.'

'That's right.' He isolated another document. 'This one here. From B Section, A Company, Third Leinster Rifles. Standard report. Canadian patrol vehicle checked at their crossing point at Pergamos. What the Turks call Beyarmuda, twelve-seventeen hours. Registration number AV 416.'

Joshua said quietly, 'But the Canadians don't have such a patrol vehicle?'

'They don't have any patrol vehicles at all! Just Land Rovers!'

'You're sure?'

'I've checked the number, and it doesn't make any sense. Not to the Canucks, not to anybody. Mind you, I haven't fed it into the main computers. It was unofficial, you understand.'

It was so obvious. Of course that was the way they would have done it. A white-painted, high-sided UN vehicle. A couple of men in the sky-blue berets wave down the bus. Your friendly UN soldiers, the men who keep the peace. Ignore the driver, speak to Boobs. A little trouble, absolutely no danger, but better to transfer the girls to the UN truck. Sorry about this. Perhaps one of the UN men would get in the bus with the driver, to make sure they all kept in contact. All rather exciting, really. Then straight on to the check point. Papers in order, Greeks wave them through. UN troops wave through their own vehicle. Then the Turks. No trouble at all. No questions asked because it would be like being given a lift in a police car in England, only more so.

When he returned to the Greek Cypriot frontier he had already decided on a course of action. The uncertainty about what had happened was over. He knew what had happened. In some ways it was the worst contingency, but at least he knew what it was.

It was the same man on duty. He looked up as Joshua entered. 'You were quick,' he said. 'I would have thought you would have stayed for a drink. They all have duty free drinks.'

Joshua produced his JBH card, and allowed the Greek a fleeting

164

glimpse of it, making his eyes widen. 'Get me Inspector Nico Tsardanis,' he said curtly. 'And ask him please to meet me at any hotel.'

The name Tsardanis obviously meant something. 'I'll try, but . . . I doubt if he'll be available.'

'He'll be available,' said Joshua, and he didn't smile.

Chapter Twenty Four

It was getting darker by the second as they drove out of the city. In the west a huge scarlet sun was dropping behind the mountains, the sky slashed with colour like the palette of a deranged Fauvist.

'I don't think it was money,' said Nico. 'I think mebbe it was fun. You know? He's got money. Why does he want more?'

Joshua said quietly, 'Scare him.'

'Sure. I scare the shit out of him.'

'Is he married?'

'Yes. Good marriage. But mostly she is away in Greece. She's Athenian, I think. But there's this English woman.'

'The boy's mother.'

'That's right. Then there's her daughter. I think mebbe he likes them young.' Nico grinned evilly. 'I think we all like them young.'

The house was large, set back from the road down a gravelled drive. As they turned into the driveway Nico said, 'This house, he used to belong to a man call Papadakis. He had two big hotels, one in Kyrenia, the other Varosha. Now . . .' Nico shrugged. 'In Varosha there's nobody. The whole damn place is cover in barbed wire. In the hotel in Kyrenia, either is nobody there or Turk bastards. He lose everything. I don't know where he is now.'

The front door of the house was open, and when Nico rang the doorbell there was no reply. He rang again, and a woman's head appeared in an upstairs window.

'Yes?' The voice was husky and English.

Nico called up, 'We've come to see Mr Jacovides. I am police officer.'

The woman hesitated, then disappeared back into the upstairs room. They waited, and then the woman appeared down a flight of stairs. She must have been in her forties, with a strong, rather equine face. She wore a kaftan, and her hair hung long and dark down her back. Round her head there was a loop of beads, and more

166

beads dangled round her neck. The last blown petal of Flower Power, thought Joshua.

She came to the door. 'You say you're pigs?'

Before Nico could speak, Joshua said, 'My colleague said he was a policeman. May we come in?'

'Suppose I say no?'

Joshua said evenly, 'Then I will be very difficult.'

She hesitated, then turned and walked away, switching on a light as she did so. Perhaps it was authority to enter, perhaps she had simply disengaged herself from the two men. Joshua nodded to Nico, and they followed her into the house.

The woman, without looking back at them, walked into a large open room with cushions scattered over a stone floor. With unexpected elegance she coiled down onto a pile of cushions. There was a sweet smell permeating the room which Joshua immediately recoginised as marijuana.

Nico glanced at a note book he had produced from his jacket. 'You Mrs Mouzas?' he asked.

She seemed to consider the question, then said, 'My husband is dead. Most people call me Mrs Jacovides. And who are you?'

Nico said, 'I am Inspector Tsardanis.'

'You can prove that?'

As he reached towards his wallet she said, 'Forget it. I believe you. You look like a pig.' Then she turned towards Joshua and said, 'But you don't. You're English, aren't you.'

'Yes.'

'What do you want here?'

'We want to talk to Mr Jacovides.'

She looked at Nico, then at Joshua, and said to Joshua, 'He's not here. He's with them.'

'With who?'

'Them!' She suddenly flared, her mouth full of big, strong teeth. 'With you! With the pigs!'

Behind them a girl's voice said, 'Who are these people?'

They turned, and there was a sulky-looking girl of about sixteen. There was no doubting whose child she was: she had her mother's full lips, large nose. But she was noticably darker, even though the woman was heavily sun-tanned.

'They're pigs, darling.'

'Tell them to go away.' The girl walked between the two men and her mother, turned, and said very slowly and distinctly, 'My mother and I would be greatly obliged, in view of the fact that we have not been introduced, if you would fuck off.'

'Jacovides is not with us,' said Nico, ignoring the girl. 'We came here to talk to him. Now, where is he please?'

'My mother and I are not in the habit of entertaining strangers,' said the girl. Then, with some talent, she adopted the voice of a debutante. 'I mean, gosh, what would everybody think? I mean, it'd be super if you were people like us, but one only has to look, hasn't one – '

'Why do you think Mr Jacovides is with the police?' asked Joshua.

'Because he went off with them!'

'When was this?'

'For Christ's sake, I don't know! This morning!'

Nico said, 'Whoever he went off with, take my word for it, lady, they weren't policemen.'

The woman hesitated, then said, 'Of course they were police! They said they were!'

'They show you papers of identification?'

The woman looked uncertain for the first time. Joshua said, 'I want you to try to remember. When they said they were police – '

'Only one of them. One of them came to me and said they were police.'

'Yes. Now, would Mr Jacovides have heard him saying that?'

'He's not deaf!'

'Yes. But was he in the room? Was he near enough to have heard what this man said?'

Now she was beginning to be frightened. She said, 'He was outside. With the other man. There were two of them. And one came back . . .' She pointed towards open french windows. 'He came in through there and said that Jacko had been very helpful and they were all going to the police station. I asked if he'd be back for lunch, and this man said they'd give him lunch to thank him for helping them.'

'You ever before see these people?' demanded Nico.

'No. I don't think so.'

The girl, still keeping her deb accent, said, 'One has to be terribly, terribly selective, doesn't one.'

Joshua said, 'Shut up.'

The girl's mouth dropped open. For a moment it looked as though she was going to launch into a tirade, then she saw the expression on his face and turned away. Joshua thought, she's about the same age as Joanna.

'Your son. Is he around?'

The woman now looked totally bewildered. She looked at Joshua, then at Nico, then at her daughter. The girl shrugged her shoulders.

Finally she said, 'He's outside.'

The girl said, 'Playing with his goat at a guess.' Then she added, 'If I'm allowed to speak.'

Joshua nodded to Nico, and walked out into the garden. 'Iannis!' he called, 'Iannis, where are you?'

A goat on a rope bounced round the side of the house, and Iannis, running, followed. It was like something out of a Disney cartoon. As they spoke the goat was leaping up and down on the end of the rope.

'Hello again,' said Joshua. 'Now, I want you to listen very carefully, because it's very important. Understand?'

'Yes.'

'When you got back here, did you tell Jacky about what we'd talked about?'

The boy hesitated, then said, 'Not at first. But . . . But he kept asking.'

'When did you tell him?'

'This morning. At breakfast. He asked me again.'

And you killed him, thought Joshua, but he said, 'What happened then?'

'He . . . I heard him telephoning. About the bus. I just heard the word *leoforio*. That's Greek for bus. But he wouldn't telephone about a bus . . . unless . . .'

'Yes. Then what happened?'

'I don't know. He was angry with me because I'd told you about . . . So I went out to . . . play. Then the two men came.'

Joshua said quietly, 'Were they the same two men you'd seen in the garage?'

'Yes.'

'You're sure?'

'I didn't go close because Jacky was still angry with me, but I saw them. They were the same men. Then . . . Jacky went off in their car.'

'Did the men see you?'

'I was hiding. Not from them. From Jacky.'

'Yes.'

'But . . . When Jacky was with them, when he got to the car . . .

169

he said something, and then one of them pushed him into the car. I don't think he really wanted to go with them.'

Joshua ruffled the boy's hair. 'You'd better come on inside.'

'I've got to put Gladys back.'

'Your goat's called Gladys?'

'Yes. Why?'

'Just that I've never run into a goat called Gladys before. Where does she live?'

The boy led Joshua round the side of the house to where a shed leant against a wall. 'Most people just leave them out, hobbled,' he said. 'But sometimes there are wolves round here.'

Grey Wolves, thought Joshua.

Gladys was pushed into the shed and the door closed. Iannis said, 'Please, what are you doing here?'

'Making sure everything's all right.'

They walked back into the house, and Nico raised an eyebrow to indicate that he had not explained the situation. Joshua said to Iannis, 'I want to have a word with your mother. It's a bit private. I'm sorry, but – '

The boy looked towards his mother. She waved a hand vaguely, 'Go up to your room, dear,' she said. 'Then we'll have supper.'

Iannis hesitated, then walked out of the room.

'He'll sulk all night now,' said the woman. 'What is it?'

The girl said, 'It had better be good.'

'I'm not going to tell you the details.' Joshua moved so that he could watch the expression on the woman's face. He was uncertain how much, if anything, she already knew. 'But your son Iannis is in danger.'

She didn't believe him. Perhaps she was still half drugged with the marijuhana, but she didn't believe him.

'In fact, you're all in danger, but he is in greater danger than either of you. The two men who went off with Jacovides this morning are very dangerous men. Your son knows about something they did.'

'What? What did they do?'

'I'm not going to tell you. For your own sake.'

The girl said, 'If you don't tell, I'll ask Iannis.'

Joshua looked at her, then at her mother. 'I am hoping that you will allow Iannis to be kept separately, under protection, until this is all over.'

'I can look after my own child! Anyway, we don't need protection! Jacky can look after him!'

There was a pause, a pause that Joshua used quite deliberately. The silence spoke more clearly than words.

She whispered, 'You think he's dead, don't you . . .'

He thought, why should she assume that? As though she could read his thoughts she said, 'I told him. God knows, I told him.' Her voice was flat and expressionless. 'I said, it's not the pigs you have to worry about. *They* won't kill you.'

Out of the corner of his eye Joshua could see Nico. Nico had not the remotest idea what she was talking about, but he was good. His expression revealed nothing.

She went on in the same expressionless tone. 'I won't let them. They think I don't know anything, but I know enough. I may not know all the names, but I know where the pigs should look.'

The old, tired, bitter vocabulary of the sixties crept out between the ageing lips. 'He thought he was hip.'

'We don't know he's dead. All we know is that he's been keeping very dangerous company.'

Nico said, 'I want to put here two policemen. All the time, two policemen. And I want to take Iannis away for few days.'

'Take him where?'

Nico shrugged. 'Mebbe my home. Mebbe other policeman's home. Where he will be safe.'

'When?'

'I think is best now.'

The girl cried out, 'What the shit is all this?'

Her mother, grotesquely in the circumstances, said, 'You know I don't like that word.'

'But what's happening? What's going on?'

The woman rose from the cushions on the floor and went over to the girl and put an arm round her. 'Darling,' she said, 'there's a lot of things you don't understand. Daddy – '

'He's not my Daddy!'

'Jacky lost all his money in the fighting.'

'So did everybody! What's that got to – ?'

'He wanted to look after us properly. And he got involved in a lot of things that . . .'

'You mean he was on the twist? So what else is new?'

The woman turned to Joshua. 'He wasn't a bad man, you know. Not really.' Then she said, 'Why did I say wasn't, not isn't?'

She released the girl and walked over to an empty fireplace. In the faint light her hand found a packet of cigarettes. She took one and lit it.

171

'He was kind to me,' she said. 'To us. People said he just bought me, but it was kindness really.'

She drew heavily on the cigarette, the tip glowing in the dusk. 'He never involved me in anything. He could have used me, but he never did.'

She stopped, then half laughed. 'He used to tell me about when he was fighting in the mountains. He was always ambushing British soldiers. Then I found out he'd really done very little. He'd wanted to, but there was something wrong with his lungs. He couldn't keep up when they were marching. I think that was what made him feel so frustrated. All his friends had done these things, and he hadn't, and they knew it. He's a big baby, really. If he's in danger now, I think he'll probably be enjoying it.'

No, thought Joshua. He isn't with the sort of minor criminals you're thinking of. If he's been very lucky, he's scared stiff. If he hasn't been lucky, he's already dead.

She threw the cigarette into the fireplace. 'If you're taking Iannis,' she said, 'I'd better go and pack him some clothes.'

They left the boy with Nico's sister. Her husband, a large, powerful man with hair like a bear's all over his back was repairing the windlass of a well in near darkness. While Joshua waited in the car with Iannis there was an animated conversation between the three Cypriots, then Nico returned and threw open the car door.

'Okay, boy,' he said. 'You stay here mebbe a coupla days. *Andaxi*?'

As they drove off Nico said, 'My brother-in-law, he got brain like a pigeon. But he's big, eh? I tell him to stay home and say I pay him what he get paid. He work in the market. He thinks he's smart. He thinks I forgotten today's Saturday and he don't work anyway tomorrow, and I pay him for nothing. But I ain't forget. Just this way I know damn well he watch the boy all the time!'

Nico grinned. 'Now I take you to one night club. Is early, but for me they open. We have a drink, a little *meze* . . . You see!'

The night club was a former snack bar in a alley off Sophocles Street. Empty Coca-Cola crates, draped in red cloth, propped up the bar. A number of red-painted, naked electric light bulbs provided faint illumination, and half a dozen small unmatched tables awaited customers. The effect was some sort of compromise between a ghost ride at a fairground and a photographic darkroom.

As Nico entered, Joshua just behind him, a woman grotesquely

172

dressed in a diamanté-spangled blouse, a black suspender-belt, black stockings, lacy black French knickers and high-heeled shoes emerged through some curtains and approached them through the gloom.

In one breath she said, 'Hello lovers you wanna hot time tonight okay oh it's you shithead.'

Nico said, 'This is my grandmother.'

'Shaddap!'

Nico looked round the room. 'It's early,' he said. 'Later they get alotta customers. Mebbe three, four.'

'Shaddap!'

'Tell you what,' he said to the woman. 'You go get me and my friend a bottle of whisky. The kind you get from Akrotiri. Not the kind you get from pissing in the bottle. Okay?'

'Shaddap!'

'You do that.'

The woman disappeared back through the curtains. 'They got the best here,' said Nico confidently. 'You want anything what they get smuggle, she has the best.'

They sat at a table in the murk. Another woman, somewhat younger and also wearing a suspender-belt and stockings, but this time with a tee shirt, appeared, and pressed a switch on a music centre behind the bar. She didn't seem to look to see what she was choosing, but a cassette started to play Theodorakis.

'They have orchestra later,' said Nico. 'Mebbe say ten o'clock.'

The first woman came back holding a half-bottle of Johnny Walker. 'It's gotta seal,' she said. 'Satisfied?'

She put the bottle on the table, then from underneath the bar produced two glasses and a bowl of melting ice.

'Tell me,' said Nico to the woman, 'my friend's interested how you go get stuff across the frontier.'

She looked first at Nico, then at Joshua. Without speaking she went to the bar and returned with another glass. She opened the bottle and poured out three generous measures. Then she drank, her lipstick rimming the glass. Finally she said to Nico, 'What sort of stuff?'

'People,' said Joshua.

She laughed, a not unattractive laugh. 'Whisky, okay yes,' she said. 'Money. They tell me drugs, but I don't know for drugs. Also I don't know for guns. But people! People, nothing!'

Joshua persisted. 'All right. Forget about people. Other things.'

173

She shrugged. 'Is no way for Greek peoples to go to north. Or Turk peoples to come here. So perhaps you pay for United Nations man. Or day tourist, mebbe. But is most times from north to south. Nobody has got no money in north. So is from them they comes.'

'What sort of things?'

She said carefully, 'I don't know. I hear antiques.'

'Antiques?'

'Ikons from churches. They make them mosques, no Turk peoples want the icons, the crosses, I hear they bring them here for selling. I hear.'

Nico said, 'And you're up to eyes in it.'

'Shut your face.' She poured herself another drink. 'Is also easier to come from north to south. Mebbe a small boat. Is a lot of coast in south. Lot. In north . . .' She shrugged again, and drank half the whisky. 'In north is not many coast, and everywhere Turk soldiers.'

The tape changed abruptly from Theodorakis to an old Johnny Halliday number. The other woman came on to the small circular dance floor and started to dance alone. It seemed to be some sort of Pavlovian reaction to the music, for after a few bars she tugged off her tee shirt, to reveal a tasselled brassière, and the dance developed into a strip routine.

'Five pound,' said the older woman to Nico.

Nico pulled out his wallet and gave her three. She seemed satisfied, and rose, walking past the dancer, and disappeared into whatever lay behind the curtains.

Joshua said, 'Do you think you'll ever find Jacovides?'

'No.' Nico refilled the glasses. 'Is easy for hide body in the mountains.' He paused, then said, 'You still think they are in the north?'

'Yes.'

Nico nodded. 'I think so too. Is impossible, but I think so too.'

The girl unclipped her brassière and threw it towards the two men. It fell, unnoticed, on the floor under the table.

Nico leant forward. 'You find them,' he said. He had lowered his voice. 'You find them, and I give you special men to fight. Special!'

'Special?'

'Trained special. I find men who know the houses.'

'I don't have any idea where the houses are.'

'Doesn't matter. I have men from every place! They fight good! They fight good because they are their houses!'

The girl dancer came swaying over to them. 'You now take down my pants,' she said.

Nico reached out and started to tug at the underwear. Underneath there was a *cache-sexe* with a mop of black hair curling out round it.

'I want to get men into the north,' said Nico. 'Is good that they go back there. Mebbe they have to come back after, but is good they go.'

The girl bent down and stepped out of her pants. 'You give me five pound,' she said.

Joshua said, 'The Turks would slaughter you.'

'They think they are tough! Before, was all fixed so we could not win! Next time we see how tough they really are!'

'Five pound and I go upstairs with you. Jigajig.'

It would be an ideal excuse for the Greeks, Joshua saw that immediately. They would return to what the British recognised as their own land to save the lives of British children. And what would the Turks do? Would they dare come between the Greeks and the terrorists? Would they be prepared to be presented to the world as men who sacrificed English children in order to keep their illegal hold on the north of Aphrodite's island?

'Good jigajig. Ace jigajig.' The girl scratched herself unappetisingly.

'I tell you privately,' said Nico. 'We have men special trained. Some is in army, some not. But when is chance, we are ready!'

Joshua finished his whisky and rose to his feet.

'Jigajig?' asked the girl without showing any signs of expecting, or even wanting, a favourable answer.

'Understand this,' he said to Nico. 'We do it my way. I want your help, and you've promised that.'

Nico nodded.

'But I don't want anybody on either side of the bloody frontier making decisions on my behalf! Okay?'

'Sure. Okay.'

'I'll let you know.'

He turned and walked out of the bar into the night. Nicosia was coming to life, the electric lights seeming brighter and clearer in the soft air than he was used to in England. There was a confused, not unattractive, jumble of music from radios and records: Greek pop, English and American pop, from somewhere a Haydn sonata, and weaving through all the music on the radio a man singing to some reedy pipe, the music of the Levant, the music of Byzantium, the music that stretched from Asia to Spain. He walked down Ledra

Street, past the open shops, the cafes and restaurants, the street traders. The people brushing past in white open-necked shirts or summer dresses of flamboyant colour were animated, talking, laughing. Then he reached the point where he could go no further, past the sign reading IT IS FORBIDDEN TO TAKE PHOTOGRAPHS BEYOND THIS POINT, the point where the wall stretched across the street and divided the city. He turned and walked slowly back to the Hotel Romantica.

Chapter Twenty Five

He woke to the sound of bells, and remembered that it was Sunday. It was a week since Joanna had been taken. A week ago he had been at home and she had been about to step ashore, excited, onto Aphrodite's murderous island.

There was nobody at reception as he walked past on his way to the dining room for breakfast. As he entered he noticed a pile of magazines and newspapers on a trolley by the door, mostly back numbers of *Country Life*. On top was the previous day's *Cyprus Mail*, and he picked it up as he passed. Over his coffee, bread, butter and jam he read about the life of the island as seen by the tiny staff of the paper through the limited facilities at their disposal. It was the second lead that caught his eye. *No Change in UK Govt. Support*, read the headline, then, *Turk Proposals 'Unacceptable'*.

He read the story, and realised how insignificant it must seem in Britain. Indeed, although Joshua did not know it, only *The Times*, *The Guardian*, and *The Independent* among English newspapers carried it at all, in no case giving it more than a few column inches on an inside page. *Britain's position over Cyprus remains unchanged*, he read. *Cyprus is part of the Commonwealth, and the Turkish occupation of the north can never be recognised.*

He skipped a paragraph to find out reasons for the item. It appeared that the Under-Secretary of State for Foreign and Commonwealth Affairs, addressing something called the Anglo-Cypriot Friendship Association, had taken the opportunity to reassert the British stand. The story went on, *While the Turkish citizens of Cyprus undoubtedly have had justifiable grievances, it would be quite unacceptable for any changes to be enforced while Turkish troops illegally occupy large areas of the island.*

If he had been in London, with access to JBH, he would have been able, within a matter of minutes, to find out the background to the story. What the hell was the Anglo-Cypriot Friendship Association? Was it a well-meaning, long-established body of ex-colonial do-gooders, or a cover organisation? And if a cover organisation, a cover for what? Was the Under-Secretary instructed to make his speech because he was senior enough a figure to be used for a government pronouncement without making too much of it, or because he was junior enough to be disowned if the position changed? What had provoked this particular non-event of a statement at this time? To whom was the Under-Secretary really addressing himself? To the Greek Government? To the Greek Cypriots? To the Turks?

To the terrorists?

Perhaps it had all been a coincidence. The annual speech by the annual not-quite-entity to the annual dinner. It didn't say, in the article.

Either way, thought Joshua grimly, it didn't help. He checked the dateline. The speech had been made the day before the paper's date, i.e. the day before yesterday, on Friday. On the Saturday the Turks had denied all knowledge of the death of Boobs who had, presumably, been killed the previous night. Unless she had been killed some time earlier, and her body kept elsewhere until they wanted to move it to Bellapaise. It couldn't have been lying at Bellapaise for long, unnoticed. Not in this climate. But speeches like that were released to the press long before they were delivered, with a release time. Sometimes days in advance.

In London, he would have had all the facilities for finding the answers to the questions that troubled him. Here, on the spot, he felt helpless.

He wiped his mouth with a table napkin, folded up the paper and tucked it into his pocket, and left the dining room. In the foyer outside he was momentarily taken aback to see the looming figure of Mike Berrisford, checking in. Berrisford wore a spotlessly clean long-sleeved white shirt which immediately set him apart from the short-sleeved Cypriots, cream slacks held up by a belt in the colours of the Rifle Brigade, and not-quite-right tan and cream coloured shoes. His cream linen jacket was casually but carefully draped over his shoulders, and his suitcase had a large label reading Saga Holidays. Joshua momentarily wondered why Berrisford always got it slightly wrong. On a Saga Holiday he would have stood out like Trotsky in a Women's Institute. But he was professional enough when he said, 'Room nine, then?' to Katherina behind the desk, in a voice soft enough to be reasonable and loud enough to tell Joshua where to find him. Then he picked up his bag, nodded to Joshua with exactly the right reserved friendship of two English strangers meeting in a foreign land, and briskly trotted up towards his room.

Joshua strolled out of the hotel and savoured the morning air. All those people who spoke about the benefits of getting up early in the Mediterranean were absolutely right. The day undoubtedly deteriorated after about ten. But it was difficult to change the habits of a lifetime.

He waited until he was certain that Katherina had seen him ignore his compatriot, then wandered back into the hotel.

'Are all the shops shut on a Sunday?' he asked.

'Many open after the church,' said Katherina.

He nodded as though it all meant a great deal to him, and went upstairs to his room. There were no sounds of anybody in the passage or otherwise displaying any interest in him, so after a couple of minutes he emerged and walked along to room nine.

Berrisford was sitting on his balcony in the sun. The bed had not been made since last night's occupant. It only needed bathing costumes drying on the balcony and a two-day old copy of the *Daily Express* to give the complete picture of the English middle class on holiday. He rose, came back into the room, and shut the window.

'Good morning, sir,'he said. 'Got in yesterday. We've got an SBS section on stand-by locally.'

Berrisford always started a conversation as though he was standing vibrant to attention, reporting to a commanding officer.

'Where?'

'On HMS *Brazen*, moored at Limassol, sir. She was on patrol off Lebanon anyway, so it fitted in rather well.'

HMS *Brazen*. Frigate. Complement two-thirty, give or take. Joshua tried to remember if he had ever been on her. But she carried a helicopter, he knew that. That might be useful.

'Shouldn't be too difficult, sir,' said Berrisford cheerfully. 'Good briefing.'

'We don't know where the girls are being held.'

Berrisford looked surprised. 'Oh. Must have misunderstood. Thought we did.'

'No.'

'Oh. Anyway, sir, I gather the idea is to find out exactly what the position is, not necessarily establishing contact unless they insist, best they don't know we're there, then move in, in collaboration with the forces under the command of the military on the spot, through the local administration.'

Then Berrisford noticed the expression on Joshua's face, swallowed, and said, 'Sir.'

Joshua said quietly, 'Sit down, Berrisford.'

Berrisford swallowed again, and sat down on the edge of the bed. He still managed to sit to attention.

'Sir?'

'What you call the local administration does not officially exist.'

'I know that sir, but – '

'And even if we were to establish contact with them, which would be contrary to orders, they certainly wouldn't put their troops at our disposal.'

There was a pause, then Berrisford said, 'Actually, I admit London seemed a bit hazy about the exact position.'

'Yes.'

'I gather that a lot of the trouble stems from the fact that all the official gen comes through the Greeks who have an axe to grind.'

'Yes.'

Berrisford was finding it difficult to keep his part of the conversation going. He said, 'But I gather there's a first rate source there. In the north. I was going to rely on him.'

Joshua looked round. 'Who's this?'

'Chap called Colonel Peacock.'

Joshua said, 'He's pushing eighty and half mad.'

'Oh.'

There was another pause, and then Joshua said, 'Why are you here?'

'Various things. I'm setting up the ops, if and when. And I've brought a WTS so we have direct safe communication with JBH.'

Joshua looked grateful. 'Good. Do the Cypriots know you've got it?'

'No, sir.'

A moment of alarm. 'They don't know you're operational, do they?'

'Oh, no. They think I'm a traveller. In contraceptives, actually.' He laughed uncertainly. 'On my papers.'

It was encouraging that one of the girls in Documentation had kept her sense of humour. Joshua said, 'Congratulations on getting the set into the country. Disguised as packets of Durex, was it?'

'No. I picked it up at Akrotiri. They have quite a number.'

'For God's sake! Are you saying they've spare sets on the bloody island, and don't tell me so I have to work through the Consulate?'

Berrisford said, 'I asked about that. It turned out they weren't on JBH lists. They were partly on MI5, and a couple with RAF (I). It was an admin balls-up really.' Then he laughed again. 'But I'm afraid you'll still have to work through the Consulate. I've put the set there. It seemed the only safe place, without knowing the island.'

Joshua thought, Berrisford may be something of a joke, but at least he's efficient. And brave. One could have a worse colleague.

'Have you run into the man in charge there?' asked Berrisford. 'Called Earnshaw.'

'Yes,' said Joshua grimly.

'Thought you must have done! When I sent a coded telex saying I was coming and would need him to be available at any hour, the reaction read like stark terror! Never seen type turn white before!' He laughed, a braying, strangulated laugh. He was obviously feeling more at ease.

'Why have the Turks stopped cooperating?' demanded Joshua.

The question surprised Berrisford. 'Didn't know they had, sir,' he said.

'There was a British citizen killed by the terrorists. The Turks denied knowing about it.'

'Perhaps they didn't know about it.'

'Her body is in their bloody mortuary!'

For some reason, Berrisford seemed to be trying to find an innocent explanation. 'I don't know, sir. I mean, did they know who she was?'

'No. I doubt it.'

'Well then, if a woman dies, there's no reason – '

'She didn't die, Berrisford. She had half her head blown away with some large calibre handgun.' He went on coldly, 'There was only the jaw and the face up to around the sinuses till recognisable as human. If I had been put before a court of law I would not have been able to swear that I could identify her from what was left of her face. I was only certain who it was because of the peculiarities that earned her her nickname among the girls she taught. Her nickname was Boobs. Do you understand me, Berrisford?'

'Yes, sir.'

'Next question. Who put the Under-Secretary up to making speeches?'

'Sir?'

Joshua produced the paper from his pocket and thrust it at

Berrisford. Berrisford read the headline, pursing his lips, then skipped through the article, and handed the paper back.

'See what you mean. Bit cats and pigeons.'

Once again Joshua checked himself. He had to view this problem as though it were just another of the incidents that had cropped up in his career. His main responsibility was to be the calm at the centre of the storm. Authoritative, reliable, emotionless, a little boring even. He had done it many times before, and he must do it now. He must not allow himself to think of those children as in any way different from all the other hostages he had released. Or tried to release, and it hadn't quite worked. He must not think of them even as children, and he must totally ignore the fact that one of them was, to him, unique and different, and the only human being on earth he really loved. If he allowed himself to become emotionally involved he would be as embarrassing as those Israeli women who had scratched his face until he was streaming blood because he stood between them and the men who held their children. As embarrassing and as useless.

'Berrisford,' he said.

'Sir?'

'So you understand. Let us assume that we find where the hostages are being held.'

He noticed that without thinking he had said, hostages, not, children. That was correct, that was the way he had to think.

'Sir.'

'Unless the political situation changes between now and then, we will be unlikely to enjoy the cooperation of the Turkish authorities.'

'Couldn't we use the Greeks, sir?'

He said irritably, 'Not unless you want to start a bloody war, no!'

Berrisford coloured, and bowed his head.

'This means that we are unlikely to be able to employ any of the standard techniques. We won't be able to sit round the terrorists and gradually get on their tits. We won't be able to communicate with them. Or, at least, it'll be a turn up for the book if we can. If it comes to a fire-fight, it's got to be straight in, straight out.'

'There is one thing,' said Berrisford. 'It won't be like that shambles outside Khalaf. From the UK point of view, this must be about the best-mapped place on earth outside Surrey!'

Joshua looked up sharply.

'Not just all the maps we made when the place was a normal

colony,' said Berrisford, 'but the maps we prepared during the fighting against EOKA in the fifties! I brought out a mass of it – it's in the Consulate at the moment – and the SBS people have copies, too!'

God bless Berrisford, with his Rifle Brigade background and his subtly non-U voice. God bless his basic efficiency, and we'll all forgive his lack of style.

And remember, Joshua told himself, you don't always have to take full responsibility for everything. Despite its shortcomings, there is a machine back there that you can use. There was no need to spend those hours poring over those obsolete maps. You don't have to invent the bicycle every time. You don't have to play at being God.

Then he thought, we don't know where to look on the maps. We don't know where the children are.

At that moment the bedside phone rang. Berrisford picked it up. He looked surprised. 'It's for you.'

Joshua took the phone. 'Yes?'

It was Katherina's voice. 'Sir, there is gentleman here to see you.'

'What's his name?'

There was a silence while, presumably, Katherina asked with her hand over the mouthpiece, then she said, 'He say he is from United Nations.'

Cooney. Cooney, worried about giving his name and being associated with him.

'Send him up.'

Before Joshua had a chance to brief Berrisford, there was a bang on the door and, without waiting for a word from Joshua, Cooney entered. He saw Berrisford and stopped.

'I thought you was alone.'

'It's all right. This is Mike Berrisford.'

Cooney said quickly, 'My name's Paddy. Just call me Paddy.' He glowered at Joshua, then said, 'I want to speak to you alone.'

Joshua said, 'Don't worry. He's with me.'

'I'm talking to you alone!'

'Don't be tiresome,' said Joshua coldly. 'I'll only have to tell him later.'

Cooney thought for a moment, then shut the door. 'If I do you a favour,' he said, 'then I'll be wanting a favour in return. Is that understood?'

'Yes.'

'I'm taking a risk!'

'Life is full of little dangers. What is it you want?'

Again Cooney looked distrustfully at Berrisford. 'I want to be fockin' left alone!'

'I'll do what I can.'

'That's not good enough!'

Berrisford said, 'Major Cooney . . .'

Cooney whirled on Joshua. 'How the hell does he know my name? You swore to me you wouldn't be telling anybody! Who is he? Is he British Embassy, or what?'

'He's JBH.'

'I might have guessed!'

'More to the point,' said Berrisford, 'We happen to know how Sligo Lodge comes into your life.'

It was as though the huge man had been punctured. He seemed almost visibly to shrink.

'Jesus . . .'

He looked at Joshua. 'Don't you ever let go? Would you use that, then?'

Joshua said, 'Let's just hear what you have to offer.'

Cooney breathed out, very slowly. 'Right,' he said. 'And I'm trusting you. You understand?'

Joshua, who had no idea what Berrisford had meant, nodded.

Cooney said, 'You said you was interested in a vehicle. A UN vehicle.'

'Yes,'

'And I found you a vehicle that crossed the frontier, but didn't exist. Right?'

'Yes.'

'Well! Now I know who was in it!'

It was as though the temperature in the room had suddenly dropped. Joshua said quietly, 'Who?'

'I want your word! If I tell you what I've found out, I want your word you'll fockin' leave me alone!'

'I give you my word.' Promises were not binding. Not promises made under duress in Cypriot hotel bedrooms. Not even promises signed before a group of sworn witnesses, not even promises made on the Bible at a high altar, not in the world of JBH. If they wanted the services of Major Cooney in the future, they would secure them.

But he'd do his best.

'Right then,' said Cooney. 'Right. Now you remember I told you that the troops manning the check point were Irish.'

'Yes.'

184

'I made it my business to run into the man who was in charge of that section. And I asked him about the vehicle, and he remembered it. He happened to be there when the vehicle arrived. Right?'

'Yes.'

'He's a Company Commander, no reason why he should have been there, but he was. And he remembers this Canadian vehicle. It was a high-sided thing, like a Saracen. He didn't know it, but there's a lot of different sorts of vehicle on this fockin' island.'

'Yes.'

'Every bloody army has its own.'

Joshua said quietly, 'You said that you know who was in this vehicle.'

'Yes.'

'This is very important. The vehicle, you say, was Canadian.'

'Right!'

'Why do you say it was Canadian?'

'Because it was full of fockin' Canadians!'

Take it carefuly. No possible misunderstanding. 'How did this Company Commander know they were Canadians?'

'How the hell should I know? He just said they were Canadians! From their uniforms!'

Joshua said, 'You can buy uniforms.' He was clutching at straws.

'Oh, sure,' said Cooney. 'I could take you to places here in Cyprus where you could buy any uniform you like to name. But he'd have known that. He's an old hand! He'd have told from the way they spoke!'

'Their accents.'

If they were Canadians, he was wrong. If they were Canadians, then everything Joshua had been basing his theories on was incorrect. A fallacy.

'Sure. Their accents.'

'Broken,' Joshua muttered, 'Yes. The way they were speaking English.'

'Who said they was speaking English? That was how he knowed! They was French Canadians! Every one of them in Cyprus now, the Canadians, they're all from Quebec!'

Be careful. Be sure. There was too much at stake. There was everything at stake. Joanna's life.

He said, 'Your friend. How fluent is his French?'

'How the – ? I told you! He's an Irishman! From County Limer-

185

ick! He's a professional soldier! Why should he be supposed to be a fockin' linguist?'

'What I'm asking,' said Joshua, keeping his voice calm, 'is whether he could tell the difference between a French Canadian speaking French and a Frenchman speaking French. Perhaps a Frenchman pretending to be a French Canadian.'

'Don't ask me, for Christ's sake! You said you were interested in this vehicle, and I found out for you!'

'Yes. Thanks.'

There was a long silence, then, rather slyly, Cooney said, 'There's something else.'

'What?'

He looked hard again at Berrisford, then said, 'I was telling you why this Company Commander remembered the vehicle at all.'

'Because he was at the post at the time. Yes.'

'That's right. There's only a few men on detachment at any one time, but he happened to be there. That's right. But there was another reason.'

'What reason?'

'I could be getting someone into trouble,' said Cooney. 'You're sure he's all right?'

Berrisford visibly stiffened. Cooney moved over and stood in front of him. Berrisford was over six feet, but Cooney towered over him. 'I don't want word getting back,' said Cooney.

'He's all right,' Joshua assured him.

Cooney looked again at Berrisford, then lumbered across the room and sat down on the bed. Joshua thought, inconsequentially, for the rest of my life I will always associate this man with unmade beds.

Cooney said, 'The other reason he remembered that vehicle was the girls.'

He found he could hardly speak. His voice came out as an absurd hoarse whisper.

'What girls?'

Cooney also lowered his voice, but his susurration was deliberate. 'Girls. You see, I told you, it was one of those armoured vehicles with high sides. For troop carrying. And this feller, when it was going through, he heard these girls who was in it.'

'There were girls – !'

'In the vehicle. Yes. Nurses.'

Joshua controlled himself. He made it sound casual, checking up on information received. 'They were nurses?'

186

'That's what he said. What else could they be? If they were attached to the United Nations, then they'd be able to go into the north without all that trouble. It's only if they were with the British. They could have been with the RAF or something, but he reckoned most likely they were nurses. The Canucks were taking them over for a bit of fun.'

Relax. Keep questioning as though it was just another incident, just a few total strangers who'd run foul of terrorists. Don't lead. Get the facts out, just the facts. 'Why should he think they were British?'

'I told you! He could hear their fockin' voices! He couldn't hear what they were saying, but you can tell! If you know a language, even if you can't hear the words, you can tell when somebody's speaking it!'

Suppose one of them had screamed for help. What would have happened then? Would the Irish infantry have been alert enough to react before there had been crashing and clanging of small-arms fire inside the armour of the vehicle? For in the world of terrorism death is better than pity, suicide preferable to anti-climax. Or perhaps, at that stage, the children still didn't know. It was still a thrill, something to describe on the first postcard home.

Cooney was still talking. 'He didn't put that in the report, you see. It would have got the Canadians in the shit, and there wasn't any harm in it. Only with the British, sometimes it isn't that easy for them to go to the north.'

Berrisford spoke for the first time. 'You said the vehicle wasn't UN.' He sounded confused.

Cooney looked at Berrisford, wondering whether to include him in the conversation. He solved the problem by answering Berrisford's question, but addressing the reply to Joshua.

'I asked him about the vehicle. He said he reckoned it was one left by one of the troop contingents that have been here and gone home. We've had all sorts. And some of them, if their equipment breaks down, then they've nobody really to repair it. Not if it breaks down just before they're due to be shipped home. Wherever home is. No time, you see. And again, mebbe some fockin' Cypriot arranges to pick it up before it's been abandoned because it's broken down, if you see what I mean.'

'I see.'

'There's enough stuff on this island. I'm no expert, but I reckon, give me forty-eight hours and a few thousand dollars, and I could lay my hands on an unregistered AFV.'

Joshua said, 'And neither the Greeks nor the Turks would worry about a white-painted vehicle they weren't expecting?'

'Why should they? It's none of their fockin' business!'

'No.'

'But I'm telling you this in confidence,' said Cooney earnestly. 'I'm relying on you not to drop that officer in it.'

'He'll be okay.'

'Only you can't blame a few squaddies for picking up some nurses and offering them a treat, because they know where there's a vehicle they can use. It can get fockin' boring here!'

'Yes.'

Cooney rose to his feet. He really was a very powerful-looking man.

'I'm relying on you for two things,' he said. 'Keeping that officer out of it, and telling your people to let me alone!'

'I told you, I'll do my best.'

Cooney moved towards the door, and unconsciously Berrisford stepped aside, though there was room enough for him to pass. 'It's not that important,' said Cooney. 'But you keep your people off me, because I've done what I said I'd do! It isn't my fault if all that happened was that a few French Canadians took a vehicle to the north hoping to have a bit of fun with a few nurses! That's not my fault! I did my share!'

He started towards the door. 'It isn't fair, coming after me all the time! I've paid you off! Now leave me alone!'

He opened the door and stomped out, Berrisford shutting the door after him.

Berrisford said, 'Sorry to use the bit about Sligo Lodge, sir. But I saw your message in London, and checked the info myself. The point was, he didn't just pinch some money. He got it from a Stateside hand-out to the Provos when he was working with one of our SAS people. It was pretty smart in that nobody could complain, not even the Yanks. But the SAS man got caught over something else, and spilt. Then we looked into Cooney, and found he'd used his share to set up an abortion clinic in a place called Sligo Lodge. I mean, he'd be absolutely finished if that came out in Eire.'

But Joshua was hardly listening. He was thinking, now it fits. At last it fits. Cooney's compatriot had seen it all happen, and he had misunderstood just two things: there were no nurses in that vehicle, there were schoolgirls, and the men were not French Canadians, they were French.

It had happened before, and it would happen again, and every time it happened the statesmen of the world would tut-tut in incredulity because in their departmentalised world terrorists could be classified like orthodox political parties, or minor religious sects, or football-team supporters. The idea that terrorism existed across boundaries in its own right and for its own sake was not an idea they could accept, although the evidence was before them.

Berrisford said, 'The French. There's been reports of *Action Directe* trying to move into the Near East.' Berrisford, for all his short-comings, lived in the real world.

'Yes.' Joshua was clearly conscious in his mind of what he believed in order to assess what he knew. 'Tell me. If you wanted to lay your hands on a vehicle you could pass off as an a UN troop carrier, where would you look?'

'Round here?' Berrisford considered. 'It wouldn't be that much of a problem. Even if you didn't run into one in Cyprus, the Lebanon's only a hundred miles away.' He gave his braying laugh. 'They sell AFVs in used car lots there! With trade-ins!'

'Odds are the vehicle would be camouflaged. So they'd have to paint it white. That would take time.' Joshua was really talking to himself. 'Suppose it was the Lebanon. Suppose they'd got it ashore here. They needn't have got it for this operation. They could just have it, ready for when they had a use for it. Right?'

'That's logical, sir.'

'At least two of the terrorists were Greek.'

'Sir?'

'Something you don't know about. The adopted son of the man who disposed of the bus – '

Berrisford was looking more and more confused.

'Sorry,' said Joshua. 'You don't know about that either. But take my word for it. Two of the terrorists involved were mainland Greek.'

'Working round here, most likely one of the new left groups, sir,' said Berrisford.

'Yes. They have contacts with the Grey Wolves because the original message was released through the Grey Wolves in Ankara. At least some of the men in the vehicle were French. Or spoke French well enough to convince the Irish. The documents they'd need would be no trouble. Presumably now they're holed up in a house, and whoever is guarding the children there could be of any nationality. But if they've planned it this well they'll certainly have a lingua franca. Planned. That's the point.'

'Sir?'

The more he thought about it, the more certain he was that he was on the right lines: and the more dangerous it appeared. 'It's a very neat job,' he said. 'Cooperation between a range of terrorist groups, the maximum humiliation to the largest number of governments, and the perfect victims.'

'Children,' said Berrisford, then remembered.

'Children of the power that claims Cyprus as a part of its Commonwealth.' He forced himself to go on deducing from the facts, even though every conclusion seemed to be leading towards the unthinkable. 'They had this vehicle hidden away somewhere on the island. And somewhere another group learnt about it. Not a group on the island, but from somewhere else. Most likely in Britain, because they were British children who were kidnapped, and the British would be the most vulnerable. They knew about the schools' cruise. They knew where that damned ship was going and they knew when it would dock. It wasn't a question of hanging around on the road hoping something would turn up. They knew that, give or take five minutes, such and such a bus – and they'd have found out which bus was taking the British children – I don't know how, but I bet there's a schedule in somewhere like Sunswept's headquarters – they knew all this! They'd planned all this from England!'

'The safe house!' exclaimed Berrisford. 'They'd have laid that on long before! You're right, sir! It only makes sense if it was planned bloody ages ago! And they'd be checking the whole thing! They'd have someone at Limassol when the ship docked, they'd have had somebody in Athens or Piraeus to make sure there weren't any changes to the schedule, they probably even had someone watching them when they started off in England!'

Suddenly, as though he could step outside himself and watch himself as in a film, a black and while film, he saw Victoria bus terminal, and his last glimpse of his daughter. Who was there? He tried to remember, but there were people coming and going, the bustle and confusion, the noise and the fumes of the buses. But the odds were that among all those boring, scurrying people there had been a terrorist, just making quite certain it was all going to plan.

He breathed out heavily, and pulled the *Cyprus Mail* from his pocket. *Her Majesty's Government will never compromise the rights of the people of Cyprus*, said the Under-Secretary of State for Foreign and Commonwealth Affairs. Joshua looked out of the hotel window, over the ridiculous wall a few hundred yards away to where a scarlet flag was mocking the Right Honourable Gentleman's words. You're playing their game, Joshua thought. Sod you. Leave it to those of us who know what we're doing. You're playing their game.

'I love you, daddy,' she'd said. He would never forget that.

Chapter Twenty Six

The fat man in the doorway was watching him when he checked in at the Turkish guardhouse. As he strolled towards the suburban house which served as immigration headquarters he sensed the man hurrying towards the phone inside the guardhouse. Berrisford had gone ahead, with instructions about hiring a car: there was no point in becoming conspicuous with a series of one-day hirings.

When Joshua entered the crowded little room, the telephone was already ringing. One of the girl clerks answered it, and looked round the room. There were two English families with children, taking advantage of the open Sunday shops in the Islamic north, and a couple of Turkish officials. It was impossible for Joshua to pretend he belonged with either family, so he put on a vacant, harmless expression and waited while the English tried to form a queue.

The girl replaced the receiver and, her eyes on Joshua, started talking urgently to a man in a khaki shirt and green slacks. He looked up sharply, then disappeared through a door leading to an inner office.

At this point one of the English women started to argue about the fee being imposed on a two year old who was whimpering in a pram.

'Baby,' the woman said in a Home Counties accent, slowly as though talking to an idiot. 'Baby. This is baby. Not child. Baby. No pay money for baby. Last time, no money for baby.'

'*Malum*?' asked her husband, inexplicably talking Urdu. '*Kutchne* money baby.'

'Money! You pay three pounds!' cried an official. He turned to the girl for the printed sheet that would prove his case, and Joshua took the opportunity to slip out through the door. He was now without the document authorising him to enter the north, but in his previous two visits nobody had particularly asked to see it. He looked cautiously round the side of the house. The fat man was standing across the street. Momentarily the fat man turned to look back towards the border crossing, and Joshua vaulted the low wall that separated the house used as the headquarters from the deserted one next door to it. Its overgrown back garden led to another, parallel, street, and not even the garden gate was locked. Within five minutes he had reached the corner of Irfan Bey Street, and there Berrisford was waiting with an Opel, its engine running.

They took the road towards Kyrenia. Berrisford glanced up into his mirror.

'Nobody following us, sir,' he reported. 'Let me know in advance if you want me to turn off. Only we're a bit conspicuous.'

Indeed, in the poorer north, there was a shortage of traffic that had obviously struck Berrisford immediately, but which Joshua now accepted without really noticing.

'Best we're not associated unless we have to be,' said Joshua. 'You know where Peacock lives?'

'Yes sir,' said Berrisford smartly. 'Bray House, Kyprianou Road. It's just as you get into Kyrenia.'

'I know,' said Joshua pointedly. 'I've been there.'

'I checked up before I came out.' Berrisford seemed to think that a map check was more reliable than a visit. 'Do you want to go there?'

'No. But if we get separated and want to make contact again, that'll be our rendezvous. And don't tell Peacock any more than you have to.'

He was already regretting having told him about Joanna. Then he realised that he had had to tell someone.

The road started to climb as the mountains loomed ahead. At the side of the road a new sign indicated a road junction to the right, leading to Dikmen. Dikmen. The name sounded familiar. Then he remembered. Dikmen had been Agios Khrysoumos, the village of Anna's family. He'd often noticed the way in which tension served as an aphrodisiac. He wanted her. If she had been with them he would have turfed Berrisford out of the car somehow, and had her. Had her in the back of the car, in a field, anywhere.

But, of course, it was impossible. She could never be with him in a car beside the road that led to her village, because she was a Greek Cypriot and this was Turkish Cyprus.

He made it sound casual. 'Take the next to the right,' he said.

Berrisford slowed and turned. He was a superb driver, because he had been trained to be. The side road wound away parallel to the mountains and the coast beyond, and it occurred to Joshua that it must be virtually parallel to the road he had taken before when he had been stopped at the road block. Indeed, there was an identical notice, warning that the area was out of bounds to UN forces. Berrisford saw the notice and glanced sideways at Joshua, but as Joshua did not react continued towards the east.

The land around seemed deserted, and such crops as there were on the sparse hot soil looked untended and unlikely ever to be harvested. They passed three small houses, all empty, the doors long ago kicked open, and contents looted. On one of the houses there were Turkish slogans written in dark red paint.

'Ankara rules, OK!' said Berrisford, and laughed.

There was a small hill, and the road continued straight over the top of it. As they came over the brow of the hill they saw Dikmen; below them, and about a mile further on. It looked like any other Cypriot village, but perhaps a little richer and smarter than some. Even from here Joshua could recognise what must have been Anna's house. It was exactly as she had described it, and he realised how hungry he must have been for her even then, before he had known her, because he could remember exactly her words, the tone of her voice, the desperation. There was the square, and yes, the church was just off the square, and next to it was the big house, the big white house with gates, the house of Anna to whom he had made love only minutes after she had told him of the house. Suddenly, inexplicably, the car smelled of Anna, of woman, of lust.

They came into the village, and Joshua sensed something unusual about it. At first he couldn't place it, then he realised. It was too tidy. There were no old men dozing in the shade, no women putting out washing, no chickens at the side of the road, no goats, no children. The walls were neater than usual, freshly whitewashed. Berrisford also realised that the village was unnatural. Neither of them recognised why, until a soldier standing outside what had once been the village bakery started on seeing the car, snapped to attention, and presented arms.

Joshua lowered Anna's camera from his eyes, and tucked it under his seat. 'Go through the village,' he said. 'Keep the speed level. When you get to the square, circle and we'll go back the way we've come.'

Berrisford nodded. They reached the dusty square, with the church and the big tree under which, in the old days, the men had met for coffee and backgammon, and on Sundays the whole village had met. Now there were only three tables out instead of two dozen, and the only people using the shade of the tree were four soldiers. They watched the Opel approaching, and exchanged words. They looked puzzled. Then one of them rose, and unshipped his rifle. Berrisford slowly circled the square, dropping down into second in case he had to accelerate away. As they passed, for a moment Joshua could see between the white pillars of the gateway, past the sentry on duty, up the short drive to Anna's house. Two men were standing in the doorway, one a senior officer in uniform, and the other in civilian clothes, with his back to Joshua. As the man turned to walk towards his car, parked at the side of the house, Joshua recognised him.

It was Pamir.

The noise of the car attracted the officer's attention. He straightened, then pointed and shouted something. Pamir turned. There was no time for Joshua to duck out of sight, and for a moment he and Pamir stared at each other. The officer shouted again and turned to run into the house.

'Move!' cried Joshua. 'Get the hell out of here!'

Berrisford slammed his foot down on the accelerator. The Opel leapt forward. In the mirror Joshua saw the soldier by the table frantically loading his rifle, then the car swerved away up the village street. As they roared towards the bakery the sentry looked up and down the street for orders, and made a half-hearted move into the road, leaping back as they passed him.

'What's going on?' asked Berrisford.

'I know the man who was outside that house! He's the man who interrogated me last time!'

'Did he recognise you?'

'I don't know if he could see me. Perhaps the sun was reflecting off the window. But he knows damn well we shouldn't be here. Get the hell out of here before they throw up a road block!'

'Police?' asked Berrisford, his foot flat to the floor.

'Intelligence. His name's Pamir.'

The Opel's speedometer was reading over ninety m.p.h. as they left the village, and Berrisford was still accelerating. 'Doubt if they'll get anything ready before we hit the main road, sir,' he observed. 'And then they won't know which way we'll be going.'

But Joshua was not hearing him. He was, slowly, beginning to see the possible meaning of what had just happened. It wasn't certain, because he didn't know all the truth. But it was possible, just possible, and the idea was intolerable.

Berrisford slowed as the main road appeared. 'Nothing,' he said happily. 'Not a soul. Which way, sir?'

'Right. To Kyrenia.'

He was beginning to think clearly again. If Pamir had seen him, then it could be that the frontier would be barred. If he had had the chance he would have stopped the car and tried to work out if, at that time, that angle, someone outside a car would be able to recognise someone within. But that had been impossible. The fat man on the border had looked as though he had known him, or known about him. How? Surely to God they didn't have a photo of him in Cyprus. But they would have photos in Ankara. Intelligence would have photos, and Pamir was with them, and Pamir knew he was in Cyprus. It had been Pamir who had told him that for him the north was closed.

Did Pamir expect him to take any notice of his banning?

'I've changed my mind,' he said. 'We'll call on Colonel Peacock. See if he'd like a house guest.'

As they breasted the hill Berrisford caught his breath and then said, 'My God, isn't it beautiful!'

The sea, such a powerful blue that the eyes couldn't look at it without watering, stretched away from the little harbour. White fishing caiques lay on water so clear that their shadows could be seen on the sand under them. The beaches sparkled, white roads threaded through the inland streets like a kitten's unravelled ball of wool, and by the shore the Dome's swimming pool, glittering as the odd swimmer broke its surface, was a pale blue imitation of the sea just beyond it.

'Yes,' said Joshua quietly, but he was thinking, we've passed the other road that leads off to Bellapaise where they had found Boobs, and beyond which, or near which – he was sure of it – was Joanna.

'Peacock's road is the first on the left,' said Berrisford. Then he realised and added, 'Sorry, sir, I forgot you've been here before.' He laughed and said, 'Culture shock!'

They rounded another corner, and Joshua said, 'That's Kyprianou Road, there.'

Then he stopped and motioned to Berrisford to slow down. Berrisford leant forward, peered, then drew the car into the side of the road. From his safari-jacket pocket he unexpectedly produced a small, but very powerful, pair of opera glasses. He lifted them to his eyes and watched. His lips moved silently as he counted, then he said, 'Military police, sir. Three cars and a truck you can't see properly. Sixteen men, I think. Forgotten how many there are in a Turkish MP Section. Should know. Only just arrived because there's still dust in the air from their movement. Yes, they're closing in. Chap in an open truck, he's got a radio. Using it. Ah. Old chap coming out of the house. Would that be Colonel Peacock? Thin, can't see his hair, he's got a handkerchief over it. Just hit a Turk who's trying to get him to put his hands up from the look of it.'

'That'll be Peacock.'

'They look as though they're taking him away. Should we intervene?'

'Under no circumstances.'

'No. Thought not.'

Berrisford lowered his glasses. 'Poor old bastard,' he said.

'It won't be the first time the Colonel's been arrested by armed men.'

'No.' Berrisford exhaled. 'Still, one has to feel sorry for him at that age. You know he's got the D.S.O.?'

'No, I didn't.'

'D.S.O. and the M.C. Shall we push on, sir? Only as there's damn all traffic. and we're stopped just by a notice saying we can't – '

'Quite right. Push on.'

Berrisford put the Opel into gear, and they rolled down towards the little town. 'Any particular place, sir?' asked Berrisford.

'Anywhere we don't run into Peacock,' said Joshua. 'He's the sort who'd think it socially necessary to hail a fellow Englishman.' Then an idea struck him. 'You know Weinstein?'

'The Jew boy who blew the whistle on the Oman business?'

'Yes.'

'Never met him.' Then Berrisford said bitterly, 'But I'd like to. The damage he's done.'

'You can have the chance. He's staying in something called the Jolly Bungalows.'

'Here?' Berrisford sounded totally amazed.

'Yes.'

'Good God!'

Joshua was apprehensive, but there seemed to be no sign of any new check points in the town as they entered it. There was a noticeable number of Turkish soldiers, but they looked as relaxed as usual, like any conscript army in a fairly cushy posting. Berrisford drew up in a narrow street leading down to the port.

'If you're known here, sir, best I find out where the Jolly Bungalows are.'

Joshua nodded. Berrisford said, 'If you really think it's a good idea we find Weinstein.'

He waited, but Joshua said nothing and Berrisford climbed out of the car. He returned a couple of minutes later.

'No sweat,' he said as he settled back in the seat. 'Along the coast, about half a mile, and there you are. Got it from a memsahib.'

When they reached them, the Jolly Bungalows made Berrisford grin happily. The bungalows themselves were some half dozen, modest, paint-peeling, down-at-heel wooden shacks; but the sign announcing their existence was thirty feet by twenty, and completely blotted out the view of the sea from two of the bungalows. Weeds were growing around and over the bungalows, the concrete between them was cracked and in part missing, and two seemed never to have been completed. Only one was inhabited, or indeed habitable, and a new Mercedes stood beside it.

Berrisford swung the Opel round into a place from which he could make a quick exit in two directions. Joshua thought, old SAS training. When he's long retired, a golf club bore, he'll still park his car where he can most effectively make a sudden run for it from the eighteenth fairway.

Weinstein had obviously seen them arriving, and opened the door with a cynical smile as Joshua was raising his hand to knock.

'Hi,' he said. Then to Berrisford, 'I don't think we've met.'

'Mike Berrisford,' he said rather stiffly.

'Oh, I know who you are.' Weinstein vaguely waved them into the bungalow. 'Just that we haven't actually been formally introduced.'

Berrisford said, 'But I know all about you,' and smiled menacingly.

'And I have a file on you too. Isn't that cosy? I've just made some coffee. Like some?'

Joshua said, 'Thanks,' before Berrisford could work out a way of reasserting his position in the pecking order. He entered the bungalow and glanced round. It had once had a certain holiday brochure chic, a gaiety exemplified in bright scarlet cotton bed covers, yellow curtains, and painted pine furniture. But since its former owner had fled to the south there had been few tourists, and for most of the year now the place accomodated nothing but mice and spiders. There was a dark patch on an outside wall, the paint on the chairs was chipped, the fabrics were perforated with moth holes, and the colours were patchily fading.

As Weinstein poured out the coffee he said, 'I was expecting you to be back.'

'Why?'

'Because this is clearly the place to be. People being killed. You know about the Turkish hit squad?'

Berrisford looked about to assert that JBH knew everything, but Joshua said, 'No.'

'Last night. They flew in last night. About thirty men my source told me. I'm surprised you don't know all about it. Milk and sugar?'

'Both,' said Joshua. 'Neither,' said Berrisford.

Weinstein carefully put two mugs of coffee on a plastic-covered table in the middle of the room. 'Sit down. Make yourselves at home. It's something everybody else has failed to do for three thousand years in this island.'

He looked at Joshua and said, 'The person who was killed was a woman, not a man.' Then he sat down on a sofa and said to Berrisford, 'But, you know, I think he knew all the time. I think he knew it was a woman but he didn't tell me. Isn't he a mischievous little imp, your boss?'

Joshua picked up his coffee and sat down on a divan. The bungalow obviously included two divans among the three beds it offered to visitors. Berrisford hesitated, then sat on the second divan, unconsciously placing himself between the window and the door.

'So I asked around,' said Weinstein. 'And I really was very, very surprised at everybody's attitude. They were so anxious to tell me! In all my career, I've never met so many people so anxious to help. Honestly, if life was normally as easy as this, I'd have retired long ago. So I asked myself, why is everybody being so nice to me?'

'And . . .?' Joshua was thinking, the Turks want some intelligence to leak. But what? And why?

'And I was hoping you might tell me.' Weinstein grinned, his ill-assorted teeth like the stones on top of a Derbyshire wall.

Joshua was thinking fast. Weinstein had not known about the kidnapping. He had known a little about Boobs' murder, but not about the kidnapping. Did he know who Boobs was? Had the Turks decided to let the information out because of that bloody speech by the Under-Secretary? And if so, how far had they gone? And at what level had the decision been made?

'You're right,' he said, 'It was a woman.'

199

'A woman called Elizabeth Enid Bessemer,' said Weinstein. 'Like the furnace. Profession, school mistress.'

Joshua thought, he knows more than I do. He can remember her name. But how much more does he know? He said, 'Who killed her?'

'The trouble with chatting to you,' said Weinstein, 'is that you always say you know nothing while expecting the rest of us to be terribly well informed. It's like having a book of quizzes, and when you turn to the back to find the answers, all you get is more questions.'

'Let's try a question you're bound to know the answer to.' They had had this sort of conversation many times before, and normally Joshua got a certain pleasure from them: but not this time, because what he was really talking about, though he never said the name and tried to avoid thinking about it, was Joanna. 'Who told you?'

Weinstein seemed to consider for a moment, then said, 'Oztek.'

Oztek. Colonel Oztek of whatever branch of whatever organisation he really belonged to. A man who had a reputation that when he got involved the papers disappeared along with the people. A professional's professional. If Oztek had told Weinstein, then he had meant to, and it mattered.

'What did he tell you?'

'He said that the woman who was killed had been in charge of some school children.' Weinstein smiled. 'There. I've told you what I know. Now it's your turn.'

'Did he say what had happened to the children?'

'Questions, questions, questions. I said, it's your turn.' Weinstein had stopped smiling.

Joshua said, 'I'll tell you that I knew that already.'

'And you knew the children had been kidnapped?'

'Yes.'

Weinstein leant forward and scratched his scalp. Specks of dandruff fell into a shaft of sunlight that transfixed the room. 'Oztek managed not to tell me what nationality the children were. I assumed that with names like Elizabeth Enid the dear departed was most likely English. I dare say that if I spoke Turkish well enough I could have used some phrase that implied the children were English too, and see if Oztek corrected me. But I don't. Anyway, as you know Oztek prefers to speak in French which he speaks really rather badly. But perhaps you could tell me. Were the children English?'

Joshua could sense Berrisford watching him. 'Yes,' he said.

There was a pause and Weinstein replaced his cup onto a saucer, carefully centering it and turning it round so that the handle was parallel to the edge of the table. He combined an irritating precision in his movements with an all-pervasive squalor in his appearance. 'That still doesn't explain you,' he said at length. 'You don't make sense.'

He leant back and there was a rasping noise. 'Sorry,' he said. 'I always fart in the mornings. I was saying, you don't make sense. Quite apart from the fact that I don't see JBH sending you out here just because of a few kidnapped children – '

He checked, and smiled at Berrisford. 'I'm sure you won't mind my saying it, but they'd be far more likely to head their team with you.'

Berrisford flushed, but didn't speak.

Weinstein continued, 'JBH wouldn't send you because you're too senior, and perhaps, forgive me, a little old. In any case, your expertise is in working with equivalent organisations in other countries. But you can't do that here. There are plenty of equivalent organisations, God knows there are, but there's nobody here the British Government recognises. And while the British Government is very concerned about children – I mean, look at the trouble everybody went to to get Mark Thatcher out of the Sahara – I don't see them risking their entire political position by sending you here to work with, say, Oztek, who has no power here at all as far as the British are concerned.'

He waited, then asked, 'Well . . .?'

'I'm here,' said Joshua. 'But I told you before, and I'll repeat it, I'm not here in connection with any business of JBH.' Poker-faced, he added, 'Whatever that is.'

'Let's play pretend,' said Weinstein. 'Suppose the British Government wants to change its position over Cyprus. Suppose it has already come to some arrangement with the Turks. There's this agreement. All arranged. Use of the airport at Nicosia, Intelligence stations up in the Karpas panhandle, everything. So that if Greece goes Communist, and Cyprus duly follows, it's business as usual for us. It's all in the agreement which is signed, but not dated. Okay? All that is needed is an outbreak of fighting in which, this time, no question, the Greeks started it and the Turks didn't. The British, acting under their treaty obligations, intervene.'

Joshua thought, that's just what Nico would like. A chance to have one more round against the Turks.

'All that is needed is this small, not too dangerous war. And that would need a dramatic, not too sanguinary incident.' Weinstein leaned back and grinned. 'If by any chance you were here to organise such an incident for such a scenario, from my point of view it is one hell of a story.'

Joshua said, 'It would be a totally untrue story.'

'As far as you know.'

'Yes. As far as I know.'

He knew so little. Would they really do that? Would they set up a kidnapping, knowing that his daughter would be involved, knowing how he would react, so as to provoke an incident? Would they do all that and not give him any hint of how he was being used? Could they have got away with it?

Weinstein went on talking, his flat, unattractive voice belying the precision of his thought. 'A few more ideas. Don't bother to deny them, and then I won't have to explain why I don't believe your contradictions, and between us we'll save a lot of time.'

He spread out his large hands with the bitten finger nails, and ticked off the questions. 'One. What is a man from JBH – let alone two of them – doing in Kybris? And I don't believe you're secret lovers who choose to spend your holidays together.'

For a moment Berrisford looked dangerous, but Weinstein went on. 'Two. Is JBH really interested in the death of a spinster school mistress, and if so, why? Three. Why would the Turks think it necessary to bring in an elite squad of paratroopers to round up whoever killed this poor woman of whom they know nothing except her name which they got from her passport which was thoughtfully left on her body? Or so they assure me. Four. Why is it that when I phone – with some difficulty – first the *Daily Mail*, then *The Times*, then Reuters in London, not only has nobody heard of her prior existence, they haven't even heard of her death?'

Joshua could sense Berrisford waiting for a lead, for an indication that he should leap into some conditioned reaction, but it was all up to Weinstein what happened.

Weinstein asked, 'More coffee?'

'I've still got some,' said Joshua, and Berrisford grunted.

'Five,' said Weinstein. 'Question five. What would happen if I phoned all my contacts in Britain saying that two men – one very senior – in a terribly, terribly secret British Intelligence organisation are in north Cyprus.'

'Nothing,' said Berrisford gruffly. 'Not a bloody thing. Nobody would print it. It isn't a story.'

Weinstein grinned. 'Not as such, no. But I do have a reputation. I really have. They know I don't waste people's money phoning collect unless I want questions asked. And even if the people I phoned couldn't get a story in the papers they work for, there's always those dreadful rags like *Private Eye* . . .'

'There's still no story,' said Berrisford. 'Nobody would be interested.'

There was a long silence before Weinstein said, 'The Greeks would be interested.'

The Greeks. Joshua was thinking hard. Weinstein was wrong. There'd been a stick proffered, and he'd taken the wrong end of it. But who had interested him in the first place, and why? The Greeks might be grateful for a flare-up, crack British troops in the north as Greek troops attacked from the south, all to save British children. But Weinstein hadn't been across the frontier. He hadn't met any Greeks. He had got his information from the Turks.

'You said something about English school children.' Joshua made his voice sound casual.

'Yes.'

'Did you gather that the Turks knew where they were?' It was a long-shot, but it made some sort of sense.

Weinstein grinned. 'I didn't ask. If you're talking to Colonel Oztek you don't say much, except thank-you sir, and you don't ask questions at all. He's telling you something he wants you to know, and that's it. But yes, I got the impressison that he knew where the children were.'

'Then why isn't he doing anything about it?' It sounded sharper, harder than he had meant it to, sharp and hard like he felt.

'As I said, one doesn't ask questions of Oztek. Tell me. Can I help you in any way?'

It was not an offer, and none of the men thought it was. It was a basis for negotiations.

'Yes,' said Joshua. He was being pushed into moving faster than he would have chosen to, but his instincts told him that time was not on his side. 'Yes, you can. I'd like to use your car.'

Berrisford looked round, surprised, but Weinstein hardly reacted at all.

'Why not?' said Weinstsein. 'It's a hire car, but I presume you have reasons for not wanting to be seen hiring cars yourself. Like not being seen to be staying overnight illegally.'

'Something like that.'

'The only thing,' said Weinstein, examining his coffee cup then rejecting it, 'is that I have these ideas about reciprocity. Like if you're going to buy Manhattan from the Red Indians, it's only fair you give them a few beads or something in exchange.'

'In exchange,' said Joshua, 'assuming it's possible, you will have the story of what happens.'

'An exclusive? Just little me?'

'Just little you. Assuming there's a story at all, and that it can be told.'

'That doesn't sound like a great many beads . . . I mean, if I just sent off what I already know . . .'

Joshua said, 'That's not a good idea.'

Weinstein grinned. 'I like the way you said that. That makes me sure. It may not be a good idea, but for reasons I don't yet know it's one hell of a good story. What would happen, do you think?'

What would happen, thought Joshua, would be that the Turks would have their hand forced, the Greeks would see their opportunity, and somewhere along the line, almost unnoticed, some children would probably get killed. Including my daughter.

But it wasn't Joshua who answered the question. It was Berrisford. He stood up and said, very formally, 'At a guess, Weinstein, Mr Doyle would break your neck. And if by any chance he didn't, even if I had to follow you to the far ends of the earth, if he didn't, I would.'

Chapter Twenty Seven

Joshua watched as Berrisford disappeared towards Nicosia in the Opel, then turned left towards Dikmen: towards Agios Khrysoumos, Anna's village. He thought, at last Berrisford can set about the work he understands and is good at, work that ends in noise and violence. He won't have to worry about things that he tends to get wrong, like implications and innuendos, understandings and human relationships.

He drove Weinstein's hired Mercedes gently along the rough road. He wanted them to see him coming. He wanted them to be ready for him, but he didn't want to be taken by surprise himself. Already that day one unfamiliar car had come down this road. The sentry who had presented arms indicated that, normally, an unfamiliar car meant an unfamiliar General. It was unlikely that he would be greeted again by a salute: but he didn't want to be greeted by a fusillade of small-arms fire.

Thirty-five miles an hour, he decided. The sort of pace that would get him to the village quickly enough so that, with any luck, they would not have time to throw up a check point at its entrance; and slowly enough to indicate goodwill, presenting no obvious threat to anybody.

It seemed to work. As he passed the straggling houses on the edge of the village soldiers were taking up positions on both sides of the road, but nobody stopped him and nobody fired a warning shot. He thought, they haven't had suicide car bombers here, fanatics who will drive their lethal loads of unstable explosives towards, they hope, certain death in the assurance of martyrdom for whatever is that year's cause.

Joshua reached the square. If there had been anybody sitting at the tables outside the *cafeneon* they had all disapeared inside. He circled slowly round, past a few deserted houses, past a building that had become some sort of military stores, past the church, now emptied of the ikons and trappings of one God to admit the bare purity of another, up towards the pillared entrance to Anna'a house. The sentry remained motionless at the At Ease position, but two other soldiers, sub-machine guns tucked under their arms, walked slowly and purposefully down the drive. He stopped the car and as he did so they glanced at each other, then, still walking forward, changed the postion of the weapons so that, in one further move, they could spray the car with bullets.

He pressed the button to lower the front passenger window so that he was clearly visible, then switched off the ignition. All the time he moved slowly and regularly, wherever possible keeping his hands visible.

The two soldiers, uncertain, halted, their hands along the trigger guards of the weapons.

It seemed hours, but it must have been less than a minute before Pamir appeared.

He stood in the doorway of the house, Anna's house, then came slowly down the drive towards the car. Joshua thought, for Christ's sake, it's like one of those old Westerns. He's coming down that path like John Wayne down the main street when everybody else was wisely pretending nothing was happening. Or was it Gary Cooper? Except that I'm not going to throw myself sideways and open fire, starting the battle. I'm going to wait and let him make the move.

Even the music of the film came into his mind. *Do not forsake me, oh my darling, on this our we-he-ding day*.

Pamir stopped between the soldiers, and said something Joshua couldn't hear, and wouldn't have understood had he heard it. They nodded, and waited where they were.

Behind the car, in the mirror Joshua could see a dozen or so men filing out, quite slowly, to block the road to the west.

Dum dum di dum dum, dum dum di dum, a something cow-ward, a something cow-ward, to my grave.

That wasn't right, and still the irritating half-remembered lines thudded at the back of his mind as he watched Pamir coming towards him. Pamir had moved to one side of the drive. It might be an accident, but it gave the two soldiers an uninterrupted line of fire on the car. There was a scuffling sound, and Joshua, by moving slightly, could see in the wing mirror that another soldier, crouching, had taken up a position behind the car, covering the driver's door.

The important thing now was not to change the tempo. He must not make a move that could be interpreted as a threat. He slowly put his hands on the steering wheel, where everybody could see them, and waited.

Pamir still walked at the same steady pace. He was wearing a white, short-sleeved shirt and fawn slacks, and didn't appear to be armed. He reached the entrance of the drive, glanced round as though checking where his men were or looking for his dog, then came over to the car, round the front to the driver's side.

Through the open window he said coldly, 'I ordered you not to return to Kybris.'

Joshua said nothing, and waited.

'You were here before,' said Pamir, 'In an Opel, registration number KT 47941.' He even remembered the number. 'You cannot read perhaps? You did not know that this is a closed village?'

Joshua lied. 'I wanted to find you.'

'Why did you come to this village?'

Because of Anna. Because he had made love to a woman and she had told him of this village. But he couldn't say that. He lied again. 'I was told you might be here.'

'Who by? By your friend Peacock?'

Thank God for the suggestion. 'Yes,' he said. 'Peacock thought it was a likely place.'

'He has been arrested.'

'He meant well.'

Pamir shrugged. 'I will probably have him released. After he has been a little hurt. Perhaps we will fine him. He will do anything for money, because he has very little of it. Sometimes he is useful.'

You don't understand him, thought Joshua. Of course Peacock can be used to send intelligence to the south. And of course he needs the money. But he would never betray his concept of his country, out-dated and ludicrous though it is. He would die for his country. The only thing that would break him would be for him to go back to it, and see what had become of it.

Joshua said, 'I came here because I wanted to talk to you.'

Pamir seemed to be considering the idea for a moment, then nodded, turned, and walked back towards the house. He snapped an order in Turkish, and a soldier Joshua had not noticed, who had been standing behind the car, stepped forward and opened the car door.

Uncertain, Joshua got out of the car. The soldier shut the door, reached through the open window and took the car keys, then indicated that he was to accompany him up the drive.

The house was elegant and spacious, one of the older houses of

207

the village, and the largest. It was cool and gracious, but now there was the angular equipment and furniture of an army in the wide corridors and visible through half-open doorways in the rooms leading off them. Nothing remained of the previous occupants except a large, rather gloomy oil painting of an elderly man, presumably a former owner of the house.

Pamir was already seated in a spacious room occupying a corner of the house when Joshua reached it. French windows opened onto a balcony, which in turn led down to an ornamental garden, now neglected and overgrown. The room was sparsely and functionally furnished, strictly an office, though a camp-bed jutted out into it. A large military map of Cyprus had been fixed to a wall, nails brutally driven into panelling.

Joshua's escort saluted, then turned and left, closing the door after him.

There was a chair opposite the desk behind which Pamir was sitting, but Pamir made no gesture that Joshua might sit. Pamir pulled open a drawer and extracted a packet of cigarettes and a lighter. He lit a cigarette, the click of the lighter clearly audidble in the hot silence.

Finally he said, 'You have five minutes to explain what you are really doing here.'

Joshua moved towards the seat, and Pamir snapped, 'I did not tell you to sit down!'

'I told you. I want to see you.'

'Why?'

'Because of the Grey Wolves who are holding the children.'

'And I have told you, that is none of your business. It is the business of the Republic of Kybris. When your Government recognises what has happened here, then yes, we can discuss problems like this. But they have lately been making it very clear that they do not recognise us.'

The Under-Secretary's speech had not gone unnoticed in the north, any more than in the south.

'And now,' said Pamir, 'you will tell me why, of all the villages in Kybris, Colonel Peacock recommended this one.'

Joshua tensed. The fear that had been niggling at the back of his mind, the conclusion he had fleetingly, in horror, accepted, and then rejected because it was unthinkable, came back again. You were used, he thought. She seduced you like a whore, and you fell for it, and you trembled on the edge of love, and she used you.

208

Careful. Careful what you say. Remember Peacock has to *live* here.

He adopted a casual voice. 'Why? I can hardly remember. I think I was discussing what the parts of Cyprus that were under Turkish occupation were like – '

He deliberately used the Cyprus Government phrase, *under Turkish occupation*, and Pamir fell for it.

Pamir growled, 'The Republic of Kybris.'

'I was discussing what the various places were like with someone, and later, when I met Peacock I was asking the same questions, and when I said I'd like to meet you again, he mentioned this village. Just as a possible sort of place.'

He realised, almost as he was speaking, that he had made a mess of it. The times didn't fit. He couldn't have asked Peacock about Pamir because he hadn't met Peacock after he'd met Pamir. Not unless he was prepared to admit that he had made a visit to the north that Pamir didn't know about, after Pamir had specifically forbidden him to do so.

Then he understood why Pamir wasn't picking it up. He knew perfectly well about the second journey. He probably knew about the visit to Bellapaise and the search in the mortuary. Pamir knew because he had been expecting him to come back, relying on it.

Pamir had used him too.

Pamir puffed on his cigarette. 'This someone you were talking to. Where was it?'

'Let me think. It must have been in my hotel.'

'And you are staying, where?'

'A place called the Hotel Romantica.'

'By the frontier.'

'Yes. It's convenient for that.'

'And this person at the hotel just mentioned this village among all the others?'

'As far as I remember.'

There was half a smile on Pamir's face. 'We know each other. We've known each other for a long time. You've seen this village. You've driven through it. Twice. What do you make of it?'

Joshua laughed. 'It's a bit like one of those villages on Salisbury Plain where the signs don't say cattle crossing, they say tanks crossing.'

'It is obviously a military headquarters.'

'Yes. Now I've seen it.'

Pamir seemed deceptively relaxed. 'And I'll tell you something else,' he said. 'If you got a chance to look at the insignia on the uniforms of the soldiers, you would see that a disproportionate number of them are Intelligence. Does that surprise you?'

'I wouldn't know. I don't know Turkish army insignia.'

'So. Who asked you about this village? Who suggested you might visit it?'

He said, 'I can't remember which of them it was. I think it was a woman. But her family used to own a house in the village.'

'Which house?'

'As far as I remember her description, this one.'

Pamir suddenly burst out laughing, a laugh of sheer triumph. 'Of course! I believe you! Of course! And when you are in Moscow, you go into Dzerzhinsky Square and take photographs of Number Three because you happened to run into a woman who lived there under the Czar!'

He suddenly stoped laughing. 'I warned you before, and I tell you one more, last time. You do not have to leave Kybris.'

Joshua said, 'It is true. A woman told me her family lived in this house.'

'And you believed her?'

'Yes.'

God forgive me, he thought. Yes, I believed her. I believed her because I wanted her, and I wanted to believe her. I wanted her body, and for that I wanted to believe what she was telling me. What's that thing they say about the theatre? The suspension of disbelief. Not actually believing, just suspending disbelief. And I did it for her. My job, my training, everything I know is not to believe, because that is what the world is like. But I believed her.

'Yes,' he repeated. 'I believed her.'

Pamir rose and walked slowly round the room, looking sideways at him. 'I am not sure,' he said. 'I am not sure if you are lying all the time or only a part of the time. But I will tell you something. The Hotel Romantica is a safe house for Greek Intelligence. You told me before that you were put in there by a tour operator. Should I believe you?'

Joshua shrugged. 'Does it make any difference what I say?'

Pamir put the cigarette down in an ash tray and looked at it thoughtfully. The smoke rose vertically in the still air until, unexpectedly, he swung his hand across his body in a gesture of resignation.

'It is because you keep coming back that I am interested in you,' he said. 'Nothing else. Your Government has made it plain that they are not prepared to negotiate with us. But you keep coming back. You should have gone home by now. You know you will achieve nothing. So I will ask you one question before I decide what to do with you.'

He picked up the cigarette, drew heavily on it, then carefully stubbed it out.

'You said before that you were here because of the kidnapped English children.'

'Yes.'

He didn't ask the question Joshua was expecting, the one he was uncertain how to answer. Pamir said, 'Do you still think the children are here in Kybris?'

'Yes.'

'Why?'

'Because I know how they were brought here.'

For a moment something that might have been surprise showed in Pamir's face. But he said nothing, and waited.

Joshua said, 'They were stopped by a United Nations patrol vehicle outside Limassol. The troops in the truck seemed to be French Canadians. They told the driver of the bus, the teacher in charge, and the children – '

He stopped, and said, 'I don't know what they told them. But they persuaded them to get out of the bus into the UN vehicle. Out of sight of the others they shot the driver. Then they took the teacher and the children into the north. It is under twenty miles. As far as I know the prisoners had no reason to suspect that they had been kidnapped until they were well inside . . .' He hesitated, then said pointedly, 'the Republic of Northern Cyprus. The Turkish occupied zone.'

Pamir said, 'You can prove this?'

'I think so. I know the number of the vehicle, and it doesn't exist among UN equipment. I know they crossed the frontier at Beyarmuda, at a quarter past twelve.' He used the Turkish name. 'I haven't checked, but I believe that the men masquerading as United Nations were not French Canadians, but French from *Action Directe*.'

Pamir nodded. 'We have reports that they are engaged in the Near East.'

He paused, then he said brusquely, 'We will deal with it. If they are working inside our country, it is our conern. It is nothing to do with the British Government. We have explained what we want, and they

211

have rejected our suggestions. Very well. It is up to us.'

Joshua said, 'I am not sure that the British Government would agree.'

'I know very well they would disagree! But what does that matter? There is nothing they can do!'

There is a British warship that is about to receive orders, thought Joshua. Depending on how long it takes Berrisford to get through, on whether it is ready to sail, if the orders can be confirmed quickly. Pamir was wrong. There was something the British Government could do.

Joshua asked him, 'Do *you* still think the children are in Kybris?'

His use of the word, Kybris, was another gesture, another leaf of an olive branch.

'Yes.'

Pamir reached for a cigarette. As he lit it he said, 'Now I am almost certain I know where they are. I had thought for some time that I knew, but I didn't want to make an issue of it becasue I felt I ought to be able to prove that it was posssible to bring them into Kybris in the first place. There are . . . colleagues . . . here who say it is not possible.'

Careful. He realised that Pamir was on the edge of confiding in him.

'You mean,' said Joshua, 'people from mainland Turkey, when they saw the frontier controls for themselves, they said it was impossible for anyone to bring the children in from the south.'

Pamir shrugged, but didn't speak.

Joshua pressed on. 'Senior people, they overruled you. Is that it?'

If he was right, perhaps he'd found a chink in Pamir's armour. He realised that he should have thought of it before. In Cyprus, Pamir was a man of authority. There was nobody in his normal work who would be in a position to contradict him. But to the men from Ankara, Pamir was just another provincial. A talented provincial, but a provincial.

He said, 'I know that Oztek and Kemal Ozal are here.'

Pamir growled, 'You know too damned much,' and puffed angrily on his cigarette. Then he said, 'They came when they got the first message. I showed them how the checks worked. Separately. You know they are hardly on speaking terms?'

'No. I didn't.'

'Then they said that it was all a hoax, and then the girl's body was found.' He added cynically, 'I presume you know about that?'

'Yes.'

For a moment Pamir's lips twitched in something like a smile. 'I was hoping you would deny it.'

'Who tipped you off? Or shouldn't I ask?'

'Who do you think?'

'It has to be Peacock.'

Pamir said nothing, but didn't deny the deduction. He said, 'We are ready to move. You are sure about the way they were brought into Kybris?'

'Yes.'

'You see, we were assuming that they must, somehow, have come through on the blasted bus. Sunswept are involved in talks about opening up a branch in the north. Without telling the Greeks, of course.'

'The bus has been cannibalised. And the man who did it is probably dead.'

'You have been working well.' The compliment felt patronising.

It was the time to press. Joshua said, 'I have told you how it was done. Now you tell me where they are.'

Pamir looked surprised. 'Why should I tell you that? It is of no interest to you.'

'I don't believe you know.'

Pamir fell for it. Joshua watched the momentary flash of anger in the eyes, the expression of a man whose competence was being challenged. 'Of course I know. I have known for two days, and suspected for five. I have even told the British!'

'Then why the hell didn't you act?'

Now Pamir was genuinely angry again. 'I will tell you why! There are two reasons why! One, because I had to be absolutely sure, and I had to be certain that when I moved the operation would be a complete success!'

Joshua interruped. 'It doesn't take five days to move in a unit to take a handful of terrorists in a country that's to all intents and purposes under military rule! That woman died because you didn't act! For all we know they may have killed another one by now!'

They may have killed Joanna, he thought.

'No,' said Pamir. 'They haven't killed another. There would be no point in killing one of the girls unless they were going to exhibit her body. I have the place under observation all the time. Nobody has left the houses since the last time. With the woman.'

'You mean, you knew all the time that they were taking that poor woman's body into Bellapaise?'

213

'No. At that time the hamlet where they are was only one of three possible places I had identified. I had not been given the men to cover all three properly.' He added bitterly, 'Most of the military had been placed under General Eldem, the anti-terrorist police and the Jandarma are under Ozal, and the special forces are under Oztek. All I have are the men normally under my command. The woman was taken by night, on a donkey. My men heard the donkey, but they couldn't see it, they weren't sure what it was, and they daren't intercept it in case that provoked a fire-fight and all the girls were shot.'

Joshua nodded. Play for time, the oldest axiom of the tactics against terrorism.

'But they saw the donkey coming back,' Pamir continued. He seemed calm again, and relit his cigarette which had gone out. 'It was after dawn. One assumes that the terrorists were city people and didn't realise how long it would take. But through binoculars the saddle cloth looked as though it was soaked in blood.'

Joshua asked quietly, 'How many men were there with the donkey?'

'A man and a woman. Young. I was told they both looked like tourists. The woman was wearing jeans.'

'You could have gone in then! That night!'

He remembered the times when he had waited, checking every tiny element, waiting only for the one thing he could not control, could not influence – night.

Pamir said contemptuously, 'I told you there were two reasons why I have waited. You appear to have forgotten the other.'

Joshua swallowed the rage that rose in him and asked meekly, 'What was it?'

'Your Government!' Pamir was spitting out the words. 'Your Government had the perfect excuse for re-establishing links with the Turkish Cypriots! We made it so easy for you! And you did nothing except fart in our faces!'

'I don't see it.' He did see it, he understood exactly how Pamir saw it, but he had to play the innocent, let Pamir vent his anger.

'We told your Government that their citizens were being held in Kybris! We told them that – on my word! – even before we were absolutely certain! We risked humiliation, if we had been wrong, so that your Government would have the excuse it needed! All it had to do was to offer to cooperate with our forces! That is all! A gesture! We would have done the work for you! *We* had found out exactly

214

where the terrorists were, where the girls were, everything! In the village where they are being held there are four houses that are separate! Four! And they are in those four houses! The girls in one house, the terrorists in two houses, and one used for stores! We know everything! There is even the truck they came in, and it has a tarpaulin over it! I did not know until now that it was a United Nations truck, but I know to within a centimetre where it is!'

He strode to the map and banged his first angrily against it. 'There! There are the houses! One, two, three, four!'   .

Joshua was thinking fast. North of Bellapaise. About a mile inland. From the time they land, given that sort of terrain, if the SBS came ashore in boats it would take them an hour to get into position. No. An hour and a quarter, allowing for the mountains and delays.

'We told the British Government!' Pamir was shouting. 'We told them through the Embassy in Ankara and through Intelligence!'

But nobody told me, thought Joshua. Not the Turks, not the Consulate in Nicosia, if they knew, not even JBH. I was being used too.

'It was a perfect arrangement! We would allow your special forces to take part in the operation! SAS, SBS, whatever you want! They would work with my men, and together they would capture the terrorists and release the children! Together! All we asked was that the terrorists were handed over to us! We would try them, we would execute them! We demanded that the SAS didn't kill them on our soil! And do you know what the British Government did?'

'No,' said Joshua quietly. He could see what it meant. The acceptance of Turkish law in Cyprus.

'They did nothing!' Pamir smashed his hand down on his desk. 'Nothing!' Smash. 'They didn't give a damn what happened to the children!' Smash. 'All they did was get some damned junior Minister to make a speech which made it absolutely impossible for us to work with them!' Smash.

Pamir didn't know. He didn't know that the British had not been as inert as he thought. They had sent a frigate and a Section of SBS. The British were preparing to act on their own, and it was fortunate that Pamir did not know that, or he might have moved earlier: he could have stormed those four houses before the British were ready.

Joshua tried to sound relaxed, impersonal, just making an enquiry, one professional talking to another. 'What are you going to do?'

'Do!' Pamir shouted. 'We will do what we have to do! If the British refuse to act with us, then we will act alone! If the British are afraid of the Greeks, we aren't!'

'When?'

Pamir looked about to speak, then checked himself. Finally he said, 'Soon.'

'When?'

'Why should I tell you? It has nothing to do with you! We extended our hand to the English, we invited the English, we spoke nicely to the English, and you did nothing. Now this is a struggle for the people of Kybris, and nobody else.'

He was thinking furiously. The *Brazen* had a top speed of around thirty knots, if he remembered aright. Suppose Berrisford has reached the frontier, suppose at this moment he is crossing into the south. Say five minutes to reach the Consulate and his WTS. How long would it take to get the bloody ship under way? How long would it take to sail round the point, round to the northern coast?

He realised that Pamir was still speaking. 'Now, it will be a victory for our people. Not as the English pretend, for the Turks, but for the Turkish Cypriots! For Kybris! If the English girls – any of them – are killed, the fault will be entirely and exclusively the fault of the English! I tell you one thing! By then the terrorists will be dead! If there cannot be a trial which proves who is in charge in Kybris, then, believe me, there will be no trial at all! Nobody wants a trial in which all that happens is that terrorists make lying propaganda before all the press of the world!'

It sounded like a distorted recording of the lectures he had listened to when he was a very junior officer, how – to quote the old Italian anarchists – terrorism is propaganda by deed, how it could revert in court before the world so that propaganda became the arm of terrorism. He remembered it all, then he remembered that, later, it had been he who had given the lectures.

Pamir was shouting. 'If there are deaths among the English girls, then so be it! It will be the English Government that killed them!'

Pamir stopped abruptly, and Joshua realised that there had been a tap on the door. Pamir shouted something in Turkish, and a young officer entered. He saluted, looked curiously at Joshua, then handed Pamir a message.

There was a silence as Pamir read it, then he nodded to the officer, who saluted and stamped out of the room. It had been an unexpected intrusion of formal discipline.

Pamir said quietly, 'I was uncertain what to do. I will be honest with you. I was wondering whether to send you back just, on chance, if you had listened to me and would use your power through JBH.'

'I've said it before,' said Joshua wearily. 'I don't have that sort of power. None of us have.'

'In any case, everything is decided.' Pamir carefully folded up the sheet of paper and put it down on his desk. 'I was wondering whether to give you one day, so that we would attack the terrorists tomorrow night. Together. The forces of the Government of Kybris, and the forces of the British Government. It is now too late.'

Pamir tapped the paper. 'This has just come from Ankara. There has been another message from the Grey Wolves. They are as impatient with us as I am with you. They say that unless the British Government announce the formal recognition of the State of Kybris by midnight tonight Greenwich Mean Time, that is two o'clock Cyprus time, they will kill a girl at dawn. They will then kill another girl every hour after that. Until the statement is made.'

He picked up the paper again, opened it, then said, 'Or, I presume, until they have run out of girls.'

'You believe them?'

'Yes,' said Pamir. 'But in any case it decides what I do. There is no longer any time for anybody to get action out of the British Government. They will have had this message by now – '

He scowled and said bitterly, 'They tell London before they tell us.'

'What will you do?'

'It is prepared,' said Pamir confidently. 'The moon tonight goes below the horizon at about two-thirty. Dawn is around four-thirty. I have two hours of darkness.'

'Let me come with you.'

Pamir looked up sharply. He sucked at his cigarette, but it had gone out. He tossed the stub out of the window.

'No,' he said. 'Why should you be there? If you had a position, if you were an officer in uniform, then perhaps I might allow it. To show that, even though the English ignore our offers, because I have known you for many years, you might be allowed to come. At least it would mean one step towards British recognition of Kybris. But you are not in uniform, and you have no authority.'

He smiled, a fleeting, half-lost smile. 'Instead, for old time's

217

sake, I will let you leave Kybris. You will stay here under arrest until after I have killed the terrorists, then I will have you escorted to the frontier. I will ignore the fact that you have broken our laws, and disobeyed my orders to stay out of our country. You may go back and join your Greek friends. But I warn you, if you ever want to come back into Kybris, you must come back legally, through Turkey! Do you understand?'

Joshua said, very slowly, 'I'm not talking as a representative of the British Government.'

'It is because you are not a representative that you will stay here!'

'I'm asking for a special reason. I'm asking to come with you.'

Joshua was suddenly aware that, even though he was talking about something that mattered more to him than anything else had ever mattered in his life, he was still standing back, watching himself, calculating how best to influence the man facing him. What was passion, what was acting? How could he believe himself when all his training over all those years had been to get his way by truth, half-truth, lie, it didn't matter which, so long as it worked? For him, Pamir was simply another of those people he had faced when lives depended on it: terrorist, government spokesman, colleague. It had been his skills that had turned the incidents the ways he had wanted. It was the same bland skill he had to use now, when everything mattered.

He said, 'You remember when you were hiding in the forests from the Greeks?'

Pamir looked at him suspiciously.

'When you were frightened, not so much for yourself as for your family? Frightened because you were not certain you could do what you thought you had to do to save them?'

Pamir growled, 'What are you talking about? Why are you saying this?'

'And the important thing to you then – as she is still the most important thing to you now – was your daughter?'

Pamir was angry. Joshua watched the reaction, judging exactly how far to go, and hating himself for having to do it. Pamir said, 'It is not for you to talk of my daughter! I forbid it!'

Joshua said, 'I'm asking you if I can come with you because I am a man like the man you were when you were hiding in the forests. The terrorists are holding six girls. One of them is Joanna. My daughter.'

Chapter Twenty Eight

It was so beautiful it seemed almost unnatural. The sea was a deep blue that only the almost imperceptible swaying of lazy waves saved from being black: the mountains around him were purple against a sky encrusted with stars as though the nymphs had poured them out of their Horn of Plenty in some drunken revel: the pale gossamer clouds were frosted by a crescent moon, the moon of Islam, as it dropped towards the sea.

For a moment Joshua felt the memory and couldn't place it. Then it came to him, the only other night of his life when he had seen nature quite as peaceful; quite as misleading.

It had been the second night of their honeymoon – the second night, for the first night had been a shambles. It had been the Mediterranean, the same sea – but had it, even then, been quite as perfect? (Capri, chosen because a colleague had a rich brother-in-law who had lent his flat for a fortnight in exchange for his place in Islington, plus the car.)

Capri, where he had believed that he and Barbara would love, honour and cherish each other as long as they both should live. Except that it hadn't turned out that way.

'You see the houses,' said Pamir in a voice so quiet that had it not been for the total stillness of the night he would have been inaudible. 'One, two, three, four. The near one, that is the store. They do not have anybody in there. The next, that is where the prisoners are. Then the two for the terrorists. They sleep in the far one and eat in the nearer. We have seen smoke from the chimney.'

The houses had once been a family's small farm. The furthest house was the largest, and the one with the prisoners, the one that, please God, held Joanna, was newer than the others, built when a son had married and where he had set up his new wife, waiting for his father to die, or hand over the farm. It was difficult to judge how far they were away, because the brilliant clarity of the moon-

219

light made them appear much nearer than they were. Perhaps a quarter of a mile, he thought. No more. Between them and the houses there was another cluster, nine cottages and a ruin, and a little chapel. There was a pinpoint of light from the house where the terrorists ate, but none from the rest of the farm or from the hamlet.

They had hobbled him, a rope loosely binding his ankles, so that he could walk, but not run. Then they had tied his thumbs together, but not the tough way: his hands in front of him, not behind his back. He sat a few feet from Pamir, and from a distance they must have looked like two romantics sharing the night. He raised his bound hands and indicated the little village.

'Who lives down there?' he asked. It was one way of approaching the terrorists, but if the houses concealed people or dogs, then they could betray any movement.

'Nobody,' said Pamir, 'Nobody lives there. Nobody has lived there this century.'

It was the first time that Joshua had caught Pamir lying. Round the newer house, and again at the back of another one, there were walls that, although they were beginning to tumble had clearly been built within the last twenty years. But it was impossible for Pamir to say that Greeks had lived there until they had fled, because that would mean that now there weren't enough Turks to take over the empty houses.

He lowered his hands and glanced at his watch. Twelve thirty-seven. About another two hours.

'You see all my men?' asked Pamir.

'No.'

Pamir grinned, his white teeth matching his white hair in the moonlight. 'I damn well hope not! But I have forty-two men within three hundred yards of the terrorists.' He gestured. 'Over there. You see a cave in the hills?'

'Yes.'

'In there is a machine gun. Ranged. And in the corner where the two fields join the road, another. They run that way – ' He flung out an arm dramatically. 'The first machine gun. They run the other, then straight to the second. They have no way they can escape.'

Joshua thought, it won't be like that. It never is. Unless it's over in seconds, and for that you don't need forty-two half-trained men, you need half a dozen experts, unless it's over in seconds, they'll try to make a get-away. They'll use the girls as cover, either cover or the last resort, you fire on us and I will kill this girl, look, I have my gun to her head. That was how it would be, because he'd seen it before, and that was how it always was.

And he knew what orders Pamir would have given. He would have ordered that under no circumstances were the terrorists to be allowed to escape. These would not only have been his orders to his own men, but they would have been the orders that came down to him from Ankara. Once the decision had been made in London not to compromise, Ankara had had no choice. It would be quite impossible for the Turks to risk a trial when the defendants were pleading for the official policy of the Government of Turkey. Worse than impossible. Ludicrous.

The terrorists would have to die, and that would mean that whoever was between the terrorists and Pamir's forty-two men would die too.

He didn't ask Pamir what orders he had given, because there was no point in making him lie again. The hope, his only hope, was that despite everything, somehow the terrorists could all be wiped out in one, overwhelming, initial onslaught.

'The forty-two men,' said Pamir, 'That does not include the men at the machine guns.'

'They all know their orders?'

'Of course. They have been waiting for two days. Everybody knows exactly what he has to do.'

But it won't be like that. It won't work out. It might, just, with the SAS or the SBS, and only then if every possible precaution had been taken. It won't work like that with Turkish Cypriot gendarmerie.

'Will you be leading them?'

'No. I will go down there to watch, but I will leave it to others to kick down doors. You and I, we are both a little too old for that.'

Joshua said, 'I want to take part.'

Pamir looked genuinely surprised. 'Why?'

'You know why.'

Pamir crawled over to him, carefully keeping below the skyline.

'You don't listen!' he hissed. 'You are being stupid, and you do not try to understand! We gave the English the chance! We gave them all the intelligence we had, all they needed to cooperate! We gave them a unique chance to settle, once and for all, the future of the Republic of Kybris! And they refused! And you! You! When I asked you to use the power of JBH, you said you could do nothing! And yet, you tell me, your daughter is in that house! Of all the people on earth, you are the last man I would permit to take part!'

He moved away, growling from the back of his throat like an angry cat.

221

There was a long silence, and then Pamir said quietly, 'I will tell you something. I tell you something. I tell you because we knew each other a long time ago when things were different. I am a Turk, but I am also a Cypriot. I hope that one day the Greeks will learn, and we can all be Cypriots again.'

There was a flash of white teeth. 'That is not perhaps the dream of all the administrators from Ankara, or all the immigrants they are settling on this island.'

'No.'

Pamir went on, 'What I want is that this will be a victroy for the Turkish Cypriots. For the people of Kybris. For us, not for our brothers from the mainland. We will show them that we can rule ourselves if we choose to.'

Joshua was puzzled. There was a nuance, something implicit in what Pamir was saying that he didn't understand. But he knew that if he asked a direct question he would not get an answer.

There was a another long silence. Pamir said, 'I would give two years of my life for a cigarette. But the light . . .'

Then, quite casually, he said, 'This attack will be our attack. Our victory. The victory of the people of Kybris. We will kill the terrorists, who are demanding what we are demanding, but who are still our enemies because we are honourable men and they are not. We will kill them while the people who still, sometimes, despise us are wasting their time.'

Now he could say it. Joshua asked, 'Why are they wasting their time?'

Pamir turned to him in the moonlight. 'While we are winning the victory, the forces under General Eldem and Commissioner Ozal, they are facing the wrong way. They think that we might be betrayed, so they are facing the wrong way.'

'I don't understand you.'

Pamir waved a hand towards the sea where the moon was carving a glittering track towards them. 'Down below us, on the other side of the ridge, there is a brigade of infantry and a special airborne unit. They think that the English will try to land on our soil without our permission. They will drive the English off, and then, they think, come up here and kill the terrorists.'

There was a soft chuckle from Pamir. 'But that will not happen, because by then we, the Cypriots, will have killed the terrorists. Do you know why I am telling you this?'

Joshua could feel his muscles tensing. 'Because I'm tied here like a bloody goat and can't do anything?'

222

Pamir was smiling. 'No,' he said. 'I am telling you because of the old times. Because there is still a bond between the Turk and the English, and between the Cypriot and the English. Because you are an English gentleman. I can rely on you not to tell my brothers from the Turkish mainland that I am arranging things so that the people of Kybris free themselves from the terrorists, and are not dependent on . . . on . . .'

'Big brother?' suggested Joshua.

Pamir laughed softly. 'Perhaps.'

Behind them there was a scuffling sound, and somebody swore quietly in Turkish. Pamir rose to his feet, reaching for the automatic in the holster at his waist. Doubled up, his hands clasped on top of his head, Berrisford stumbled into view, a Turkish sergeant prodding him forward with a bayoneted rifle.

'Good God,' said Joshua.

'Hello sir,' said Berrisford, then to Pamir, 'We haven't actually met, but I recognise you from the village. Dikmen.'

The sergeant stabbed him viciously, and Berrisford said to Pamir, 'I'm afraid I don't speak Turkish, and this sergeant doesn't speak any language I speak, but I'd be grateful if you'd tell him to stop sticking his bayonet up my arse. It's not as though I'm going anywhere.'

Pamir grunted something to the sergeant, who stepped back, then sat on a rock, his rifle still covering Berrisford.

'Thanks,' said Berrisford. 'He has no idea how bloody near being a eunuch he was, when I'd got half a chance.'

Joshua said, 'What the hell are you doing here?'

'Got back from Kyrenia, and started looking for you. No sign. Even our friend still has visitors.'

Presumably Berrisford meant Peacock, because he seemed to be waving his fingers above his head to indicate a peacock's tail. He went on, 'So I asked, but nobody said anything, and as I had this hire car I went back to this village where . . .'

He hesitated, waiting for a lead.

'Where you'd seen Pamir,' said Joshua. 'As I told you, in Intelligence.'

Berrisford nodded gratefully. 'Yes. Village called Dikmen. Just that you said you knew him, and I thought he might . . .'

He nodded towards Pamir, then said to him, 'I must say, they're pretty sharp, your chaps! I got out and said I was looking for an English friend I'd seen with a Mr Pamir, next thing I knew, up against a wall, hands tied behind my back to start with, then blind-folded, into a truck, thrown out about a mile back, and Shanks's pony with the sergeant here all the rest of the way.'

He added pointedly, 'A hell of a lot of trouble to go to, just to find a chum.'

Pamir said, 'Who allowed you back into Kybris?'

'Yes,' said Berrisford affably. 'I suppose I ought to apolgise. Only I wanted to get back into the south. Had to make a phone call. And I knew it would be a bit tricky explaining, particularly when I don't speak Turkish. But by sheer good luck I ran into this United Nations chap who gave me a lift in. Seems they can do these things.'

Berrisford looked at Joshua and said with an inflection as unsubtle as a wink, 'Irish chap, actually. Major Cookie or some-thing. So I picked up the car again, and here I am.'

He turned again to Pamir. 'Could I take my hands down, do you think? Only it's really quite uncomfortable having them up all the time.'

Pamir nodded, and Berrisford lowered his arms, flexing his fin-gers. The sergeant rose menacingly, but sat down again, this time on his haunches, when he saw Pamir's expression.

The sergeant doesn't understand a word of English, thought Joshua. Remember that.

He had somehow to talk to Berrisford. There were so many questions he had to ask, so much he had to know, and it was impossible with Pamir present. Had Berrisford managed to contact the *Brazen*? What contingency plans were the SBS drawing up? Where *was* the *Brazen*? Had it already sailed, or was it waiting in Limassol for orders from the Admiralty?

His mind was whirling, trying to work out what must be the situation. The British had been given all the Turkish intelligence. That's what Pamir had said. So had it reached the *Brazen*? Had it reached the SBS?

Suppose it had. Suppose the SBS knew about the four houses, and even though they weren't going to have a chance to do a proper reconnaissance, they had adequate maps.

The important thing was that they had to get in before the Turks. If, somehow, he could stall Pamir's attack until the SBS were ready . . .

Then he remembered, and his skin felt cold. It was not a question of delaying Pamir. It was the terrorists who were imposing the time limit. They would start killing the girls at dawn.

Pamir looked round, and motioned to Berrisford. 'Sit down,' he said curtly. 'You are in danger of being seen.'

Berrisford, with surprising grace, coiled to the ground. Pamir said something to the sergeant and then said in English, 'I have told him that if either of you moves at all he is to shoot you.' To Joshua he added, 'If you think I would not do that because the shots would rouse the terrorists, they often hunt at night in these mountains.'

The four men sat in silence as the time crawled past. Joshua looked down on the little cluster of houses and thought, is she asleep? Is she down there, or have they go everything wrong and she's somewhere else? Is it already too late, and she's dead?

But he didn't believe that. He could imagine her, lying there with one hand's fingers entwined in her hair as she had always slept since she was a small girl. Who was guarding them? For somebody must be guarding them. For a moment he thought of the other thing that could happen, what had happened to Patty Hearst, what had happened in Sweden, which is why they called it the Stockholm Syndrome, that already Joanna was corrupted, willing, that she was lying with one of them beside her, on top of her, inside her.

He forced the thought from his mind, and glanced again at the luminous dial of his watch. Twelve minutes past two. He looked up and the moon had dropped dramatically since he had last checked. Not long to wait now.

Pamir noticed his move, and glanced at his own watch. Then he rose to his feet, unzipping his fly. He said something to the sergeant, and strode off behind a rock.

Joshua waited, listening intently. There was the sound of several footsteps, retreating, then silence.

He turned and smiled at the sergeant. 'On the word, you take the sergeant,' he said, quietly.

The sergeant rose heavily to his feet and kicked him hard in the back, just below the ribs, then retired back to his rock. The blow half rolled Joshua over, bound as he was, but he was sitting normally again by the time Pamir returned.

'I'm going down,' he said. 'In a quarter of an hour the moon will be below the horizon. Then we go in.'

He spoke to the sergeant, who rose to his feet. Joshua thought, that sergeant, he's hard all right, but he's getting on. Second line, not assault. Then he realised that, in all probability, he would be a part-timer, not a regular solider at all. Otherwise he would not come under Pamir. The thought momentarily encouraged him.

'I've told him that you are to stay here until I come back. You are not to be allowed to move. He understands.' Pamir straightened. 'I will see you later.'

Joshua stretched out. 'Could I have my hands untied?' he asked.

'No.'

'Only it's bloody painful with them bound together.'

'If you had your hands free you could untie your legs,' said Pamir sharply.

Joshua nodded towards the sergeant. 'With him here?'

Pamir hestitated, then said, 'If I untie your hands, will you give me your word that you will not try to escape?'

'Escape to where?'

'Your word that you will not try to take any part in what is going to happen? Your word that you – both of you – that you will not interfere at all with what we are going to do?'

'All I want is to get some circulation back into my hands! Yes, I'll give you my word!'

'Your word as an English gentleman?'

'My word as an English gentleman, if that's what you want!'

Pamir knelt beside Joshua, and produced a pen-knife from his pocket.

'Funny, really,' said Joshua, as Pamir opened the blade. He sensed Berrisford watching him. 'Funny, after God knows how many years we should find ourselves like this.'

'Keep your hands still,' said Pamir. 'Or I will cut you.'

'No, but when we were at Charminster House all those years ago, I don't suppose either of – go!'

As he swung his feet into Pamir's face he could feel the moment when the jaw crumpled. He spun himself up and round. There was a grunt from somewhere to his right, but he had no time to check. For a moment he saw Pamir's face, the expression of total disbelief, as his hands reached the mouth and the gushing blood. Joshua smashed the side of his own hand against Pamir's neck, then was sitting astride him, the newly freed thumbs pressing down on the carotid arteries.

'Sorry,' he muttered as he pressed. 'But there aren't any English gentlemen left.'

Pamir's eyes rolled upwards, and at the last moment Joshua straightened up, taking his hands away. You don't kill a colleague, even an ex-colleague, not unless you have to. But as he glanced round, the body of the sergeant at Berrisford's feet looked ominously still.

'The SBS has a section, sir,' said Berrisford, picking up the sergeant's rifle. 'They intended to come in as soon as the moon's down. Usual routine. Rubber boat. Then they're sending the helicopter in to take the girls out.'

'They've got to be stopped!'

Berrisford looked blank. 'Stopped?'

'There's half the bloody Turkish army covering this bit of coastline! Ten SBS! They'd be slaughtered! They'd never even get ashore!'

Joshua crouched, and wrestled the belt off Pamir's inert body. He pulled the automatic out of its holster. A Browning. Bit old-fashioned, but reliable enough and it was always useful to have a decent magazine, like the Browing's thirteen rounds. He said, 'You get down towards that beach and stop them trying to land! I don't mind how you do it, but stop them!'

'Sir.' Then, a little tentatively, 'Where will you be, sir?'

He nodded curtly towards the houses. 'Down there. I want to find when they're going in, and get in first. About ten seconds first. But – listen – '

'Sir?'

'Don't let the SBS get taken by surprise. But the longer I have to work before there's a fire-fight on the beach, the better. Right?'

Berrisford nodded. Joshua got a fleeting impression that Berrisford was really rather looking forward to the next half hour. He straightened up, and fastened the belt round his own waist, keeping the automatic in its holster, but the holster unbuttoned. As a last thought, he picked up the sergeant's cap, and put it on.

'Go! Go! Go!'

Berrisford ran, crouching but fast, vaulting a low stone wall. Within seconds he had disappeared into the night. Joshua looked slowly round him. He thought he had taken in the details of the landscape that he would need during the preceding hours when the moon had illuminated the hills, but he had to accustom himself to what it would look like as the darkness deepened. Then, breathing easily, he started to walk down towards the deserted village, keeping in the long shadows as he did so.

Ahead of him a man clutching an M16 doubled across the road. It was hard to tell in the moonlight, but from the way he moved he didn't look young, or highly trained. Then, from the shadows into which the man had disappeared, three others emerged, facing up the road.

One of them saw Joshua, and for an uncertain moment it looked as though he would be challenged. With an imperious movement Joshua waved them back into the darkness, and strode past. He heard a low mutter of Turkish as he walked on, but there was no further movement.

He was now near the buildings in which the girls were supposed to be being held. He crouched behind a wall, and looked carefully through a gap where, in the Greek days, there had been a gate. At first he counted five buldings, four roughly the same size, and one smaller. Then he realised that the smaller shape was a vehicle with a camouflaged tarpaulin drawn over it.

The vehicle would hide his movements both from the nearest house and also from a light machine gun post he could just discern to one side of the farmyard, its crew with their backs to him. He crawled to its cover, and tried to assess the position.

Forty-something men, Pamir had said. Plus the machine-gunners further out. If Pamir had planned the attack, how would he have conceived it? He'd had police training; he'd had Intelligence training. But had he ever had any normal military training? In Turkey presumably they had conscription. But not in Cyprus under the British. Would he have attended any army course in the years since '74?

Would he know the basics of storming a building full of terrorists and hostages, let alone the subtleties that had been learnt only recently, learnt the hard way, of attacking with such momentum and violence, with so much noise that the terrorists were thrown into a calculated state of shock and were dead before they had even reacted to being threatened?

No, Pamir would know nothing of that. And worse, the men under him would not even be the equals of normal infantry, let alone of the world's elite. They would be the equivalent of Britain's Territorials.

But it would not be Pamir in charge. Pamir was lying, hopefully undiscovered, unconscious by a fallen wall. The attack would be in the hands of a Cypriot officer who, in all probability, would lack any of Pamir's basic flair and intelligence. A part-time professional leading part-time amateurs.

Joshua considered what he knew. He knew the positions of the two machine gun posts. They were both covering the far side of the village, so Pamir had presumably intended to attack the obvious way, the shortest way, the way the terrorists would be expecting an attack. Except they were not expecting an attack. Please God.

228

Carefully he reached up and pulled aside a corner of the tarpaulin over the vehicle. In the faint light he could make out where it had been painted white. The white of the United Nations, of the Peace Keeping Force.

In the darkness there was a greater darkness in the lee of the vehicle, and he used it to edge up to the building. There was a window high up in the wall, but he was not prepared to risk standing up to look in. Then he saw a narrow ventilation slit further along the wall, and only about eighteen inches above the ground. He crawled along to it and listened intently. He didn't believe that Pamir and his men really knew what was happening in the houses. To get that sort of intelligence without detection required far greater expertise than they would have had, training they were not up to, equipment they would never have heard of. He listened, and heard a rustling from within. Silence again, then more rustling, then a squeak.

He breathed out softly. Rats. Pamir was right about that house at any rate. If a house had free-ranging rats, then it wouldn't have unsleeping human beings.

The moon had now completely disappeared, and the night seemed almost preternaturally dark, because it had been so luminous only a few minutes earlier. He wished he knew exactly when Pamir had decided that his men should attack. He glanced at his watch. Two forty-seven. Say three. They were not experts, they wouldn't have the sophistication to pick a moment that would be meaningless to their enemy, say two fifty-one, or four minutes past three. More likely to pick the hour or the half hour.

He looked cautiously round the side of the delapidated building. The next building, only about thirty yards away, according to Pamir was where the prisoners were. Where Joanna was. If Pamir was right, if they were there at all, if they were still alive. There was the remains of a hen coop to one side of the building that offered concealment from anyone inside the house who happened to look out. He was conisidering it when there was the creak of an ill-fitting door, and from the house beyond, the one that Pamir said was only used for eating, which should have been empty in the middle of the night, a man emerged.

It was the moment of recognition. Until that second the terrorists had been a concept, ideas that were assessed in terms of known probable connections, possessions, associations, motives. They had not been human, they had not had shape and weight and life. Now he could see the terrorist, and the terrorist was real. He was a tall

229

man, over six foot, and as far as Joshua could see in the new darkness, lean and muscular. He was quite naked. He stood outside the door, and started to urinate.

Who was he? Where did he come from, what had brought him here? Who was he to Joanna? Her torturer? Her captor? Her lover?

The man finished, and for a moment it looked as though he might take it into his head to go for a stroll in the night: but after glancing round he went back into the house.

As the man disappeared there was the sound of a piece of wood snapping. It came from somewhere to Joshua's right, one of the gendarmerie, not one of the terrorists. They were closing in. Odds were the attack was timed for three. He hadn't long.

There was a real danger that one of the Turks might see him and mistake him for a terrorist. The threat then was not so much the chance of being shot, because the Turks were still some distance away, and in the near darkness, so long as he avoided silhouetting himself against the sky, he doubted if he would be hit by amateur marksmen. The real danger was that the moment a shot was fired, the attack would have to begin. The first shot, and the terrorists would be awake, alerted, murderous. One shot, and the hostages would – what would they do with the hostages? Massacre them? Use them as a screen to try to escape, driving them towards the waiting machine guns? Force them out of the house, one by one, each with a terrorist behind her and a gun in her back?

The door of the far house creaked again, and the naked terrorist emerged, now smoking a cigarette. He stood a yard or two from the doorway, puffing luxuriously in the warm air, the tip of his cigarette glowing brighter as he inhaled.

From somewhere there was the sound of a man suppressing a sneeze. The terrorist checked himself, the cigarette in his hand held away from his mouth as he listened. Then a night bird gave a half-hearted cry and got no answer. The terrorist paused, waiting, then, satisfied, turned and walked slowly back into the house. The door creaked shut.

The Turks would still be watching the far house, and Joshua doubled across to the hen coop beside the other house. From where he now was he could see a faint glow of light from inside the house, thin slivers of orange visible through cracks in the old, closed shutters.

He tried to work out what the light would be. A candle? An oil lamp? A torch? The light seemed steady, so it was not a torch in somebody's hand, a torch being used by an unsleeping terrorist to check that all was well. Sinking down to the dusty earth he made his way until he was directly below the window.

There were people in the little house, there was no doubt about that. He could hear faint sounds of heavy breathing, then a girl's voice said *not take it with us* in the loud monotone of someone talking in her sleep. A girl's voice, and English. Then another girl gave a little sob, as though she was crying under the sheets.

He had worked out the likely form of the house while he had been on the hill above it. There was a door in the centre of one wall which had been the front door, leading, presumably, into a main room which had a bedroom off it. At the back of the house there was a septic tank some distance away, so presumably there would be two more doors leading off the main room to a lavatory and kitchen. The house was not on the mains, and there was a well that must have been used by the whole family in the old days. For a moment he was puzzled that Pamir had not mentioned seeing people going to the well for water, then he realised that they would have laid in enough water in advance. They had laid it in before because they knew what they were doing, and it had all been planned. Expertly planned over a period.

The main door would be locked, no doubt of that. Perhaps it might break if he threw himself at it, but it was too risky to consider. They would have grenades, apart from automatic weapons. They must not have time, that was the main thing.

He crawled round to the back of the house, the side he could not see from the hill, and found another door. To his surprise it was ajar. He was wondering whether to risk the noise of opening it when he heard a muffled cough from the darkness behind him. The Turks were coming in faster than he had expected, and he gritted his teeth as he heard the unmistakable sound of a military boot crunching over loose stones.

If he didn't move now, the Turks would have roused the whole group. Their priorities were not his priorities. They were striking a blow for their right to nationhood. He was trying to save the life of his only child. He took out the automatic, cocked it, and crouching, pushed his way into the house.

He found himself in near total darkness, and reached cautiously round. There was a door to each side of him, and another in front. He reached down and felt a stone-flagged floor. He was in some sort of added-on back section, an entrance porch with a kitchen to one side, judging by the smell a lavatory to the other, and the main house straight ahead.

231

He was still considering what to do when there was the sound of a shot, violently loud in the stealthy night, from outside the next building. He threw himself at the door. Something shattered, and he found himself in the main room. There was now the crashing of shots all round the farmstead. He could see that the room was packed with girls, still half-asleep, bewildered, awaking to terror. A bullet smashed through a shutter, whined across the room and buried itself in the wall opposite.

'Keep down!' he shouted. 'Keep flat on the floor!'

He looked round, crouching, his gun held out before him, for the terrorists who must be guarding the girls. He edged away from the door, so that he could not be silhouetted against the sky by anybody lying on the floor. Against the main door, they'd be guarding the main door. In the faint light of an oil lamp he watched.

'Keep down and don't move!' he cried. If he could stop the girls, just for a moment, from becoming hysterical, stop them from moving, he still had a chance.

His mind was racing, but he knew he had to be rational, he had to behave as though the girls were just any hostages, unknown to him. There must be two guards, at least, because there were always at least two guards. But in the darkness, in what must have been less than a second but dragged and dragged, nobody moved. The shock was total.

Then to one side of the main door he saw a movement, as someone who had been sleeping on the floor began to sit up. It was a girl, he could just make her out in the glow of an oil lamp. A girl with long blonde hair.

It was instinct, the conditioned reflex, the result of all the training, that made him fire. One, two, three shots. The third bullet got her in the neck. He saw her head thrown sideways, then a gush of blood spurted out, splashing over the lamp.

For one appalling moment he thought that, simply because They had made him what he was, They had trained him for what he had to do, he had killed one of the hostages. Killed his own daughter. Then, as she fell back, he saw her face and she was older than the girls, in her twenties, and beside her hand, where she had been reaching out, there was a gun.

Two guards. There would be another, he was certain. At the last minute he realised, and spun round. A huge figure holding a Skorpion had entered behind him from the lavatory. He fired as the man levelled the weapon. He was so close he could not possibly miss. The first bullet struck in the groin, the second directly into the heart. He jumped to one side, but there was no answering fire from anyone else in the room.

From the moment he entered the room until the moment the big man was thrown backwards to bounce off the frame of the door and begin falling forward had taken no more than two and half seconds.

Then suddenly a girl screamed, then another, then it seemed as though the whole room was an intolerable echo chamber of screams. He tried to shout over them, but he could not be heard. He ran to where there was a shuttered window facing towards the house where the terrorists had been sleeping, and smashed the shutters apart, throwing himself to one side as he did so. He saw a man run across the front of the builiding next to his, the one where the naked man had been, but held his fire as he saw the man kick in the door and toss in a grenade. With inexpert haste the man managed to grab the door and close it before the grenade exploded. Then another man ran forward, his hands above his head, and there was a fusillade of shots as he was cut down.

Joshua went over to the door through the screaming girls. The girl he had shot had her head thrown back like a puppet whose string had broken, and the blood was still pumping out. To her right was the Beretta she had been reaching for when he had fired. He picked it up, checked that it was loaded, then tucked his Browning back in his holster. He was thinking coldly and professionally. A Beretta and an MP5, he thought. Different weapons, but they take the same ammunition. Italian connections, French connections, German, PLA – could have come from anywhere. All the same, they'd known what they were doing.

He returned to the back door, and looked cautiously out. Nobody in the area of the farmstead was still firing, but there was no point in getting shot in mistake for a terrorist. On the other hand, what looked like a major battle had erupted over the ridge. Flares were curling skywards, machine-gun tracer laced the night, and there was the intermittent crump of grenades. For a moment he was baffled, then he remembered Berrisford. God bless Berrisford. If you needed a man to create a confusion into which nobody, let alone experts like the SBS, would dream of setting foot, Berrisford was your man. Just give him the chance of finding the odd grenade or a flare or two, and Berrisford would create mayhem in a matter of minutes, with everybody firing on everybody else.

233

He hoped that Berrisford would manage not to get himelf killed, but reflected that Berrisford had always been a lucky man, considering.

A short burst of sub-machine gun fire cut across the farmyard a few feet away, and spattered stone off the storehouse. He turned and pressed back into the house, where the screaming of the girls had mostly subsided into choking exhaustion.

'Hello,' he said. 'Don't worry any more. It's nearly over. I'm English, and it's all nearly over.'

He thought, they must think I'm a raving lunatic. I tell them it's over and any moment some half-trained Turk is liable to charge in shooting in panic, and I'm having to make myself heard over the First Battle of the Somme half a mile away. He went on, 'Just relax, and we'll wait until it's all settled down.'

And for Christ's sake, don't scream. I couldn't take that.

Then a girl spoke, and he suddenly thought, this is the best moment of my whole life. The girl said, 'It really is all right. He's my father.'

Chapter Twenty Nine

They obviously still hadn't found Pamir and the sergeant by the time the helicopter arrived, flapping noisily through the sky. Otherwise, they'd probably have opened fire on it. Otherwise they would be unlikely to leave him sitting there on a wall outside the storeroom, sitting with Joanna. There had been a middle-aged officer who spoke reasonable English, and who seemed to accept that Joshua had helped in the operation, and had not been a terrorist in disguise – though it occurred to Joshua that it might have been more difficult to explain had it not been for the presence of Joanna.

Father and daughter hadn't talked about what had happened: partly because he realised that she, and the others, were in a state of shock, partly because he knew that, whatever had taken place, it would be better for her to tell someone else first. They sat on the wall holding hands like adolescent lovers.

The firing by the coast had stopped, though a questioning flare still rose from time to time. The gendarmerie seemed bewildered, in that they had done what they had been told to do, the bodies of the terrorists were in body-bags waiting to be taken away, and they had run out of orders. Nobody was telling them exactly what should be happening *now*. As the chopper dropped to the ground an officer came over to Joshua, waving, and shouting in Turkish above the noise. He realised that Joshua did not understand him, but instead of looking for an interpreter shrugged, and walked away.

With enviable expertise, a group of Marines leapt out of the helicopter and in seconds had taken up firing positions around it. Then an officer rose and shouted, 'Is there anybody here speaks English?'

'I do,' called Joshua, rising from the wall.

The officer doubled over towards him, pistol in hand. Behind him, a Marine ran crouching, his weapon trained towards Joshua. At a given point he stopped, dropped to the ground, as the officer continued forward.

Joshua murmured to Joanna, 'See that? Remind you of anything? Sheep dog trials!'

She giggled, and Joshua realised it was the first time she had giggled since he had found her. She had laughed, she had laughed hysterically, but that had been different.

The officer, difficult to see and place in the night, stopped about four feet from Joshua.

'I am British officer,' he said, very slowly. 'I come in peace. We are here to help you. Do you understand me?'

'I have to tell you,' said Joshua, 'that my English is a lot better than my Turkish. Even better than my pidgin English.'

The officer looked uncertain, and Joshua added, 'My name's Chief Superintendent Doyle.'

'Oh! I say, that's good!' The officer laughed. 'Thought you were – well, no idea who you were, actually! Your chap Berrisford, he told us you were here in the north somewhere, but I didn't expect to run into you quite like this!'

He thrust out a camouflaged hand. 'Truscott's, my name. Lieutenant Gerry Truscott. Glad to meet you.'

They shook hands, and Truscott said, 'Have you any idea what's happened to Berrisford, sir? Only he said he'd be trying to get back here.'

'He was last seen setting up the special effects for World War III.'

'What? Oh, I see! The fireworks!'

'Yes.'

'Damned impressive!'

'Did it work?' In a way he was surprised to find that he was concerned about Berrisford's fate. 'Did the SBS get the message?'

'Oh, indeed they did! You mean, one man stage-managed all that?'

'Yes.'

'Well, he did a damned good job! You don't normally see the SBS high-tailing it for home, but with all that going on, nothing else to do!' Then Truscott suddenly became the efficient young officer again. 'The drill sir. Did Berrisford tell you what the plans are?'

'No. We didn't have much time.'

He was too busy killing a Turk twice his age, while I was garrotting a man who trusted me as an old friend. As an English gentleman.

'Well,' said Truscott, 'we're going to take the girls out on the helicopter. These Lynxes can easily take the seven of them plus the crew.'

'There's only six now.' Boobs will not be coming back.

236

'Better still. Then there'll be room for you. They're going to check them on the *Brazen*, then fly them on to Limassol. Debriefing – it'll be gentle, you understand.'

'Yes.' It'll be gentle, unless it has to be otherwise.

'And then fly them back to England. Only we weren't sure if there'd be any casualties.'

Joanna said, 'No. Nobody was hurt.' Then she said quietly, 'Unless you include their people.'

What happened to you? Have you changed for ever? Can it ever be like it was between us? Will you ever be able to tell me what happened?

Truscott seemed not to have noticed Joanna before. He flipped a finger towards his beret. 'Sorry, miss. Didn't realise you were there. Were you . . . one of them?'

'Yes,' said Joanna, very quietly.

It doesn't matter what happened, so long as you can tell me.

Truscott glanced over his shoulder. 'Ready when you are, sir,' he said. 'Only I expect Johnny Turk will be heading this way when he realises we're not landing, and we don't want a fire-fight. Not if we can help it.'

'No.'

Truscott raised his voice. 'Would the girls please go to the helicopter. We'll be taking off any moment.'

He indicated, and two Marines ran off to the house round which the girls of St. Hilda's were still crouching, wide-eyed, mostly still too shocked to speak.

'The other chaps,' said Truscott. 'They seem to be taking it very quietly. The chopper, I mean.'

'They are looking for the man in charge of them,' said Joshua. He thought, I hope I didn't kill him. He was a good man, he meant well, and he didn't deserve to die. But I don't think I killed him. 'They haven't got anybody else to give them orders, not now the firing's over.'

Girls hurried past him towards the helicopter and two or three Marines materialised behind them. It was difficult to be certain of the number for they wore night camouflage, and disappeared into patches of darkness as they moved.

One of the Marines came up to Truscott, and muttered something that Joshua didn't catch. Truscott hesitated, then turned to Joshua.

'Just been told. Bit of bad news. Your chap Berrisford.'

'What about him? He's not – '

'No. Oh no, just a couple of flesh wounds, the Marine says.'

'Where is he?'

'By the helicopter.'

Joshua ran, stumbling over the rough ground, towards the chopper. Berrisford was lying on the ground under it, a Marine Sergeant beside him.

'Hello, sir,' said Berrisford. 'Damned silly. You know who got me?'

'Who?'

'Bloody SBS! I was covered from one side, then I got shot in the arse from the sea! Never can trust the Navy!'

'He's also got a bullet in the hip,' said the Sergeant.

'Same one!' said Berrisford cheerfully, but the Marine glanced at Truscott and shook his head.

Truscott looked at Joshua and said tentatively, 'We have plasma in the chopper.'

'Of course.'

'What I mean is, he'll take up a place – '

'He takes mine,' said Joshua curtly, and turned away.

Truscott gripped Joshua by the shoulder, the grip of a young man, an athlete.

'With respect, sir, I'm in charge here. And I'll be staying with my men. You'll be leaving with the other non-combatants.'

Non-combatants. Children, women, those too young or too old to fight.

Then Truscott grinned. 'I expect we'll meet up pretty soon. Pretty quick turnaround. But if it does get tricky, better to leave it to the experts.'

For a moment Joshua felt a surge of pride, a surge of anger. Then he thought, how would I have felt at twenty-two if some civilian near-geriatric had tried to assume my command?

'Okay,' he said.

First Berrisford was loaded, then the girls, two of them crying, one giving little helpless laughs. Then, as the blades began to rotate, Joshua climbed in. At the other end of the dark cavern of the helicopter someone was attaching Berrisford to a plasma drip feed.

Joshua looked out as, to an irregular crescendo, the wind swept round the men on the ground and in its strangely prehistoric way, like one of God's failed designs for a pterodactyl, the helicopter clattered up into the dark, moonless sky.

238

He edged back towards Berrisford, whose eyes were closed.

A Marine was crouched beside him.

'Gave him a shot, sir,' said the Marine. 'He'll be all right.'

Joshua nodded, then he felt arms round his neck.

'Oh, daddy, daddy, daddy!' she said. He put his hands on hers.

The Marine asked, 'Your daughter, sir?'

'Yes.'

'I didn't realise.' He nodded towards Berrisford. 'He didn't tell anybody, as far as I know.'

'He wasn't allowed to.'

'Oh.'

A flare came up, swept lazily past them as they crossed the coastline.

'You know,' said the Marine. 'You've got to hand it to them. The way they took it. Most people, try to load them under stress . . .'

'Yes.'

'They should be proud of themselves. I don't think I'd have done as well, not at that age.'

In the faint illumination inside the helicopter Joshua looked at the face under the proud green beret. At that age, he'd said, and he didn't look as though he'd need to shave more than twice a week.

The Marine grinned at Joanna. 'Quite a story,' he said. 'Tell your friends what really happened. Not what they read in the papers.'

Joshua said, 'There won't be much in the papers.'

'Oh. Really?'

Joshua thought, Weinstein won't get much of an account from me and nobody else will get a thing. It isn't one of those stories. Nobody comes out of it very well, not the English, not the Turks, not the Cypriots, nobody. It'll hardly get in the papers at all. Nobody will want it in the papers.

The Marine pointed, and below them, just ahead, HMS *Brazen* was waiting. Joshua turned, and he could still see the dark mountains of Aphrodite's island.

As the helicopter started to shudder down towards its pad, the Marine said, 'The main thing is, the children are all right.'

'Yes.'

He looked at Joanna, her arms still wrapped round her father. 'Soon be over! Get you on an aeroplane, straight home! This time tomorrow you'll be back home with your mother!'

239

With her mother. With Barbara.

Joshua turned away, blinking to stop the tears running down his face.

We're going back home to Barbara.